KILLING PRETTIES

DS Malice Series
Book 1

By

Rob Ashman

To Gemma and Holly, for keeping my feet on the ground
whether I needed it or not.

Also by Rob Ashman

The Mechanic Trilogy

Those that Remain

In Your Name

Pay the Penance

The DI Roz Kray series

Faceless

This Little Piggy

Suspended Retribution

Jaded

Preface

'I encourage you to take a moment ... take a moment to imagine what it must be like to wake in the morning and have the world smile back at you. Imagine floating through your day on a kaleidoscope of beaming faces; each one happy to be in your presence; each one hoping some of your sparkle will land on them.

'Imagine a life where no one is interested in your competence or your conduct, not your beliefs nor your personality. The only thing that's important is the way you look. The way you shine.

'Imagine being born with a privilege that paves the way to a lifetime of success and riches. Success you don't deserve and riches you have not earned.

'That is the life of a Pretty.

'Pretties are everywhere. I see them at work, in the supermarket, in bars and restaurants. All of them ghosting through life with an effortless façade with which to dazzle others. Unlocking opportunities with a flash of a smile.

'In a world that values looking good above all else, being ugly is a raw deal. I should know.

'Pretties are the focus of my psychosis. The passion that gives the demons in my head purpose and direction. But not all Pretties are the same. Some are imposters, hiding talents beneath an attractive wrapping. These people run their own businesses, speak several languages, play musical instruments, paint amazing pictures or race cars for a living. These are not true Pretties. They have something to offer; something valuable to contribute; something to enrich the life of others.

'The Pretties I loathe are the ones that have nothing to offer. The ones that are guilty of breathing air that is meant for others. These are the ones that make the cut. Male or female, it doesn't matter. I'm all about equality.

'My name is Damien Kaplan and killing Pretties makes me happy.'

Chapter 1

Victims are like buses. You wait for ages for one, then two turn up at once. I know Callum is a Pretty but Elsa hasn't finished playing with him. I have no choice but to wait.

The headboard thumps off the wall like the bass drum in a rock band. I had fixed blocks of polystyrene to the wall to deaden the sound, but Callum's energetic performance has made short work of them. Elsa is moaning and panting like a pack of bitches on heat. I know I should be horrified. But I'm not.

Three hours earlier Callum had rapped sharply on the front door, the sound echoing around our vaulted hallway. I had butterflies in my stomach the size of condors. This was his fourth time and his second visit to our house. Tonight could be the night.

I'd answered the door to the tall man dressed in a jacket and jeans, his white shirt gaping open to reveal a well-sculptured chest and silver chain. He was late twenties and greeted me with a dazzling smile.

'Sorry I'm a little early,' he'd said, giving me the full benefit of his perfect teeth while handing over a bottle of red wine.

'No problem. It's lovely to see you again. Please come in. Elsa's in the lounge.'

We'd shaken hands, a ridiculous ceremony given where his hands were going to be in a short while. I had ushered him inside and he disappeared through the archway towards the sitting room. I'd glanced outside to see his car parked next to ours in the driveway. My heart skipped a beat as I imagined myself disposing of it.

I closed the door and followed him into the lounge. Elsa was on her feet greeting him with a kiss… a lingering kiss. She was dressed in a long maxi dress with a split running up the front. I had watched her dress for the occasion, so I knew the only thing she was wearing underneath was body lotion and Chanel No.5.

I watched as Callum ran his hand down her body, letting it rest on her hip. Now he knew as well.

'I'll fix us some drinks,' I'd said. 'Dinner will be ready in thirty minutes.'

'That's great,' Callum replied, peeling himself away from Elsa.

I had gone into the kitchen and filled three glasses with champagne. When I returned, Elsa was sitting in the armchair opposite Callum. I handed over the drinks and parked myself next to him.

'Cheers,' I'd said, raising my glass. 'Here's to us.'

'Cheers,' Callum had replied, holding his glass in the air.

We both settled back into the soft cushions. Callum was looking across at Elsa whose skirt had fallen either side of her legs. If he had been in any doubt about the underwear situation before, he wasn't now. Elsa smiled at me and raised her glass.

'How have you been?' asked Elsa. It was my cue to leave.

I returned to the kitchen to prepare dinner: baked sea bass with braised vegetables followed by individual chocolate soufflés. I could hear her giggling in the other room. My heart had been beating so hard in my chest I couldn't concentrate.

This could be the night ...

This could be the night when Elsa says 'yes'.

The night when it's my turn to play.

I'd tried to focus on making food but my mind kept wandering, fantasising about what lay in store for Callum. All I needed was for Elsa to give me the green light. All I needed was one small word — Yes.

I could hear the pair of them laughing. I went into the lounge to refill their glasses. Elsa was next to Callum, he had his arm draped around her shoulder.

'Top up, anyone?'

'Yes please,' Elsa said unwinding herself from his embrace. Her one hand held up her glass while the other rested high on his thigh. I filled her glass and she settled back against his chest, leaving her hand on his leg. He held out his glass and I did the honours. She reached up and whispered in his ear. They both laughed. It was time for me to leave again.

Back in the kitchen I downed my drink in one. My hands were shaking. How the hell I managed to cook dinner I'll never know. I went to tell them food was ready to find her straddled across his lap, kissing him hard. Callum's hands were inside her dress.

'Dinner is ready if you'd like to…' I struggled to tear my eyes away as she ground her hips against him.

'Let's eat,' Elsa said climbing off. 'It smells gorgeous.' She picked up her drink and then stroked my cheek with her hand as she wafted by. Her perfume was more intoxicating than the wine.

By some miracle dinner had turned out to be delicious, even if I do say so myself — the soufflé the crowning glory. The conversation around the table had been light and airy, confirming what we both knew — Callum had nothing to contribute, save for his electric smile and chiselled physique. He was a classic Pretty.

By the time we'd finished the main course, Callum's eyes were beginning to glaze over. I could tell that Elsa had been running her foot up and down his leg under the table. When I returned from the kitchen with two plates of dessert, her half-reclined position told me she'd reached his crotch.

More drinks had followed and Callum was fit to burst.

'I'll clear up,' he'd said, eager to move things along. Elsa had flashed me a look.

'No, no, I'll sort the dishes,' I replied, stacking the plates and taking them into the kitchen. After all, it was my job to do the dishes, his job to do my wife.

I returned to collect the glasses just in time to see Elsa take Callum by the hand. She led him out of the dining room into the hallway. They began climbing the stairs hand in hand. I held my breath.

This could be the night…

Elsa smiled at me as she made her way upstairs. She shook her head. The answer was 'No'.

'Shit,' I muttered under my breath, downing the last of the red wine. I had been sure that she had grown tired of this one and it was my turn. But no, she wanted more.

The banging and wailing continues unabated. I roll over and look at the clock on the bedside table: 1.25am. The one thing you can say about darling Callum is the boy has staying power. I have to be in court in eight hours' time and I'm not sure what's keeping me awake the most – the sound of Elsa coming like a train or my cock standing to attention.

Chapter 2

Khenan Malice smashed his gloved right hand into the bag and snorted through his nose. Then he pivoted his broad shoulders and slammed his left fist into the heavy leather. A straight right completed the combination. His skin glistened with sweat under the harsh lights.

'And again,' a short wiry man with a face the same beaten complexion as the leather bag barked an instruction. Malice's right hand hooked once more. The wiry man rocked back on his heels under the force of the blow. The next two punches landed hard.

'Time!' the man holding the bag yelled. He unwrapped a towel from around his neck and tossed it at Malice. 'The power is there but you're too damn slow. But then, you were always too damned slow.'

'Yeah and you've always been a miserable bastard,' Malice wiped his face and arms.

'Piss off.'

Malice doubled over with his hands on his knees, sucking air into his bursting lungs. The miserable bastard had a point. There was a time when his hands were a blur, but then there was a time when he was two stone lighter and twenty years younger. The wiry bloke had coached him to an ABA Championship belt and a shot at turning professional. But an ankle injury during training and a botched medical procedure had brought the curtain down on his fighting career and his time in the limelight was over. He could punch a hole in a brick wall but he moved about the ring with all the balance and grace of a drunk pensioner.

Malice glanced over at the clock on the wall – 6.15am. The morning sun was trying its best to break through the grime on the windows. It was time to get a move on. He had a busy day ahead; things to do, people to scare.

He went to the changing room and pulled on jeans, trainers and a black hoody. He called out a 'see ya!' and left the building. In the carpark he looked up at the sign emblazoned above the door. It read Jim's Gym. In the twenty-seven years he had known him, it was his friend's one and only attempt at humour. Which was probably just as well.

He gunned the motor and sped away.

The streets were still waking up and the traffic was light. He had plenty of time but seemed to spend his entire life in a permanent hurry. The traffic lights turned red, causing him to cruise to a stop. He saw Burko leaning against the wall under the flyover. He was partially hidden in darkness but his ridiculous hat gave him away, a choice of woollen headgear that gave his head the same profile as Marge Simpson.

Malice was not due to squeeze him for a couple of days but it paid to keep them on their toes. The lights turned green and Malice shot across the junction, screeching to a halt against the kerb. Burko jerked his head up, panic spreading across his face. He ran on the spot trying to decide his best escape route, but before he could orientate himself Malice was out of his vehicle, bearing down on him. Burko stopped dancing, resigned to his fate.

'Hey man, how's it hanging?' Burko said with as much bravado as he could muster, trying to mask the fact he wanted to be anywhere but here.

'Hanging low, brother. You been busy?'

'Yeah, it's been a long night, if you know what I mean.' Burko nodded like a dog performing for a treat. His towering hat bobbled around.

'You got something for me?'

'Hell no, man. Today is Wednesday, you said Friday!'

'Friday... Wednesday... what's a couple of days between friends?'

'Oh, man, give me a break.'

'I'll break something...' he raised his hand and Burko flinched. A shard of light caught his face. Malice could see an angry bruise under his left eye and his lip was split.

'You been upsetting people?'

'Oh, it's nothing.'

'Is someone leaning on you?'

'It's nothing I can't handle.'

'Looks like you handled it by putting your face in the way.'

Burko fingered his swollen cheek. 'Like I said, it's nothing.'

'If you say so. Now, let's pretend it's Friday.'

'Okay, okay, but it isn't going to be the full amount.'

'That's fine, I'll see you at the end of the week for the balance.'

Burko pulled out a roll of notes from the side pocket of his combat trousers. He peeled off five twenties. Malice eyed him and wagged his finger. Burko reeled off another two plus a tenner.

'That's it, man. I gotta stock-up,' Burko said, shrugging his shoulders.

Malice snatched the notes, balled them up and stuffed them in his pocket. He seized a handful of Burko's tracksuit top and pulled him in close. Malice could smell the remnants of cheap alcohol and kebab sauce on his breath. Burko looked away and jigged from one foot to the other like he needed a piss. He forced a smile in an attempt to diffuse the situation, treating Malice to the full glow of his yellow crumbling teeth, the product of too much crystal meth. He wondered how much longer Burko was going to be around.

'See you Friday. Look after that eye,' Malice touched his right hand to his forehead in mock salute and walked back to his car. 'You stay safe now.'

He could hear Burko cursing. It was always good to keep them off balance.

Malice spun the car around in the road and roared away. The clock on the dashboard read 6.40 a.m. He shoved his right foot into the carpet and the big six-cylinder engine lurched the car forward.

The houses and shops flew by as Malice powered his way out of town and onto the dual carriageway. The morning commute was starting to build and he kept having to jump on the brakes.

Come on, come on!

He could see the building up ahead in all its glory. The white cladding of the new office block fluoresced in the first glow of sunshine. He screeched to a halt and held his card against the black box. Nothing happened. He repeated the process but the barrier remained down. So he pressed the intercom button.

After what felt like an age, a disembodied voice cracked into life.

'Helloooooo.'

'Stop dicking about. My card's not working again.'

'I told you to get that fixed, Mally.'

'Yeah, well why don't you fix your bloody barrier.'

'It's not the barrier, it's your damned card.'

'Are you going to let me in?'

'Say please.'

'Please.'

'Say pretty please.'

Malice buzzed down his window and stuck out his arm. He flipped the middle finger on his right hand into the cool morning air. The security guard hunched over the CCTV monitors, laughed and raised the barrier.

Malice parked the car and leapt out, running across the concourse to the main entrance. He opened the big glass door and took the stairs two at a time to the second floor. He yanked on the handle and was enveloped with the smell of steam and deodorant. A couple of men were getting dressed in the changing room.

'Morning,' Malice said opening his locker. He was greeted by another smell, the odour of festering week-old clothes. He pulled out a suit and shirt. His watch read: 6.55 a.m.

Shit. No time for a shower.

He stripped down to his underwear, throwing his jeans, trainers and hoody into the locker to join the others. He tugged the shirt over his head and wrestled with the trousers. His shoes and socks were next. In his haste he pulled too hard on the lace and it snapped.

'Bollocks,' he muttered, tossing the broken shoelace onto the floor. He tucked in his shirt and pulled the jacket from the hanger, then fished a tie from the inside pocket and forced the knotted loop over his head and around his collar. He scraped his fingers through his closely cropped hair. The dreadlocks of his teens were long gone, having hit the floor in his mother's kitchen floor when she'd declared that he had to smarten himself up. Now the barber's clippers kept the unruly mess under control.

Malice dashed out the changing room and up the stairs to the conference room at the top. The sound of voices drifted down the stairwell, telling him the briefing was already underway. He opened the door and walked in. Fifteen faces turned to greet him.

'Yaay!' someone said as he took his seat. He looked at his watch – 7.04 a.m.

Shit!

'As I was saying,' Detective Superintendent Samantha Waite, a woman in her late thirties, was standing at the front. She'd been with the force for around nine months and was forging herself a formidable reputation. She was uncompromising and blunt to the point of rudeness and was certainly making a name for herself; but not one which could be used in polite conversation.

Behind her, a large TV screen was mounted on a stand, showing a street map with two houses highlighted in yellow.

'We believe both the properties will be occupied, so please be sure we don't lose anyone. As far as we know there are no minors involved. There could be anything up to fifteen, maybe twenty people in each house. Remember, they could be victims of trafficking and forced labour so they must be treated as vulnerable adults. We also have a translator on hand. Is everybody clear?'

'Yes, ma'am,' the room replied in unison.

'We have five vehicles on standby to transfer the occupants to the processing centre. There will be four teams; two for each property. DS Beech has a list of who goes where. Are there any questions?' A collective shaking of heads told her they were ready. 'Okay let's go.'

The men and women rose from their seats and made their way out the door. Malice joined them.

'Not so fast Mally,' Waite instructed, crooking her finger at him. 'I got a job for you.'

'Morning guv, sorry–'

'Is that the same shirt you had on yesterday?'

'Erm, no. I have two the same,' Malice lied.

'We have a missing person I want you to take a look at. A woman reported missing three days ago. The Sign of Life Team have confirmed there's been nil activity.'

'Oh, why me, ma'am?'

'Because you were the last one into the briefing. I've left the file on your desk.'

'So, you were always going to give me the missing person the job?'

'That's right. Because you were always going to be late.'

Chapter 3

It was the day I discovered the horrifying truth…

F inding body parts in the wall cavity of our house was not the worst thing to happen that day.

It was the summer of 1976. I was ten years of age and thought the blazing sun would last forever. I remember ice cream dripping onto my hand and the tarmac melting into black mirrored puddles.

My dad had passed away the summer before and we were getting ourselves back on track. Cancer took him from diagnosis to crematorium in less than six months. I'm an only child and lived with my mum in a sprawling converted farmhouse in the countryside. I had no friends, other than the ones I made up in my head, and school was a forty-minute bus ride away. Dad dying only served to increase my sense of isolation.

He'd been a high powered criminal barrister and worked away in London during the week. He would come home on a Friday night exhausted, then work all weekend preparing for Monday. The vast fees he commanded put a grand roof over our heads and meant mum didn't have to work.

My parents argued about everything. They even fought about money, which was absurd as we had more than we could spend. While they kept the truth from me, I suspect theirs was not a happy marriage.

On the days when he wasn't preparing briefs, or practising his court speeches, dad would throw himself into DIY. He always said he was secretly a frustrated builder — a stud wall here, a false ceiling there. He loved it and threw himself into the projects with child-like enthusiasm. However, even at a young age, it struck me that for someone with such a passion for home improvements he seemed to be particularly crap at it.

I would lend a hand when he went into renovation mode. It was the only time me and dad interacted like father and son. The rest of the time he was cold and distant. There was something dark about my father I could never quite put my finger on. All I knew was, for the most part of my childhood, he was not a man I wanted to get too close to.

Growing up I lived a largely solitary existence at the cottage. The friends in my head were rampant. I started setting fires in the woods nearby but my inbuilt reticence prevented me from going too far. I harboured fantasies of burning down the school, or some other public building, but never had the conviction to see it through. I trapped animals to torture and kill, which led to me thinking what it would be like to trap and kill a classmate. Despite the encouragement of my malicious friends, that never came to fruition either.

My make-believe pals would goad me, driving me to escalating heights of cruelty. I knew it wasn't right but it felt like a release every time I watched the life extinguish from the eyes of something struggling to free itself.

I would love to say that I was abused as a child and that's the reason for me being the way I am, or that I was subjected to an immense trauma, which fractured my personality, releasing my inner demon. But, none of that is true. I had to content myself with knowing I am the way I am because… just because.

When we went into town I would spend the time in the public library while mum did her shopping. I devoured every book I could find about real life killers. I wasn't interested in fictional crime novels. I wanted to read about the real thing – The Zodiac Killer, Donald Henry Gaskins, the Casanova Killer. They held me in a macabre grip of fascination.

What made them tick? How did they get caught?

All the while, searching for the answer to a question: *Why did I feel this way? Was it a phase of growing up that would pass or would it stay with me for life?*

Eventually the librarian alerted my mum, telling her that she didn't consider my reading habits appropriate for a boy of my age. So, that put an end to that. But I couldn't switch off what was raging in my head. I would sit in class wondering if the children around me harboured the same thoughts. I would have asked, had it not been for the fact that no-one spoke to me.

My earliest memory of feeling this way was when I stabbed a boy in the chest with the stem of a daffodil. I was six years of age and I didn't know it wouldn't kill him. I can remember him sitting next to me crying. He wouldn't shut up. No matter what the teacher did, he kept on wailing. The stem broke and he stared at me in shock, his eyes as wide as saucers. Even now I can still feel the intense sense of disappointment.

Mum waited a year after my dad's death before turning her attention to the house. She must have considered twelve months to be a suitable mourning period. She went through our home itemising what needed to change.

'That fireplace is so 1950's and that arch has to go,' I remember her saying. 'No-one has a serving hatch between the kitchen and the dining room anymore and that wall can come down to open up the back of the house.'

She scribbled notes onto a pad as she went from room to room itemising the work to be done. I watched her with a distant curiosity,

'We're going to do the house up and sell it,' she announced one day. 'Move to a city where I can get a job and you can make new friends. You'd like that, Damien, wouldn't you?'

How the hell should I know? I've never lived in a city and I've never had any friends. And anyway, if that's what you want to do, why not sell the bloody place?

I suppose, it was mum's way of making a fresh start, and knocking the house about was her way of exercising the ghost of my father.

I can remember one morning sitting on my swing under the tree, watching as the builders arrived. Mum was excited and her voice carried over the sound of the flatbed lorry as it parked on the drive. The workmen bundled wheelbarrows, drills and toolboxes into the house. I envied them their hand tools and my mind turned to the damage I could inflict if I had them to play with in the woods.

A big bloke walked to the house carrying two heavy sledge hammers, one in each hand. This guy wasn't pissing about. The peace was shattered by the cacophony of thumping and banging as they were put to good use.

Twenty minutes later everything was on stop. I went into the house to find mum sitting on the sofa crying and the builders mulling around in the next room.

'What is it?' I asked. 'Mum, what's the matter?'

'Go to your room.'

'But, what—'

'Go to your room!' she snapped. I knew it was serious because mum never yelled.

I did as I was told and half an hour later I saw a police car pull up outside and two uniformed officers got out. I sat at the top of the stairs to listen to the murmured conversation. One of the coppers came into the hallway to use our telephone.

'It looks like a human femur wrapped in plastic... yes, that's right, Guv. It was hidden in the wall cavity... it fell onto the floor when they knocked a... yeah that's right, she's at the property now... I can see what looks like more body parts, you'd better get a team down here.'

Uncovering human remains was not part of the contract and the builders made a sharp exit. Mum and I were moved into a hotel in town, which was great because I could walk to school.

Two days later we were escorted back to the house to collect more of our belongings to find it looking like a giant block of Swiss cheese. There were holes everywhere, so many I wondered if the house might fall down. The police told mum they had discovered more body parts hidden in the wall cavities. I later found out that the remains of five people were lying in the morgue. I say remains because, despite the number of limbs, none of them matched to complete a full set.

I remember mum was livid, more because her long-awaited renovation project was on hold rather than the consequence of finding out her husband was a killer. After a couple of days her moral compass corrected itself and she was devastated.

Finding body parts in the wall cavity of our house was not the worst thing to happen that day. The worst thing was realising it was genetic. This was no temporary aberration. I was pre-disposed to feel the way I did.

Killing was in my genes.

Chapter 4

I'm sitting in court room number one — ready to go. Securing a guilty verdict when there's no body is always a challenge, but in this case I'm relishing the battle. It's my second celebrity trial and I have a vested interest in making this one stick.

Well, when I say celebrity, I maybe over egging the pudding. Two second-rate models with ambitions way above their abilities wouldn't normally flicker the paparazzi needle. But when one of them is accused of murdering the other it makes for great headlines.

Despite my lack of sleep, I'm feeling remarkably fresh. The defence team have the floor today and are going all out to discredit the evidence and rubbish my arguments. They have their work cut out. I'm damned good at this game, even if I do say so myself.

The judge lifted the reporting restrictions two weeks ago and the red-tops have had a field day. The best tag line to date has been to label the accused 'The Catwalk Killer' which is jumping the gun a little. After such an inflammatory start, the article was suitably vague to keep themselves out of court, though the nickname stuck. There are days when I arrive at court and have to fight my way through the forest of cameras waiting for the circus to roll into town.

The defence have done a good job under difficult circumstances but by my estimation I have my neck in front and a guilty verdict is on the cards. The absence of a body goes in their favour but their relationship background goes in mine.

Brendan and Tracey Bairstow married four years ago in a *Hello* magazine extravaganza designed to showcase two beautiful people on their magical day. However, the stunning photographs failed to depict a toxic relationship where serial infidelity was used as a weapon and physical abuse was the order of the day.

Brendan worked for Peccadillo Associates, a leading fashion designer and model agency, while Tracey strutted her stuff for Welbourn Parade. Each one trying to out-do the other, each one busting a gut to elbow the other out of the limelight. But together they were the driving force behind Brand Bairstow which supplied an extensive make-up and clothing range to the young and trendy. She was the brains of the outfit and he hung onto her coattails and enjoyed the ride. Neither of them wanted to end their marriage however venomous it became; killing the golden goose was not part of the plan.

Shackled together in the headlong pursuit of fame and fortune brought them into constant conflict from which neither shied away. That was until Brendan went missing six months ago.

Before the trial started I had made the preliminary legal arguments that their previous violent behaviour and misconduct should be heard. The defence said it was inadmissible. I won and they lost.

Strike one to me.

Brendan had been reported missing by his agent when he failed to show up for work. I can't wait to ask Tracey the question: 'So, Ms Bairstow, can you explain to the court why you failed to report your husband missing, despite the fact that you were residing at the family home at the time?'

She will burble an incomplete answer, providing me the opportunity to roast her at the stake. She'll be a gibbering wreck when I've finished.

Strike two to me.

The defence team have coached her well and Tracey is nothing like her public persona. In the courtroom she is softly spoken and demure to the point of coyness; but in the public eye she's a hard drinking, coke sniffing diva who flaunts her infidelity for all to see. In a society where woman-power is lauded over like a new religion, it serves to boost the brand. When she was snapped kissing her latest acquisition the headlines read 'You Go Girl!'. Though I suspect a lot of what's been reported is for show, a great deal of it is genuine. It would appear that blatant infidelity is the true badge of female empowerment.

Brendan on the other hand has had to keep his tit-for-tat dalliances out of the papers. A man caught doing the same would be subject to a media flogging which would do the brand no good at all.

The couple have had a field day playing out their pantomime of a life together in the full glare of the press while watching their brand develop a cult following. But their relationship hides an even darker side. Hospital admissions and police records tell a history of physical abuse on both sides and while her defence are trying to paint Tracey as the victim, it's impossible to discount the evidence.

In her statement Tracey will say that Brendan left the house one Saturday morning and she hasn't seen him since. My guess is the jury will remain stony faced and not buy a word of it.

My argument will be that she attacked her husband in a jealous rage, killed him and disposed of his body and his car. Her catalogue of violent behaviour will provide a background and context that will be hard to deny.

Strike three to me.

The trial is in its fourth week. I've been practising my closing remarks for some time and I'm confident I can sway the jury in my favour. The defence want to paint Tracey as a wronged-woman but it's not working. I know it, and they know it. But they're ploughing on regardless. She is due to take the stand in the next few days – I can't wait.

It makes my heart sing to see two people so deserving of their misfortune. She is beautiful, calculating and clever. He is equally beautiful and fucking useless.

It's important for me to convince the jury to deliver a guilty verdict even though I know Tracey Bairstow is an innocent woman. I can, hand on heart, confirm that Brendan left the family home fit and well on that Saturday morning and was a million miles way from being dead.

In many ways Tracey Bairstow is as much of a victim as her dork of a husband.

She didn't kill Brendan.

I did.

Chapter 5

Malice was the product of a Jamaican mother and English father. His family had come to Britain as part of the Windrush project and had made it their home. The marriage of a black woman to a white man had not gone down well in either camp and when they produced Khenan he was one of a kind in his neighbourhood.

'So, are you white or black?' his friends would ask.

'Both I suppose,' he would reply.

'Kinda coffee like?'

'Yeah, kinda.'

'That's cool. Let's go play footie.'

His dual heritage had never been an issue until he reached his teenage years, then the racial divide bit him in the arse like a rabid dog. Having friends of both colours no longer worked, you had to pick a side. Malice chose black. Mainly because, where he lived, they were in the majority. Life was easier that way.

Malice pressed the doorbell and heard a melodic chime on the other side of the door. Waite had been right. Belinda Garrett had been missing for three days with no activity on her social media accounts, no phone calls or messages and no transactions on her bank account or credit cards — the woman had gone AWOL.

She'd been reported missing by her house mate and a phone call to her employer had confirmed she had not been to work either. Malice pressed the bell again. He looked at his watch and considered what else he could be doing right now. Mason Wrigley would be doing his rounds and he was overdue a visit.

Maybe later I'll pay…

A woman answered the door dressed in a bath robe with a towel wrapped around her head. She was in her late twenties and looked mad as hell.

'Yes?' She flung open the door. Malice glanced at the water pooling around her feet.

'Sorry were you…'

'In the bloody shower, yes.'

'Sorry about that. I'm DS Malice. I wonder if I could ask you a few questions relating to Belinda Garrett,' he said, flashing his warrant card.

'You pick your times, don't you?'

'May I…'

'Come in. I'm getting ready for work.'

'Okay, thanks.'

Malice followed her into the house, managing not to step on the watery footprints left behind on the laminate floor. She showed him into the lounge where he took a seat as she sat opposite, both hands ensuring her modesty stayed intact.

'Can I ask your name?' Malice asked.

'I'm Jenny Chase. I live with Belinda.'

'Is this your house?'

'No, we rent it. We've been housemates a couple of months. I was here first and Belinda moved in early February.'

'You reported her missing...'

'Yeah, that's right. It's not like her to simply disappear. We're not close but we get along okay and she's never done anything like this before. I'm in a rush and need some coffee. Would you like one?'

'Yes, that would be good,' Malice took out his pocket book and scribbled a few notes. 'Could she be staying with a friend?'

'She could be, I suppose. But she didn't say that's what she was doing.'

Chase busied herself with mugs in the kitchen while Malice got to his feet and started mooching around. The house was light and modern with stylish furniture.

'Is there a boyfriend on the scene?'

'Not really.'

Malice screwed his face up.

'What does that mean?'

Chase stuck her turban topped head around the door. 'Let's just say she's a bit of a free spirit.'

'So, there's no one special?'

'Belinda is not so much looking for Mr or Mrs Right, it's more like she's looking for Mr or Mrs Right-now.'

'Mr or Mrs?'

'She likes girls and boys.'

'Do you know any of them?'

Chase appeared with two hot drinks in one hand and a photograph in the other. Her dressing gown revealing a little more leg than she would have wanted. She handed over a coffee and photograph and tugged at her robe.

'I've met a few in the morning and I've definitely heard a few at night. But I don't know any names. This is a recent photograph of her, was taken on a night out.'

'Thank you,' Malice said, raising his mug. 'When was the last time you saw her?'

'Saturday morning. She said she was going to meet a friend and she'd be back on Sunday.'

'So that's Saturday, thirteenth of April?'

'That's right.'

'Who was the friend?'

'No idea. She didn't talk much about her social life. Do you think something has happened to her?'

'That's what I'm here to find out. What about family?'

'Never heard her talk about them. She did tell me once that they'd lost touch years ago after a massive argument.'

'What was that about?'

'She didn't say and I didn't ask. Look, do you mind if I get ready for work?'

'Please, you carry on. Can I take a look at her room?'

'Help yourself. It's the one on the left at the top of the stairs.'

Chase returned to the kitchen, took a plastic container from the cupboard and food from the fridge. Malice left his coffee and went upstairs.

The bedroom was decorated in neutral colours with a double bed, a wardrobe and a chest of drawers. A glass topped desk and leather chair sat in the bay window. The room was immaculate. Malice slouched into the chair and began spinning from side to side.

Tidy girl.

He wrinkled up his nose as the aroma of two-day old shirt wafted up at him. He got up and started poking around in the drawers. There were clothes and make-up but nothing of interest. A large suitcase was stored on top of the wardrobe, Malice took it down and ran the zip around the edge. It was empty. He pulled his phone from his inside pocket and called a number. A low buzzing noise came from somewhere in the room.

Malice turned his head to locate the sound. On the floor, by the side of the bed he found the vibrating mobile, plugged into the wall socket. He took out a pen and pressed a button. Seven missed calls.

Now... why would you do that?

He shook a plastic bag from his pocket and dropped the phone into it. Crossing to the desk, her laptop was next. He placed it into another bag.

A waste paper basket sat beside the desk full of discarded paperwork. He emptied the bin onto the floor and waded through it: junk mail, takeaway flyers, a rail receipt and a ton of neon coloured post-its. He laid them out and scanned the scribbled notes: Tommy, deodorant, condoms, Trixy, rent — each one written in heavy black ball point.

Chase appeared in the doorway dressed in a smart trouser suit and a white blouse. 'Are you going to be much longer, I have to go?' She was clutching her coffee cup with both hands.

'What's with the post-its? I mean, everyone writes themselves reminders now and again but this is...'

'Excessive?'

'You could say that.'

'Belinda had a fixation about forgetting things. It was like she was paranoid about it. So every day she wrote herself notes so she'd remember.'

'Why didn't she write a list and save all this?' Malice waved his hand across the multi-coloured carpet of squared paper laying on the floor in front of him.

'I don't know,' Chase shook her head and took a slurp. 'Sometimes she would stick them on the fridge door because she said it would be more in her face.'

Malice collected them up and put them into an evidence bag.

'I'll also take the ones from the fridge if you don't mind. Did she make a habit of leaving her phone behind when she went out?'

'Not as far as I know.'

'A couple more questions. Does Belinda own a car?'

'No, she doesn't drive.'

'Can you remember if Belinda took an overnight bag on the day she left?'

'Erm, yes. It was red, I think. One of those cabin-sized bags suitable to use on planes.' She turned to walk away. 'I really do need to go now, sorry.'

'Okay, I want a CSI team check out the room. Is it okay if they come round when you're back tonight?'

'Yup, that's fine,' she said over her shoulder.

Malice got to his feet and looked around. On the desk were three blocks of coloured post-its. He picked up the green one and tilted it to the window so the light caught the surface at an angle. His eyes scanned the paperwork on the floor. He did the same with the orange one. The fluorescent yellow block made him frown and purse his lips. He went downstairs to the kitchen and scanned the coloured squares stuck to the fridge door.

And... why would you do that?

Chapter 6

It was the day I had been waiting for ...

My name is Damien Kaplan and you could describe me as a bit of a catch: I'm a fabulous conversationalist, smart and funny; I am an accomplished chef, play several musical instruments, speak four languages, own three houses and I'm well sought after as a criminal barrister. But, I have one overwhelming drawback — I'm pig-ugly. There's no kind way of saying it: I make Shrek look like a model for *Maybelline*.

I've always been that way. In my younger years the difference between me and those around me was less noticeable. Then they began to mature into their teenage years, shedding their awkwardness and goofy appearance. Boy-like features were replaced with broad shoulders and square jaws, the girls developed curves and smiles that lit

up the room. Everyone was making a beautiful transition
— except me.

Why not me? What's wrong with me?

I think, looking back, that was the point when my
resentment turned to hate.

The passage of years has left me with a thicker
waistline and an even thicker neck. My receding hairline
began to gallop into the distance by the time I hit thirty and
the bags under my eyes could hold a weekly family shop.
Still, I have good teeth. But then the only person who's
passed comment on them is my dentist.

After the police investigation into the body parts had
run its course mum sold the house for far less than the
original asking price. Not that the difference made a dent
in the Kaplan finances. Mum wanted shot of the place and
would have given it away had the family lawyer not
intervened.

Mum bought a sprawling house in Winchester and I
started in a new school. She got a local office job and
thrived in her new environment. She flourished in her new
life. I didn't. I was quickly back to square one. No friends
and the same vitriolic people roaming around in my head.

I was enrolled into a top school and it was there I
excelled. While everyone else was laying siege to their
hormones, I was collecting A* results like confetti at a
wedding and getting myself bumped up to the year above
for English and History; a move which served to reinforce
the general opinion that I was a bit of a weirdo.

I immersed myself in every after-school activity, so
long as it didn't involve kicking or hitting a ball and
soaked it up. Achievement evenings became a procession
of 'And this year, the award goes to Damien Kaplan'. My
walk on stage to collect my certificate was always

accompanied with a ripple of polite applause, with an undercurrent of 'Bloody hell, not him again!'. Mum was always beaming with pride, oblivious to the furrowed eyebrows surrounding her.

The dark thoughts rumbling around in my head were still there but I felt less inclined to bend to their will. The rush of success had the effect of putting a sticking plaster on the gaping wound in my character. And the more success I had, the more I wanted. I was too busy chasing accolades that I was oblivious to mum getting involved with a bloke called Mark. He was nice enough and showed up from time to time to take her out for the evening.

I left six-form with four A levels, gaining the top grade in every one. Our mantelpiece was so crammed with academic trophies that the end-of-year award had to be consigned to the dining room. I went to Oxford to read Law and moved into digs at Jesus College. Mark came along with mum to move me in and I remember shaking his hand as they bid me goodbye. He then slipped his arm around mum and they walked to the car. I can remember thinking, *that's a little odd*, but shoved it to the back of my mind. There were far more interesting things to think about, like … *what clubs can I join?*

Freshers' week was amazing. I signed up for every society I could. It was then I found a new passion – pottery. There was something calming and therapeutic about moulding a creation out of wet clay. While everyone else was busy playing the game of 'hide the sausage' – it's hilarious the way posh kids talk about sex – I was learning about different firing mediums and the effects of different slips and glazes.

The first term passed in a blur of academic excitement, punctuated by periods of sleep-deprived study. I was in my element. Mum and Mark came to pick me up at the end of term. I didn't want to leave, the thought of returning to the mundane existence of home weighing heavily on me. That was when the dark friends that occupied my head returned with a vengeance. They were not happy at being ignored. In fact, they were furious.

One evening mum sat me down and told me she and Mark were in a relationship and he was going to move in. I shrugged my shoulders and said, 'Yeah, whatever.'

My mum's influence in my life had diminished to that of a cameo role, which occurred every now and again then went away. During my first Christmas back at home, the local wood was filling up with animal graves to satisfy my growing psychosis.

Before I knew it, Christmas was over and I was back in my student accommodation. On the first morning of the new term I remember waking before my alarm and struggling to cram my sadistic friends back into their respective boxes. I needed to focus on the packed itinerary I had planned for the week. After all, being top of the class was addictive.

The years flew by and I graduated with first class honours. I won yet another prize for academic excellence, as well as receiving an award for a piece of glazed pottery that I had entered in a national competition. I'm not sure which one I was proud of most.

In the blink of an eye, my time at Oxford had come to an end. I had excelled in criminal law and enrolled on the Bar Professional Training Course immediately afterwards. Twelve months later, and a handful of plaudits in the bag, I took a pupillage with Christie and Parsons — a well-known chamber of barristers based in London. They allowed me to defer the place for a year to join my old university professor and deliver a lecture tour in three European universities – Madrid, Berlin and Utrecht. One semester in each law school.

I was twenty-two years of age and I jumped at the opportunity. By now my pathological hatred of Pretties had crystallised into an obsession. The rigors of academia no longer kept the demons at bay and the only thing that gave me any respite was when I made pottery.

The prospect of spending ten weeks in a foreign city excited me. The prospect of repeating the experience three times over made me positively ecstatic. Not because of the opportunities they might bring. But because it was an ideal time to kill my first Pretty.

Chapter 7

I open the front door and my senses are assaulted with the aroma of lasagne and garlic bread. The hallway wall to my left is festooned with a collage of photographs, depicting a procession of law practice dinner dances and corporate events; on the wall to my right is an array of similar pictures, arcing their way up the curved staircase. A pictorial representation of our journey to success. Or that's what Elsa calls them.

The judge had called an unexpected halt to the proceedings today which allowed me to cancel my hotel and get an earlier train home. I drop my bag next to the coat stand. An evening of pottery awaits and the butterflies in my stomach have been going wild since we left London.

'Hiya, I'm in the kitchen,' Elsa calls out.

I follow the gorgeous smell to where she is standing at the worktop preparing green salad in a bowl. She turns her head and flashes me a magic smile. Her blonde hair is piled high on her head and she's wearing an apron over her dress. I wrap my arms around her and kiss the back of her neck.

'The old duffer must have had enough and needed a lie down,' I whisper in her ear.

She spins around, not breaking my embrace and kisses me on the mouth. 'It's a lovely surprise, I wasn't expecting you home tonight,' she kisses me again. 'Why don't you get changed and we can have dinner before you disappear to your shed.'

'I keep telling you it's not a shed.' I fake outrage at the suggestion then pat her on the arse and head upstairs. The bed is made up with fresh linen and the duvet cover is smoothed as flat as a billiard table. A quick glance behind the headboard reveals what I already know, the polystyrene blocks are on the floor and the paint is chipped and scuffed.

I need to think of something else ...

My suit goes on a hanger to join the others in the wardrobe, and I fish a pair of jeans and a stained sweatshirt from a drawer. A faint smell of sulphur wafts towards me, a reminder that they are overdue a wash. I shrug my shoulders and pull them on then go back to the kitchen.

'Here you go,' Elsa hands me a glass of red wine. 'Dinner's nearly ready.'

I sit at the big farmhouse table, cluttered with chopping boards, knives and peelings. 'Did you have a good time last night?' I ask.

'Oh, it was the best. That Sea Bass was amazing,' she replies, clearing away the debris and wiping the surface with a cloth.

'I meant Callum.'

'Ah, Callum,' she breathes his name with a theatrical sigh and dips at the knees.

'I wondered if—'

Elsa puts her finger to my lips preventing me from finishing the sentence. 'Are you sulking? Is my husband having a sulk?'

'I just thought…'

'You can have him when I've finished. And besides, you've not long had someone to play with. Don't be greedy.'

She plants a kiss on my lips and forces her tongue into my mouth. I grasp the back of her head and kiss her hard. She pulls away and returns to the oven, opening the door; a puff of steam escapes from the bubbling pot. The garlic bread is next.

'In answer to your question: Callum was great but then I don't suppose I need to tell you that?'

'No you don't. What time did he leave?'

'About one o'clock this afternoon.'

Elsa puts the hot dishes on table mats and hands me a serving spoon. I dig out a slab of lasagne and put two pieces of bread on my plate. My fingers dance against the hot, garlicky covered loveliness.

'Cheers!' Elsa holds up her glass. 'Here's to early finishes.'

Our glasses chink together.

'To coming home early to a sensational wife.'

Dinner is delicious and the conversation flows freely. I wolf down the food and we polish off the bottle of wine, then I gather my plate to put it into the dishwasher.

'I'll sort that,' Elsa says. 'You go and have fun.'

'Thanks.' I rise from the table and run my hand across her shoulders.

'Do you want sex tonight?' Elsa chirps.

'Oh, umm…'

'Thought you might like a little treat after your disappointment of last night.'

'I have to catch an early train in the morning, so…'

'How about something quick and easy?'

'Yeah, okay, that would be good.'

I open the back door and step out onto the patio. We have a large garden with a couple of fruit trees, a weeping willow next to the pond and a vegetable patch over to one side. At the back is a large brick building with a fat chimney poking at the sky from the tiled roof. It has no windows and a single door. I step inside and flick the switch. The place floods with light from the fluorescent lights hanging from the ceiling.

I have three potting wheels, two large wooden benches and my tools and formers are hung on a board on the wall. In the corner is my glazing station where I keep my oxides, slips and dyes. In the opposite corner is the kiln; a floor to ceiling box-like structure measuring six feet square with a door in the front wall. My kiln is my pride and joy. I built it by hand and it fires to a temperature of one thousand degrees centigrade. I had considered buying one but they weren't big enough.

In the other corner is my hotbox. This is where the clay is proved prior to going into the kiln. As a potter, you soon realise that moisture is your enemy and this room dries out the material. I built this as well because I wanted a room large enough for me to walk around inside. Two electric heaters provide me with a temperature-controlled environment. There is shelving on three of the walls which already have pots and plates waiting for the next part of the process.

I grab hold of the metal shelving and wheel a section of it away from the wall. Behind it is a stud wall which has been insulated to retain the heat. I take the hook, which is dangling from a ring, and slot it into the small hole; a twist to the right and the wall opens up. The room beyond is long and narrow with an open drain in the floor covered with a metal grid. The pipework below runs through a macerator to the septic tank buried at the side of the house. I hit the switch and a single bulb lights up the space. At the one end of the room is a chest freezer.

I rummage around inside and bring out a number of packages wrapped in paper and tied with string. Some are small, others large. I take them to one of the work benches and after several trips back and forth to the freezer I have seven parcels lined up.

Taking a pair of scissors, I cut the string and carefully peel away the wrapping. This is a critical part of the process as any contamination can ruin the effect. I carefully put the paper and string into a pile and walk over to the kiln and step inside. Brick shelves line the walls which are used to support the pots during the firing process. I put the paper and string onto one of the lower shelves and go back to my bench.

The remaining items are carefully placed on metal dishes. One by one I arrange them in the kiln and close the door.

I've won a number of awards for my pottery work. Whether it's vases, crockery or abstract sculptures, I always get a special mention for the quality of my glaze. It's become my trademark. Every firing is different, and every firing will produce a different glaze depending on the mixture of impurities and chemicals you paint on the clay.

Other potters have asked how I do it.

How do you achieve such a unique glaze? How do you get that glistening sheen of reds, blues, greens and purples? What's your secret?

Of course, I never tell them.

The kiln is loaded up and ready to go. I open the isolation valves, push a couple of buttons on the control panel and it whooshes into life. Fifteen minutes on full burn normally does the trick. To achieve the right consistency, it is important not to overload the process so a number of firings is required. One more, I reckon. Plus, a final blast to dispose of what's left.

Belinda Garrett was a wisp of a woman. A slip of a girl with the outward persona of butter wouldn't melt in her mouth. But Elsa told me stories to the contrary. I uncork a bottle of red from my stash in the corner, fill my glass and watch the temperature gauge rise.

With what remains in the freezer, I'll be done by ten o'clock. One more careful firing, then a final blast. That should do the trick.

Chapter 8

Malice glanced at the clock in the bottom corner of the screen — 18.20. He was cutting it fine. He swept the paperwork off his desk into a drawer, logged off and hurried from the office to find Superintendent Waite in the corridor.

Shit!

'Hey boss, how did you get on today?' His tactic was always to ask her a question first, in an attempt to stop her asking him.

Waite looked tired and irritable, an expression she carried around with her most days.

'We picked up twenty-six people. The interpreter said they were mostly Hungarian and Polish. It looks like forced labour but until we formally process them we won't know for sure.'

'Any idea on the gangmaster?'

'They haven't given up a name… yet.'

'When they do, let me know and I'll put out some feelers.'

'A few of them said they were in the building trade, doing up houses and flats. It shouldn't take us long to get the full picture. How did you get on with the missing person?'

Bollocks, I need to leave…

'I talked to her house mate and she confirmed that Belinda's disappearance is out of character. I spent the rest of the day doing the leg work on her last known whereabouts and tracking down her contacts and friends. I have a few items of interest with forensics and should get those back in the morning. Maybe that will shed some light.'

'Okay, I'll see you in the morning.'

'Night, boss.'

Malice cursed under his breath as he ran to the changing room. He stripped off and hung his clothes on a hanger, then pulled on his gym gear from this morning. A man turned up next to him wrapped in a towel and opened a locker.

'Bloody hell, Mally, that gear stinks,' he said waving his hand in front of his face.

'Cheeky bastard that's my best aftershave – Eau de Shitbag.'

'Phew. You're not on the pull that's for sure.'

'It's not my clothes they're after.'

Malice bundled the hanger into the locker and slammed the door, rushing for the exit.

'Have you got anything to be late for in the morning?' the guy in the towel called after him.

'Piss off!'

Malice ran down the stairs, out the building and fired up his car. The barrier went up and he roared away. The

Claxton Estate was fifteen minutes' drive away and he had an appointment to keep.

His meeting with Burko earlier had bothered him. Burko was old-school and not one to get into fights or arguments. So, how he came to be sporting a bruised eye and cut lip was cause for concern. He let his mind wander to when they had first crossed paths.

Malice had been a detective for nine years, moving out of uniform and into plain clothes on a whim. He quickly gained the rank of sergeant and that's where his career progression ground to a halt. After failing his Inspector's exams three times he decided to give the whole 'climbing the corporate ladder' a miss; choosing instead to sit back and enjoy the ride.

Then his life took a turn for the worse when his marriage fell apart. Looking back, he was a shit husband and a crap father. They divorced when his daughter was four years old and the pressures of maintaining a roof over his family's head while trying to keep one over his own had proved almost impossible. So, he decided to diversify.

Malice had recognised that the criminal fraternity were no more scared of getting caught and going through the judicial process than he was of opening his front door to a bunch of kids on Halloween. Suspended sentences, community service and cautions were the sanctions of choice — handed out like sweets to alleviate the burgeoning prison population. But without the resources to adequately enforce the court orders it was like getting a slap on the wrist and being sent to bed with no supper.

Malice decided that if the police weren't prepared to help him get on in life, then he had better make his own arrangements.

It was the week before Christmas when Malice decided Burko was going to be his first recruit. He'd followed him to Broadbent Avenue, a favourite location for the drug fraternity where anything you wanted was readily on sale. Even the cops knew this place was like going to *Asda*, but because it was in a rundown area, they chose to look the other way. Choosing instead to commit bodies to investigating internet hate crimes rather than keeping drugs off the streets.

Malice had never read the force's drugs strategy but figured it must go along the lines of *so long as the drugs don't have an adverse impact on 'decent' folk, all is well with the world.* And if the powers that be didn't care, he didn't see why he should either.

He'd found Burko lurking on a corner, bundled him into his car and drove him to a disused warehouse. Burko was babbling like an idiot on nitrous oxide, which on reflection he probably was.

Malice and Burko had history. Malice had nicked him on four separate occasions and in each case Burko had walked out of the station straight back onto the streets. Being arrested was nothing more than an occupational hazard, a temporary break in service.

When they arrived at the warehouse Malice had manhandled Burko inside.

'Don't, don't.' Burko had said, his knees visibly shaking.

'Don't what?'

'Don't do whatever it is you're going to do.'

Malice had walked around him watching the bloke crumble.

'I'm going to help you.'

'Eh?'

'That's right, I'm going to help you.'

'How do you mean?'

'The force is planning a massive crackdown on street dealers,' Malice lied, moving in close to Burko and getting in his face. 'This will go one of two ways. Either I will be breathing down your neck every minute of every day and effectively shut you down, or, I can feed you tit-bits of information which will allow you to stay out of trouble.'

'I don't get it.'

'It's easy, which one would you prefer?'

'The one where I stay out of trouble.'

'That's good, because that's the one I prefer too. But there's a teeny-weeny catch.'

'What?'

'I want a cut from what you take.'

'Shit, I can't do that, man.'

'The other option is I close you down.'

'Hell, man. I got people I need to report to and they aren't going to be happy.'

'That's not my problem. It's a good deal. I tell you how to keep one step ahead, your business flourishes and I get a little something in return. Simple.'

Burko took a while to process the information, then said 'yes' more times than was necessary to make the point.

And that was it. Malice's Christmas present to himself was that he had recruited his first dealer. Money in exchange for information — everybody wins. That was three years ago and now he had another five dealers under his belt. In a perverted way, Malice considered that he was depleting their ability to purchase drugs by relieving them of their hard-earned cash. In his head he was carrying out his own policing strategy, and in his opinion, this one was more effective.

Malice snapped his mind back to the present; he pulled his car over to the kerb, popped the boot open and dug out a long, filthy trench coat. He slipped it on and eyed the vast expanse of houses that made up the Claxton Estate. Even in his dirty gym gear he would be over-dressed for this locality.

He locked his car and set off. The regimented layout of the houses must have looked good when the designer drew them on a plan. Fifty years later, the estate looked like something out of an apocalypse movie. Every other property had its windows and doors boarded up with metal sheeting, not that it stopped people getting in. Gangs of teenagers on bikes hung around the street corners while others burned rubber on the road, wheel-spinning their boy-racer cars. The acrid smell of burned tyres hung in the air, a permanent reminder of where you were.

Malice turned into a back street that ran between two sets of houses. Half-way down he hopped over a wall into a garden overgrown with weeds and peppered with beer bottles. He reached the back door, prised the metal shuttering away from the frame and squeezed through.

The stench of stale drugs smacked him in the back of the throat, making his tongue stick to the roof of his mouth. He coughed and spat on the floor.

The room was in semi-darkness and Malice allowed his eyes to adjust. As they did the silhouettes of people came into view. Some were sat with their backs against the wall, others were curled up in the foetal position on the floor. He picked his way through the bodies and up the stairs. The same scene greeted him on the landing. A man and two women were slumped in a heap, each of them completely gone, each of them stinking of piss.

Malice walked through a doorway off to the left to find two men sitting in armchairs both of them smoking cigarettes. One of them had long hair drawn back in a ponytail, a goatee beard and sunken eyes. His bony knees stuck through the rips in his jeans. His jaw was moving in a cow-like chewing action. The second was heavy-set, clad in a leather jacket and jogging bottoms, his shaved head glowing white in the gloom.

The room had once been a bedroom but now had bare floorboards and yellow papered walls. There was a hole in the ceiling where the light fitting used to be and the door had long since departed. The floor was littered with discarded cigarette boxes, empty beer cans and food cartons. The ideal carpet of choice if you were planning to supply your runners with drugs and wanted ultimate deniability should the police pay a visit.

'Hey, Wrigley,' said Malice.

'Mally, I thought you weren't gonna show,' the man with the pony tail raised his hand.

'I got held up — you know how it is.'

'Yeah, you must be a busy man. How have you been?'

'Pretty good, I can't stay long.'

Malice sank down onto his haunches with his back against the wall. Wrigley didn't bother getting up. He blew plumes of smoke into the air and chomped on the lump of gum in his mouth. He leaned over and murmured something to the second guy who got up and walked out.

'I would tell him to shut the door, but...' Bullseye went out onto the landing and down the stairs.

'The neighbourhood has gone to shit,' said Malice, shaking his head.

'Okay. What do you have?'

'Lay low on the Turnbull estate.'

'Fuck, you're kidding me.'

'Nope.'

'That's my best patch.'

'That's why it's a target. Give it a few weeks and they'll move on.'

'Shit, that's gonna cost me a wedge.'

'They'll lose interest, then you can move back. You know the score by now.'

Malice had a sneaking admiration for Wrigley. Out of all the dealers, he was the one who treated it most like a business. As far as Malice knew, Wrigley was clean and didn't use any of his own product. He ran a network of twelve runners who distributed skunk, heroin, crack, meth amphetamines — you name it — to anyone who wanted to get high. It was a telephone only service, which operated like a well-oiled machine, customer service was his buzz word. *'If we make it easy, they'll come back for more. Maintaining repeat business is easier than finding new punters.'* Many a high street retailer would be jealous of his customer loyalty.

Wrigley fished out a roll of notes and tossed it over to Malice. He caught it in mid-air and stuffed it into his pocket. There was no need to count it.

An almighty crash came from downstairs and the sound of heavy boots reverberated against the wooden stairs. Two men carrying baseball bats appeared in the doorway.

Chapter 9

It was the day Antonio took flight ...

No sooner had we kicked off the first week of lectures in Madrid than my professor had to head home. A family emergency needed urgent attention and I was going to have to go it alone.

Perfect.

The university had found me accommodation in an old block of flats in the centre of the city. I had four rooms – a lounge, small kitchen, a bedroom and bathroom. The high vaulted ceilings gave the place a regal feel but the furniture and décor looked like they hadn't been touched in fifty years. The place smelled like an antiques shop.

When I arrived on my first day, two heavy oak doors welcomed me in from the street into the lobby area where a man dressed in a ridiculous bellboy outfit sat behind a desk. His main job was to nod to the people coming in and out and ogle the women. Other than carrying out those duties, I have no idea why he was there. A massive spiral stairwell corkscrewed its way through the centre of the building from the bottom to the top. A wrought iron bannister topped with a thick oak handrail wound its way skywards.

My place was on the sixth floor, Antonio a floor above.

I didn't know that was his name when I first met him; all I knew was his stereo was too damned loud. It was the third night in a row and the thud, thud, thud of his music was driving me crazy. I remember checking my watch — it was half past one in the morning — throwing myself out of bed, pulling on some clothes and stomping up the stone steps. The noise increased as I neared number 702 and hammered on the door.

Nothing happened. I hammered again.

The door cracked open to the extent of the security chain and a pair of glazed eyes stared through the gap.

'Si,' said the partially hidden face from behind the door.

'Do you live here?'

'Yes.'

'I live downstairs and your music is too loud.'

'Oh, I'm sorry,' I heard the chain being pulled across, the door opened to reveal a man dressed in a comedy smoking jacket and cravat. His long, tousled hair would be the envy of any woman, as would his large eyes and long lashes. 'You live downstairs?'

'That's right and I can't sleep with your music playing so loud.'

I heard a woman laugh and glanced over his shoulder. I could see several people in the lounge where the air was thick with smoke. The smell of something that wasn't tobacco wafted over me. The woman who had laughed flopped down onto the lap of a man sitting on the sofa. He slid his hand up her thigh and held his glass to her lips.

'I'm so sorry, darling. I had no idea. I'll turn it down.'

'Thank you.'

'I've just moved in and not seen my friends in ages so we like to... get to know each other again.'

I struggled to maintain eye contact with my oddly dressed neighbour, the sight of the woman passionately kissing the man on the sofa holding my gaze. Her legs had slipped open and his hand was up her skirt.

'This is not the first time—' I burbled.

'I know, I'm sorry. Would you like to come in?'

'No, no, I have to sleep. I have a busy day tomorrow.'

'Okay, the invitation is there if you change your mind.'

'If you could keep it down.'

My jaw must have fallen open as another man, who nestled in beside them and kissed the woman, joined the couple on the sofa. She turned and put her arm around the back of his neck, pulling him to her.

My neighbour turned to see what had caught my attention.

'Ah, like I said, we like to get to know each other again. Are you sure you won't...' he stepped away from the door and waved his arm to usher me across the threshold.

'No, I can't.' The second man now had his hand down her top. 'If you could keep the music down that would be good.'

'I will. Goodnight.' The door closed and I was left on the landing, my head spinning with what I had just seen.

The lecture programme was going well and in the third week I was invited to a drinks party hosted by the Law Society. My Spanish was improving at an exponential rate — being immersed in a foreign city will do that — and I enjoyed being in the company of the students and lecturers. So I went along.

I hadn't had cause to pay my mysterious neighbour another visit and, while the parties continued, the music was not a problem. I fantasised about what I'd seen. Every night I was sorely tempted to knock on his door on the pretext of wanting something. But my courage deserted me every time and I stayed in my flat.

I was chatting with the Head of Admissions when I spotted him across the room. He was holding court with five other people, spewing conversation and anecdotes as they rolled back with peals of laughter. His sharp suit, tanned skin and dazzling smile had those around him captivated.

A burly chap wearing a tuxedo lightly took hold of his arm and led him away to another group of people eager to make his acquaintance.

'Who's the guy in the blue suit, with the long hair?' I asked my host.

'That's Antonio Pérez.'

'I've not seen him around the university. Is he part of the faculty?'

'Ha, no. He's an actor and a model. I think he works for a famous brand. He's a guest of one of the professors. Do you know him?'

'Erm, no, I wondered who he was.' I watched as Antonio glided around the room soaking up the handshakes and kisses. His perfect smile greeted everyone the same. I sipped my drink and watched him work the room.

Then he clocked me with a casual turn of the head and our eyes locked. It took a second for me to register in his brain and when it did, he flashed me a smile and mouthed 'Hello'. He broke away from his group and walked up to me.

'We meet again.' His minder appeared carrying a furrowed look on his face. 'I didn't introduce myself last time. My name is Antonio.' He held out his hand. I took it and the touch of his soft, cool skin made me feel sick.

'My… my name is Damien.'

'Ah, like in the movie.'

'No not like in the movie.'

I released my grip.

'I've been trying to keep the noise down.'

'I know, thank you.'

'Are you a student here?'

'No I'm a—'

The shrill sound the ting-ting-ting filled the room as someone struck a glass with a spoon, before everything fell silent.

'Señoras y señores, permítanme llamar su atención. Ladies and gentlemen, may I have your attention. Please welcome our guest speaker Antonio Pérez.'

There was a round of applause.

Pérez leaned into me. I could smell his cologne.

'I have to go now,' he whispered.

He swaggered through the crowd, making his way to the front, touching the hands of the guests as he passed. He planted kisses on the cheeks of several of the women and they dipped at the knees in a mock act of swooning.

Antonio stood at the front with his arms outstretched soaking up the applause. He clasped his hands together under his chin and bowed at the waist, a well-practised move. The taste of bile filled my mouth.

I could only make out part of his speech. He spoke fast and animated and I struggled to keep up. I watched him as he played the crowd like a cheap whistle. One hundred smiling faces beaming back at him, confirming what Antonio knew all along — he was fucking wonderful.

It was my last day in Madrid. I wrestled my bags across the landing into the lift and down to the lobby where a taxi was waiting to take me to Barajas Airport. It was seven thirty in the morning and the rush hour traffic was building. The driver helped to load the bags into the boot and we set off.

'Parada aqui, he olvidado algo,' I yelled. The driver slammed on the brakes not happy with being told to stop because I'd forgotten something.

I apologised again and dashed from the cab, around the side of the block of flats to a set of wrought iron stairs bolted to the back of the building. The fire escape creaked and groaned as I made my way to the seventh floor. I had to catch my breath at the top. I was not built for this type of exertion.

The small stone was in place, exactly where I had left it, wedged in the door-jam. I slipped inside onto the top landing, walked up to number 702 and rapped on the door. I knocked again. I knew he was in because he repeated his daily routine like clockwork and always left his flat at ten-thirty to have coffee with his gaggle of lovelies. I knocked again.

I could hear the sound of shuffling feet on wooden flooring. The door cracked open.

'Si?'

'Hey Antonio. I know it's early but I've come to say goodbye.'

'Que? I mean what?' he opened the door wide. He was cloaked in a blood red silk dressing gown.

'I'm leaving and I wanted to say goodbye.'

It took a while for the message to land in his brain.

'Oh, okay, well, have a safe trip.'

He offered his hand. I refused it.

'I hope you don't mind, I've bought you a gift.'

'A gift?'

'Yes, to say thank you for turning the music down.'

'That's fine. No problem.'

I produced a crystal from my pocket. 'I want you to have this.'

'Thank you,' Antonio said, stepping onto the landing. 'There is no need for you—'

'I want to. Please come and look.' I stepped back against the bannister and held the crystal up to the light flooding through the glass dome above us. 'When the light passes through it, the colours are amazing. See how it glints and shimmers?'

Antonio came next to me and peered up at the crystal as I rotated it between my fingers. Shards of red, blue and green light danced across my fingers.

'It's very beautiful,' he said.

'It's pretty, just like you.'

I bent down, wrapped my arms around his knees and heaved for all I was worth. Antonio tipped sideways and his chest slammed into the wooden handrail.

'Aghh!' he yelled. 'What are you—'

His hands flailed in the air, not knowing whether to grab the bannister or me. I drove hard with my legs and he tipped over the top.

He made the entire journey to the floor below in compete silence. Landing on the tiled floor below with a slap that echoed through the stairwell. I ran to the fire escape and hurtled down the steps to the waiting taxi. My heart was thumping in my chest and by the time I reached the ground I couldn't speak.

The taxi driver was huffing his displeasure as I slid across the back seat.

'Perdone,' I rasped as the car lurched away from the curb. I opened my hand.

The crystal looked dull and lifeless — much like Antonio.

Chapter 10

I only harvest the best parts to make my glaze. Don't get me wrong, in every case the victim is a Pretty who deserves to die, but even Pretties have features that stand out above the rest. It might be their eyes, their hands, their feet, their lips, their genitals — the prettiest parts are the ones I treasure the most.

But they need to be collected when the victim is alive to achieve the maximum effect. I've tried taking them once the last vestiges of life have been extinguished from their bodies but it's never the same. To the uneducated observer, there is no discernible difference in the end product but I know... I know there's a difference.

The prettiest parts — or 'packets of joy' as I like to call them — are fired in the kiln and their ashes lovingly collected. It's essential to control the temperature and the time, it's easy to reduce them to nothing. The heat and duration of the fire must be precise to produce the desired results.

Once processed, they are mixed with other compounds to produce my signature glaze. The glaze that sets me apart from other potters. The glaze that makes the other competitors ask: *how do you do that?*

The timer goes off on the kiln, closely followed by the one on my phone. I always take the precaution of setting two. I would hate to over-cook my packets of joy. The valves close and I open the vent. There is a hissing sound as the heat rushes into the night. I watch the temperature gauge plummet and sip my wine.

The temperature has dropped sufficiently for me to open the door; the residual heat from the bricks hitting me in the face as I enter. I'm wearing heavy welding gloves and pick up the metal plates, returning to my work bench and arranging them on a thick asbestos tray. There are six in total and I put the tray into the proving room to cool down.

There are three more small packages left in the freezer. I enter the narrow room and fish them out. Belinda Garrett is next to me, suspended from a winch in the ceiling. Her body white and motionless, the stumps at the end of her legs where her feet had once been hovering eighteen inches above the grill. I poke her with my finger and she swings back and forth. The butcher's hooks in her back support her weight easily now she's drained of blood, and minus a few body parts.

I look into her face. She was once strikingly beautiful. The type of natural beauty that ripped the breath from your lungs when you met her. At least, that's what happened to me. Elsa did the same when Belinda slipped her arm around her waist and kissed her on the neck.

We used to meet Belinda in a hotel. It was always the same arrangements. We would arrive on a Saturday and book into our room. Belinda would check into the room next door and the adjoining door was our conduit of pleasure.

I would order room service of oysters and champagne and we would sit and chat while gorging our fill on both. That was until Elsa could wait no longer and started gorging herself on Belinda. As much as Elsa likes men — and she certainly likes men — the prospect of bedding a woman always fills her with an animal-intensity she finds hard to control.

I remember on one occasion we were sitting in our hotel room in mid-conversation when Elsa launched herself at Belinda, pawing at her body and tugging at her clothes. The two of them writhed around on the sofa oblivious to the fact I was there and equally oblivious to the spilled wine pooling on the cushions. After several minutes of kissing and groping, Elsa took Belinda by the hand and led her into the other room, banging the door shut, leaving me to finish the rest of the meal. I remember looking at my watch. It was at half past two in the afternoon — they fucked each other to a standstill for hours. At six-thirty Elsa re-emerged through the adjoining door completely naked.

'We're starving,' she said, walking across the room and kissing me hard on the mouth. I could taste Belinda on her lips.

'You probably need carbs. How about burger and chips?' I said.

'That would be great. And more Champagne.'

I glanced through into the other room to see Belinda sitting up in bed. In a theatrical gesture she swept the covers back to reveal her lean body and opened her legs giving me an eyeful. Elsa smiled and kissed me again.

'Give us a knock when it arrives,' she winked and re-joined her lover. Pretty soon the sound of gasps and groans were coming through the walls. My cock was as stiff as a fireside poker but I wanted to save myself for later.

Elsa had a fixation for Belinda for longer than I would have wanted. Then one day she gave me the signal, which meant she had finished with her and it was my turn.

It wasn't difficult to see why Elsa was so captivated. Belinda was a complete fucking airhead with nothing to contribute other than the way she looked and the way she could make my wife scream in bed.

As I stare into her face, it is important to remember Belinda had been strikingly beautiful. But now a hole in the middle of her face, where her aquiline nose had once been, and her exposed teeth give her head a screaming-skull look, now her pouting lips have been removed. Her fingers were long and slender like a pianist. I severed each one using garden secateurs and rolled them into neat paper packages.

I'm not sure what made it perfect, but Elsa always told me that Belinda had the perfect arse. So, I sliced her buttocks from her body and put them in the freezer. Packets of joy waiting to be used.

The rest of the carcass is no use to me. Sure, her breasts are nice and her legs are delightful, but they aren't her prettiest parts.

I press the button to lower Belinda into the wheelbarrow. Then unclip the carabiners, leaving the hooks in her back and wheel her across the room to the kiln. I heave her up and attach the hooks to two metal rods secured to a hoist in the roof of the kiln. I run the chain through my hands and she unfolds herself from the confines of the barrow.

Belinda looks very sorry for herself hanging there. I walk out, close the door and press the buttons. The kiln fires up.

I cross to my workbench and set the timer on my phone. I've cast a fabulous vase for a competition coming up next month and the glaze has to be exquisite. My confidence is high. Belinda Garrett was an exquisite Pretty.

Elsa comes in.

'Hey, how's it going?' she asks.

'Good, I'll be finished in an hour.'

'Any more of that wine left?'

'Sure.'

I fetch another glass, top it up and hand it over.

'Cheers!' Elsa chinks my glass and slurps a large slug of wine. She pushes me back into my chair and puts her glass on the table. Then she leans over me with her hands on my thighs and kisses me. 'I feel guilty about last night so I want to make it up to you.'

Elsa kneels between my legs and tugs at the buttons of my jeans.

'I thought you said…'

'I know but I thought you might like a starter before your main course.'

As I watch the temperature gauge rise, Elsa goes to work on my cock. It's not long before both are in the red.

Chapter 11

The first guy charged into the room hard and fast, wielding his bat. Wrigley flew at him, catching the attacker in the chest with his shoulder. Both men toppled over in the corner, a solid thud echoing around the room as the attacker's head thumped into the wall.

The second guy barrelled in swinging his bat at nothing. Malice was still sitting with his back against the wall, below his eyeline.

Wrigley jumped to his feet and was just about to stamp on the guy on the floor when the second attacker flattened him with a swing that smashed into his shoulder. Wrigley was once more lying on top of the man in the corner.

The second man raised the bat above his head, taking aim. Malice lashed out with his boot and swept the man's legs from under him. He cartwheeled in the air and crashed down to the floor, spilling the bat. Malice lurched forward and punched him twice in the face but the man brought his knee up, catching Malice on the side of his head. The blow sent him tumbling backwards.

Wrigley was rolling around trying to claw himself away from the man lying in the corner. The second guy found his bat and brought it down hard on Wrigley's arm. He screamed in pain.

Malice had regained his feet and launched a haymaker at the man with the bat. His fist slammed into the side of his jaw, causing the man's head to snap to the side. He crumpled into a heap.

The first guy was now on his feet having recovered from his bang on the head and ran at Malice with his head down. Malice caught him in a headlock and dropped to the floor. The man's head bounced from his grasp as it slammed into the wood. It was unlikely he would be recovering from the impact anytime soon.

Malice rushed over to Wrigley who was thrashing around, groaning.

'Fucking hell!' Wrigley clasped his right shoulder.

Bullseye appeared in the doorway, blood running down his face. 'You okay?' he asked.

'Yeah, but Wrigley got knocked about.' Malice wiped blood from his eye. 'Who the hell are these guys?'

'I don't know,' Bullseye replied, kneeling beside his boss.

'Fuck!' Wrigley yelped, heaving himself to his feet. He rushed across to the attacker laying like a starfish on the floor and kicked him in the balls. The inert figure didn't budge. 'You need to leave,' Wrigley said, nodding at Malice.

'You might want to get that looked at,' Malice replied, surveying the scene. He pulled out his phone and took a photograph of each of the attackers, then riffled through their pockets and came up empty.

'All in good time,' replied Wrigley. 'Firstly, you need to go.'

'I have my car nearby, I can drive you.'

'You've helped enough. I got it from here.'

'And you have no idea who these guys are?'

'Nope. Never seen them before. Now, let me take care of business.'

'Okay.' Malice held up his hands. 'I'll see you around,' He left the house by the same way he came in. His eye hurt and his knuckles were bruised. He sat in the car and twisted the rear-view mirror to get a better look.

'Bollocks!' Malice viewed the cut to the side of his right eye and explored it with his fingers; not too deep, wouldn't require a stitch. He pulled a cloth from the glovebox, rolled it into a ball and pressed it to the wound. He had a visit to make and turning up with blood running down the side of his face would not be good. He glanced at the box sitting in the footwell wrapped in pink paper and glanced at the clock.

Oh shit!

Forty minutes later Malice pressed the doorbell on the semi-detached property. The curtains were drawn in the bay window but the house lights were on and her car was in the drive. He checked his watch and cursed under his breath. The curtain to his right twitched.

He saw the fluted image through the glass of a person approaching the door. The safety chain was disengaged and the front door opened. The woman standing before him was dressed in jeans and a T-shirt with nothing on her feet. She was a year younger than Malice.

And for the second time today, he was greeted by an angry woman.

'You gotta be joking?' she said.

'Sorry, I got held up.'

'For Christ's sake, Khenan. It's a bloody school night. She's in bed.'

'I bought her a present,' he said, offering up the pink box like he was showing a piece of evidence.

'A present that should have been here ages ago. I thought you were coming round for tea?'

A tiny recollection went off in his head, one where he said he'd be there at five o'clock for birthday tea and cake.

Fuck it!

'Sorry. Something cropped up.'

'I don't believe you,' she said, turning on her heels and heading back through the hallway, leaving the front door wide open. Malice got the message and followed her inside.

It was strange to think about it now but there was a time when he and Hayley had been happily married. Five years they had stayed together but then the cracks in their relationship became chasms and the disagreements became stand-up rows. The biggest point of contention was Hayley wanted kids and Malice didn't — and there's not a great deal of compromise available to resolve that one.

Then one day Hayley announced she was pregnant. She swore it wasn't a trap, pleaded with him that it was an accident. But it signalled the decline. Their marriage probably would not have run the course but by the time Amy arrived, it was dead in the water.

Malice shuffled into the lounge. Hayley was sat on the sofa with her arms crossed, legs crossed, kicking her foot out like a metronome. It was a position he knew only too well. Birthday cards lined the mantelpiece and the window sill.

'Look at the state of you,' Hayley said, waving her hand in his direction. 'You turn up four hours late looking like you've been in a brawl.'

You were never normally that perceptive…

'I'm sorry, we had an incident at work.'

'There's always a fucking incident at work,' Hayley snapped back before resuming her pissed off position.

He fingered his eye and could feel a new trickle of blood. 'Do you have a plaster?'

'Oh, bloody hell.'

Hayley jumped from the settee and stormed into the kitchen. Malice wandered after her. She rummaged around in a cupboard and brought out a green first aid kit. Malice sat at the kitchen table and unpacked the box, eventually finding what he was looking for.

'How have you been?' he said cutting a plaster into thin strips.

'Amy was upset you didn't show.'

'Sorry. What did you tell her?'

'I told her you'd been held up catching bad guys at work. What else do you tell a six-year-old?'

'Thanks. I'll make it up to her.'

'You really are a piece of shit.'

Hayley swept past him into the other room. Malice peered at his reflection in a small mirror and applied the strips of plaster to the cut. He smoothed them into place and returned to the lounge. Hayley had resumed her foot kicking protest.

'Can I go up and see her?' he asked.

'No you—'

'Daddy!' Amy thudded down the stars, then raced into his arms. Malice scooped her up.

'I heard a little princess had a birthday today. You don't happen to know who it is, do you?'

Hayley sprang from the sofa and huffed her way into the kitchen. He could hear the kettle being filled from the tap.

'It's me, daddy, it's me!' Amy squealed as he swung her around.

'That's good because I've got a pressie for you.'

She squealed some more. Malice put her down and handed over the pink box. It had taken him ages to wrap the damned thing and it took Amy seconds to demolish it. Inside was a talking doll that wet herself, along with a hair dressing kit and a tea set. It was just what she wanted.

Malice spent the next twenty minutes playing with his daughter on the floor, making tea and brushing hair.

'Come on it's time for bed,' Hayley interrupted.

'Aww, mummy, can't I stay up and play some more?'

'No you have school in the morning. You can play with it tomorrow.'

'But daddy won't be here tomorrow.'

'Come on, time for bed.'

Malice lifted her up and carried her upstairs, hugging the doll tight to her chest. He kissed her goodnight and left the door slightly ajar.

He popped his head into the sitting room. 'I'll be off then.'

'Yeah, that's right. You show up four hours' late, give her a present, play with her for thirty minutes and then I'm the bad mummy for making her go to bed.'

'I'll give you a call,' he said as his fingers touched a fresh trickle of blood running from his eye.

'Whatever. You really are a piece of shit.'

Chapter 12

It was the day Elsa showed me what I'd been missing…

The first time I set eyes on her, a bomb went off in my head. Her silver-blonde hair was cut into a stylish bob with the ends flicked forwards to accentuate her jawline. Her translucent skin seemed to have an iridescent quality under the lights. She was utterly stunning.

I plucked up enough courage and walked over to her. Her smile knocked me back on my heels.

She asked my name and what I wanted, which was an odd experience for me. Women like her tended to ask what the fuck I was doing talking to them and were never interested in what I'm called, let alone what I wanted. We sat and chatted for what seemed like an eternity.

She said her name was Brie and she lived on the other side of the city. My finely-tuned senses told me she was lying — on both counts. She said she spoke four languages which was true because they were the same four I could speak fluently ——English, Dutch, German and French. But none of that mattered. I drowned in her electric-blue eyes as the conversation flowed.

When it was time for me to leave, I asked for her number and she was elusive. I didn't want to spoil things by pushing my luck. She said we could meet next week, if that's what I wanted. I let her know I'd be delighted to, then kissed her softly on the cheek as I left. The scent of her perfume floated me away.

The following Saturday we met again. She was just as beautiful and I had dressed up for the occasion. We talked and talked. She was keen to know more about me and where I had come from, but she was most interested in my aspirations for the future. No one had ever been that interested in me before, especially someone as gorgeous as Brie. She quizzed me hard about my work and my connections, her intensity forcing the air around us to crackle.

I had taken the unusual step of booking a hotel nearby so I could see her on the Sunday as well. I tentatively asked if she would like to have dinner. She declined, putting her hand on my arm. My skin fizzed beneath her touch.

I hardly slept that night and saw her the next day. She had a whole new set of questions to fire at me. I was spellbound.

I saw her the following weekend and the one after that. Then one Monday morning, when I was ten minutes into my nine a.m. lecture, I saw her sitting in the centre of the fifth row. The lecture theatre must have had one-hundred and twenty students in it, each one scribbling away, hanging onto my every word. She sat with her hands folded on the desk, staring at me. Our eyes locked and she smiled. My heart went into overdrive and beat so hard in my chest that I was sure the thud, thud, thud could be heard through the microphone on my lapel.

This was my fifth week delivering criminology lectures at Utrecht University and seeing her completely knocked me off my stride. She had never been there before and her presence had me burbling and blundering through my material. All the while she sat there, not taking any notes, just smiling. I tried to tear my gaze away and focus on the other students, but each time I did, my gaze was drawn back to her blue eye shadow. I couldn't break free from her spell. I couldn't catch my breath.

The rest of the lecture flew by in a blur and before I realised it, it was time to pack up. The lecture theatre emptied out, all except Brie who had made her way down to the front and was leaning against the front row.

'Hi,' she said. 'I'm sorry if I made you lose your place.'

'Err, well, I have to admit, seeing you there did kind of throw me.'

'I saw that.'

'It usually goes a lot better.'

'It was interesting. I enjoyed it.'

I filled my bag with notes. 'It's… it's a lovely surprise to see you.'

'Looks like it was more of a shock,' she said, cracking another smile before tilting her head to one side. 'Why don't you let me buy you a coffee to say sorry?'

'Sorry for what?'

'For turning up unannounced. And besides, you look as though you need one.'

'Yes, that would be nice. My next lecture is this afternoon. I could buy you lunch.'

She glanced up at the clock mounted on the wall. 'Don't you think it's a little early for lunch?' The clock read 10.05 a.m.

'Oh, yeah, sorry I lost track of time.'

She pushed herself off the desk and nodded towards the door.

'Come on, let's grab a coffee.'

I followed behind her like a lapdog on our way to the cafeteria.

'You get a table and I'll bring it over,' she said, joining the queue and tapping the shoulder of the young man in front. 'Hi,' I heard her chant as he turned around and embraced her.

Utrecht has a student population of twenty-nine thousand and it looked like they'd all decided to congregate in the cafeteria at the same time. The place was heaving with bleary-eyed people trying to get a big enough fix of caffeine to help them through the morning. I found a table against the wall and dragged over two chairs. My pulse was racing.

What the hell is going on?

I tried to get a grip of myself but was failing. She appeared out of the throng with two coffees in takeaway cups.

'I didn't know what you wanted, so I got a filter coffee,' she said, settling into the seat opposite. I found myself staring at her as she played with her hair, tucking it behind her ear.

'That's fine, thank you,' I replied.

'You should drink. You'll feel better. I promise.'

I took her lead and swigged from the cup. She was right. It did go some way to setting my nerves.

'What's your real name?' I asked.

'Elsa.'

'Do you study here or do you have a weird hobby of showing up at random lectures?'

'I'm in my final year reading politics and economics.'

'I'm—'

'You're on a lecture tour having completed two stints at universities in Madrid and Berlin. This is your fifth week and you have another four weeks before you return to the UK.'

I raised my eyebrow.

'Someone has been doing their homework.'

'I'm nothing if not thorough.'

I held up my cardboard cup in a silent cheers. She did the same.

'How long have you been...' I left the sentence unfinished.

'A sex worker? A few years now. The money is good. It more than covers my rent.'

'Have you always worked in Amsterdam?'

'No, I've worked all over. But while I'm in Utrecht it's an hour away and I can more or less pick my hours.'

'I'm not surprised.'

'Not surprised by what?'

'You're absolutely gorgeous. They would have you for one hour a week if you said. You're so... so...'

'It doesn't work like that.'

I sipped my coffee.

'I feel a little embarrassed.'

'Don't be. It's natural. Buying and selling sex is a part of life.'

'You do it for the money?'

'In part, the money is important but I do it for other reasons.'

'Oh, like what?'

She leaned in close and whispered, 'I love sex.'

'But you could have any guy you wanted.'

'Maybe. But if I screwed every boy in my year group I would have the reputation of being the university bike, so I chose to take my pleasures elsewhere.'

'You like sex *that* much?' The sentence dried in my mouth.

'I do. So, for five days of the week I'm on a strict diet and then on the weekend I gorge myself stupid.'

'Do you not fancy anyone here?'

'Yeah, they are kind of alright. But they are not the right person.'

'You mean man?'

'No, I mean person. I like boys and girls.'

I spluttered my coffee. She leaned back in her seat and brought her hand up to her mouth, then giggled.

'S-sorry.' I croaked, wiping the liquid from my chin.

'You are funny,' she giggled again.

'You're not in a relationship?'

'Relationships are for people who don't know what they want.'

'So you don't have a boyf– I mean… partner?'

'I consider sex and relationships the same way they viewed marriage in the time of Louis the Fourteenth, when he was at the Palace of Versailles. Sex you can have anytime, anywhere, with whoever you want. Sex is all about enjoyment – you *marry* for power. I look at it in much the same way. I want a relationship with a person who will give me power, influence and money, loads of money. Sex I can get whenever I want.'

'That's quite an approach to life. It doesn't work that way for everyone, you know?' I said pointing a finger at my chest. As if she couldn't work it out for herself.

'It works for me. Do you feel better now?' she motioned to the coffee.

'I do, but I still feel awkward that... well... you know, I knocked at your window.'

'I don't feel uncomfortable and neither should you. But I have a question.' She leaned in and I could smell the same scent that I had done all those weeks ago when she first opened the door and beckoned me in.

'What is it?' I asked.

'In my line of work, it is usual for the men to want sex — straight sex, oral, hand-jobs, foot jobs — you name it, they want it.'

'And is that okay?'

'Yeah, that's perfectly normal. What isn't normal is for the guy to pay me over the odds to simply talk.'

'I'm sorry. I just wanted to chat. You're so lovely and I—'

'It's fine. I'm trying to explain why I joined your lecture this morning. I wanted to find you because you're different.'

'Yeah, but you're way out of my league.'

'Ha,' she laughed again. 'Give me your hand.'

'What?'

'Give me your hand.' She held hers across the table and I took it softly. My head was spinning. 'Come on.' She got up from the table.

'Where are we going?'

'You said your next lecture wasn't until this afternoon. My halls of residence are nearby.'

'I would like to see where you live.'

She giggled again as she led me away.

'You're funny.'

'Funny? What have I said now?'

She stopped and stared into my eyes.

'I don't want to show you my accommodation, silly boy. I want to show you what you could have spent your money on.'

'What?'

I lurched back and gawped at her.

'In future, there'll be no need for you to go to Amsterdam. You need to keep your money in your pocket.'

'But how will I see you again?'

Elsa pulled me in close, pushing her breasts against my chest.

'Don't worry about that… you're mine now.'

Chapter 13

Court No.1 is in full session. Tracey Bairstow is sitting in the dock with her hands clasped in her lap. She looks pale and vacant. I almost feel sorry for her... *almost*.

Her husband produced a dazzling glaze of sunburnt orange and red. I think it was his eyes that created the most dramatic effect. When they were in their rightful place they lit up the room and enchanted everyone he met. Now they adorn the surface of my vase, equally enthralling for anyone who views it.

When I dug them out of his head, his body went into spasm, shaking against the bonds holding him in place. His eyes were too delicate to blast in the kiln so I rendered them down under the grill. Elsa wasn't too happy because it stank the kitchen out and she made me promise not to do it again. If only she knew that was the third time I'd used that technique. On the other occasions, she'd been out.

The defence team have called a woman by the name of Abigale Greening. She's being presented as a character witness and a close friend to both Tracey and Brendan Bairstow. I must admit, their decision to put her on the stand is a little confusing, but I'm delighted they have.

We've made a full disclosure, so they know what's coming down the track. Maybe they think her polished performance will win the day, maybe they think the jury will believe her account of the events, or maybe someone has missed it. I don't know which one. But if it were me, I would not have her anywhere near the dock. I'm going to enjoy this.

She's coming to the end of her testimony and has spent the last twenty minutes painting a warts-and-all picture of the Bairstow's relationship. Greening was once a model and as such she understands all too well the horrendous pressures and crippling work schedules that are forced onto those in the profession. The rejection, the starvation, the punishing gym sessions, the high-octane lifestyle has been skilfully laid bare for all to see.

Greening had tears in her eyes when she described how the Bairstow's relationship was tempestuous, passionate and aggressive at times. But that was all part of the fabric that held them together. The very fact that Tracey and Brendan had stayed married for so long was a true testament to their love and devotion for one another. Tracey would never murder her husband because she worshipped the ground he walked on, He idolised her in return. Yes, there was infidelity, yes there was drink and drugs; but then no couple's marriage is the same. Through all of it they were each other's soul mates.

Greening is delivering a clever portrayal, because at no time does she excuse their bad behaviour and at no time does she seek to diminish what others might find repulsive. She is, however, delivering a plausible story of two people who loved each other so intensely that on occasions it boiled over.

'No more questions,' the defence lawyer says, nodding to the judge before sitting down. I get to my feet. Greening gives me a look that says, 'Come on then, let's have it.'

'Ms Greening, you've been a close friend of both Tracey and Brendan Bairstow for how long?'

'About ten years,' she says, returning my glare.

'You were friends with them before they were married.'

'Yes, that's correct.'

'Who were you friends with first?'

'I knew Tracey before I met Brendan.'

'Would it be fair to say you struck up a strong friendship with the defendant?'

'Yes, I think so. Tracey and I have been close for years.'

'So, when Brendan came on the scene, what did you think?'

'There was always going to be fireworks but as I stated earlier, they were made for each other. You only had to look at them to realise this was a couple who were going to go far.' She turns to the jury as if to drill home her point.

'How do you mean — go far?'

'By that I mean they were always going to be successful.'

'That's right, Ms Greening. They were, and you spotted that potential straightaway. Would you tell the court what you do for a living?'

'I own a fashion gallery.'

'How long have you owned it?'

'Coming up for six years.'

'Is it fair to say that in the early years business was tough?'

'Yes. The fashion industry is a tough place.'

'In fact, you had several lean years until you began exhibiting the Bairstow-branded products. That's right, isn't it, Ms Greening?'

'It's a good partnership. My gallery and shop are in a good location and at the time their brand was taking off, so it worked. Sometimes in business you need a bit of luck.'

'Yes, luck indeed. The Bairstow brand now accounts for thirty eight percent of your revenue stream, doesn't it?'

'Yes, something like that. I couldn't tell you the precise figure.'

'Well, let me remind you. In your last set of company results your relationship with Tracey and Brandan Bairstow was worth over eight hundred and forty-five thousand pounds. That's a lot of money, Ms Greening.'

'Yes, it is.'

'What, I mean is, that's a lot of money to lose if the Bairstow brand ceases to trade.'

It's the first time I see her blink. She looks over to the defence lawyer. He's no help.

'Let me put it another way, if the Bairstow brand goes into liquidation there's a fair chance you will too.'

'It would be a blow to the company but it would be up to me to find new business and plug the gap.'

'Plug the gap… I put it to you that if you lost their trade it would hole your company below the waterline and you would sink without trace.'

'I wouldn't put it like that.'

'I suggest that replacing almost forty-percent of your turnover, when by your own admission the fashion business is a tough place to be, would be almost impossible.'

'It would be difficult, but—'

'I want to move on, if I may, and take you back to the evening of Friday, the ninth of September last year. Do you remember it?'

'Err, no.'

'Let me refresh your memory. You were holding an event at your gallery to launch a new range of ladieswear designed by Tracey Bairstow. Do you recall the evening?'

'Yes, we hold a lot of events which is why I couldn't remember that specific one.'

'You *couldn't* remember it... okay, we'll move on. Would you like to tell the jury what took place that evening?'

'Umm, the place was packed. We had about a hundred and fifty people there. I sold some product and we took a lot of orders. It was quite a while ago.'

'Sounds like a successful night. Was the champagne flowing?'

'Yes. I think we had drinks and canapés.'

'Were Tracey and Brendan Bairstow there?'

'Yes of course they were. It was her collection.'

'Would you like to tell the court what else happened that evening, apart from making sales and taking orders?'

'Tracey and Brendan had a disagreement. They had one of their rows.'

'A disagreement. I think it was a little more than a disagreement. Let me jog your memory. Tracey and Brendan had a blazing argument which resulted in him storming out of the venue. He went out into the street to have a cigarette and calm down. Five minutes later he's joined by Tracey and the argument continues. The CCTV footage shows them screaming in each other's faces. Would you like to tell the court what happened next?'

Greening is shuffling on the spot and looking down at her shoes. They aren't going to help her. She glances up at her barrister — he's not going to help either. The judge intervenes.

'If you could answer the question, Ms Greening?' he says.

'Tracey hit Brendan.'

'Sorry, could you speak up, please?' I say to her.

'I said, Tracey hit Brendan.'

'I think she did a lot more than that. She came out of your gallery swigging from a bottle of Krug champagne and smashed it across the back of his head. That's right, isn't it, Ms Greening?'

'I don't know. I wasn't there.'

'No you weren't there, but you have seen the CCTV footage. Haven't you?'

'Yes.'

'Could you speak up again, please?'

'Yes, I've seen the footage.'

'You saw the footage because the police showed it to you when you were called to make a statement. That's right isn't it, Ms Greening?' She stares at her shoes again, says nothing. 'You seem to be struggling with this part of your testimony, Ms Greening, so let me help. Tracey Bairstow struck Brendan over the head with a bottle, knocking him to the ground. The CCTV footage shows her standing over him shouting while he struggles to get to his feet. Hardly the actions of a wife who worships the ground her husband walks on. She continues to yell at him when you appear, that's right, isn't it, Ms Greening?'

'Yes.'

'You turn up and pull Tracey away. You take the bottle from her and send her back inside. By this time Brendan is bleeding profusely from the gash he's sustained to the back of his head. You remove his jacket and ball it up to stop the bleeding then flag down a taxi to take him to the A&E department of University College Hospital where you drop him off and return to the event. Is that right, Ms Greening?'

'I don't remember.'

'Sorry, say that again.'

'I don't remember.'

'That's right, you don't remember. At this point I think it's only fair for me to confirm to the jury that you are being wholly consistent in your testimony. The day after the attack the police turned up at your house for a statement and, after consulting your lawyer, you used the phrase 'I can't remember' eight times. That's right, isn't it, Ms Greening?'

'Yes, that's right.'

'There were no charges brought by Brendan Bairstow, so there was no case to answer. Your statement was never used. But I put it to you that you were lying in that statement for the sake of your business. I put it to you that you couldn't remember what happened that night because you chose not to incriminate your friends. And by saying 'I can't remember', it let you off the hook.'

'I'd been drinking... it was late... we'd all been drinking... I was pretty out of it.'

'You said you couldn't remember finding Brendan Bairstow lying in the street; you couldn't remember ushering the defendant away from the scene and neither could you remember taking Brendan to A&E. And yet… and yet — members of the jury — Ms Greening had the presence of mind to stem the bleeding from the wound on Brendan's head; she paid for the taxi with the exact change, saying to the driver 'That will make my purse lighter'; and she then asked the driver to wait and told him, if he did, she would pay him double for the return journey. Does that sound like the actions of a woman who is *pretty out of it*?'

'It wasn't like that. I don't remember.'

'Well if you don't remember, Ms Greening, how can you be so sure?'

'I can't remember. I said so in my statement.'

'Yes, you did, Ms Greening, you did indeed. You are here in this courtroom to vouch for the loving relationship that the defendant had with her husband, so your credibility is of crucial importance. I put it to you that you've painted a picture of the relationship between Tracey and Brendan Bairstow that is simply not credible. It was a relationship scarred with ferocious outbursts of jealousy and rage. You have characterised it as being tempestuous and passionate. I put it to you that it was one where violence and abuse was commonplace; and you have done everything in your power to hide that from public view. Including covering up what happened when Tracey Bairstow attacked her husband in the street causing him to have five stitches in his head. And you've done this to protect your business interests, that's right isn't it, Ms Greening?'

'No… I wouldn't… I can't remember…'

'You have painted a picture of the Bairstow's relationship that has zero credibility and you have shown yourself to have zero credibility in this court. No more questions.'

I glance across at Tracey Bairstow. Her face is two shades paler.

Chapter 14

Malice arrived at the station suited and booted. He'd not been to the gym, choosing instead to do a little early morning cruising, looking for Wrigley and Bullseye.

The events of the previous evening troubled him, not solely because he now had a cut above his eye, but because men showing up with baseball bats was out of character with the local drug fraternity. There were occasional fights and regular disagreements, but this felt different. This felt like someone was sending a message.

He berated himself as he toured the streets. His mind was occupied with Wrigley when it really should've been concerned with letting his daughter down on her birthday. He salved his conscience by telling himself he would make it up to her. Deep down, he knew this was his first lie of the day.

Tracking down Wrigley and Bullseye was a little like trying to catch vampires. These were people who slept in the day and worked at night. Once the punters had filled their veins and lungs with their drugs of choice, Wrigley and Bullseye would often get pissed on cheap lager at five o'clock in the morning. Malice had once asked Wrigley why he did it.

'Don't you like a beer after work?' Wrigley had replied. Which seemed fair enough.

Malice had stopped to ask a couple of people if they had seen them. They shook their heads and shrugged their shoulders. Either no one had seen them, or no one was talking.

Malice marched past the door marked CID on his way to the forensics lab.

'Mally!' Waite yelled from her office.

'Yes boss?' he stopped and poked his head around the doorframe.

'Got a minute?'

'I'm on my way to forensics to see what they've turned up from the stuff I took away from Garrett's place.'

'It's not about that.'

Malice sauntered in, standing in front of her desk.

'What is it?'

'We've got a new starter and I want—'

'Oh come on boss, I've got my hands full with this missing woman. The last thing I want is for you to put me on babysitting duty as well.'

'Interesting… what I was going to say, is… I want you to meet Kelly Pietersen,'

Waite stood up and waved her hand towards the back of the room where a young woman was sitting in the corner, filling in paperwork on her lap. She was in her late twenties, dressed in a navy blue trouser suit with dark shoulder length hair pulled back in a pony tail. She looked up, put her head to one side and gave half a smile.

'Kelly's joined us and I want her to work with you on the Garrett case. As you said — you have your hands full, so I thought you could do with the help.'

Malice cast his eyes to the ceiling and held out his hand.

'Sorry, I'm Khenan Malice. Pleased to meet you.'

'Hi, I'm Kelly.' She stood up and shook his hand with a firm grip. 'Here you go ma'am, I think this is the last of them.' Pietersen handed over the completed forms.

'Thanks. I'll catch up with you in a few days to see how you're settling in,' Waite said, returning to her seat.

'Thank you, ma'am.' Pietersen turned to Malice. 'Forensics then?'

Malice nodded his head.

'Forensics.'

'Have fun,' Waite called after them as they left the office. Malice stomped down the corridor with Pietersen close behind. The silence between them was deafening.

'Who's the missing person?' asked Pietersen, determined to get off the mark.

'Her name is Belinda Garrett. Her housemate called it in. I visited the property and took away a bunch of things. Forensics rang to say they've finished with them.'

'How long has she been missing?'

'This is the fourth day.'

'Any activity on her phone, bank accounts or social media?'

'Nothing. Her housemate confirmed she's never done this sort of thing before.'

'What's her last movements?'

'I don't know. That's what I'm trying to piece together.'

'Boyfriend?'

'No one special.'

'Parents?'

'Spoke to them yesterday and they haven't seen her in eighteen months. I got the impression there'd been some sort of family feud.'

'Are any of her clothes missing?'

'The housemate said she remembers Belinda had a red overnight bag, which is not at the property. Not done a check on her clothing.'

'What happened to your eye?'

'Do you always ask these many questions?'

'Normally… yes.'

Malice shook his head and pressed on. They arrived at forensics and donned a set of coveralls.

'In here, Mally,' said a voice. They went inside to find a middle-aged man dressed like a Teletubby hunched over a large monitor screen.

'Alright Jez?'

Malice went over and slapped the man on the shoulder.

'Yeah, I'm fine.'

Malice glanced over to a large table set against the far wall. On it sat the contents of the waste bin plus the other items from the house.

'What have you got?'

'My name is Kelly Pietersen,' Pietersen forced her introduction.

'Oh hi, I'm Jez Lewis,' Lewis replied nodding his head. He got up and walked over to the table. 'There's nothing remarkable about what you brought back.'

'Where did you find them?' Pietersen asked.

'The waste bin in her bedroom and this group of post-its were attached to the fridge door,' Malice said, pointing to a collection of eight notes laid out separately to the others.

'How many are there?' Pietersen asked.

'One hundred and thirty-one. Plus, these odds and sods.' Lewis pointed to the other assorted items on the desk. 'And there's this…' He crossed the lab, perched himself on the chair and produced three printouts, each one showing a black and grey square. 'Thankfully this woman writes with a heavy hand. These pictures show the imprints of what was written on the last post-it to be taken from the pad.' He spread them on the desk. They stared at the words: *Council tax; Condoms and Mexborough.*

'What *is* all this stuff?' Pietersen asked.

'Belinda Garrett was paranoid about forgetting things,' Malice replied. 'According to her housemate she wrote notes to remind herself and, presumably, when they'd served their purpose she binned them. Hence all this…' He picked up one of the pictures and walked back to the coloured notes spread out over the desk. Pietersen joined him, then pulled on a pair of gloves and started moving the pieces of paper around.

'What are you doing?' Malice asked.

'Collating them into groups. Garrett may have been paranoid about forgetting things, but not everything, just certain things. I think there's a pattern.' Malice gazed down as Pietersen moved the notes around. 'I think these are items that she wanted to buy: *Condoms, tooth paste, milk, bread* etcetera. These are people's names: *Michael, Lucy, Chis.* There is a grouping that is about places: *Kings Cross, Hammersmith, Guilfor*d and these are things she needs to do: *Pick up dry cleaning, sort phone, call Cindy* and then there are a few that don't really fit into any group.'

'This stands out like a sore thumb.' Malice handed Pietersen the picture of the post-it note pad with the word *Mexborough* scrawled across it.

'How?'

'There were three blocks of post-it notes on the desk. The last thing written on them correspond to a note found in the bin. *Council tax* and *Condoms* are here.' Malice pointed to three squares of paper on the desk. 'But *Mexborough* is missing.'

Pietersen scanned the table and looked at the image.

'You're right.'

'What the hell is Mexborough?' Malice whispered under his breath.

'It's a place outside Sheffield.'

'How do you know that?'

'I did my degree there.'

'A degree, eh? What did you do?'

'Now who asks a lot of questions?'

Malice raised his eyebrows.

'It could be someone's name?' he said.

'More likely to be a surname.'

'Agreed.'

'Does Belinda Garrett own a car?'

'No. Her housemate said she didn't drive.'

'Mexborough isn't the only thing that stands out.'

'What else?'

Pietersen picked an item from the table and walked over to Lewis.

'Do you mind?' She sat in his seat and moved the mouse around.

'What is it?' Malice asked, still studying the table top.

'Give me a minute.' Pietersen tapped away at the keyboard and various windows popped up on the screen. After a while she sat back and studied the item in her hand. 'Take a look at this.' Malice ambled over. 'This rail ticket receipt also sticks out like a sore thumb. You found it stuck to the fridge, right?

'Yeah, I did.'

'It's for an open return to Maidenhead. It sticks out like a sore thumb because this isn't a reminder, it's dated three weeks ago.'

'Let me see.' Malice took the ticket from her hand. 'It was issued from Paddington station on the day of travel.'

'That's right.'

'Why would she keep that?'

'You're going to love this,' Pietersen said, spinning the monitor around so it was facing Malice. The screen showed a country manor hotel with ornate grounds and a grand entrance. 'Mexborough is also the name of a hotel in Maidenhead. This receipt isn't a reminder. It's a memento.'

Chapter 15

It was the day I confessed my darkest desire ...

Utrecht was fast becoming my favourite European city. Not because of its history or culture, nor because of its vibrant nightlife; it was fast becoming my favourite because Elsa lived there.

The next five weeks flew by in a blaze of sexual exploration. Having sex with Elsa was like being in a gourmet restaurant where you could choose anything you wanted from an extensive menu. Up to that point the sum total of my sexual conquests had consisted of a couple of failed attempts with members of the opposite sex and a mountain of happy endings with a stack of magazines. To Elsa, my naivety was a massive turn-on and a personal challenge.

We quickly settled into a routine. Monday to Friday, Elsa ensured that by the end of the day not a single sperm was left in my body. I would drift off to sleep drained of energy and semen. On Saturday we would take the train into Amsterdam and have lunch by the canal before Elsa started her shift. She would kiss me on the cheek and whisper, 'I'll look out for you.'

I would stand on the opposite side of the street and watch her work. A steady procession of men, each one eager to sample the silver-haired beauty, each one leaving with a glazed expression and a broad smile. She would clock me watching her and pose and pout in my direction, her teasing was relentless and it drove me to distraction.

I booked us into the same hotel I'd used before to save us travelling back and forth. On our first night we were lying in bed when Elsa announced that there was a new rule.

'We need to have an Amsterdam rule.'

'What's that?' I asked.

'I never mix business with pleasure. So there will be no sex for you tonight.' She had been tantalising me all day and it was obvious from my upright cock that this was somewhat of a disappointment.

'I don't understand?'

'I don't mix business with pleasure. You will have to wait until Monday.'

'Nice to know I'm the pleasure side of that equation.'

'Don't be silly, you're the business side. You're mine now.' It was three o'clock in the morning and she rolled over and went to sleep. I must be the only single bloke to have visited Amsterdam's red-light district on ten occasions and never once had sex.

On the last week of the lecture tour we were walking back to Elsa's place when she said, 'I've been looking into the pupillage you have lined up with Christie and Parsons when you get back to the UK.'

'What of it?'

'It's the wrong chambers.'

'What?'

'You're aiming too low. They're a second-tier firm at best, with a shabby client list and low fees.'

'But—'

'I've been doing some digging and you need to do your pupillage with Warren and Partners.'

'Ha, yeah, right! Do you know who they are?'

'They're one of the leading firms of criminal barristers in London.'

'Do you have any idea how difficult it is to get a position with them?'

'I've checked their recruitment and selection criteria and you're perfect.'

'I might be but—'

'But nothing. I called and they have unfilled places on this year's intake. You need to apply.'

'But I already have a place with Christie and Parsons.'

'You'll have to tell them you've changed your mind.'

'What if I don't get a place with Warren? Then I'll be left with nothing.'

'Okay, then don't tell them. Keep the pupillage with Christie and Parsons until you have the other one in the bag.'

'In the bag? You make it sound—'

'Stop whining. We've got work to do. They have another selection board in three weeks. That gives us enough time to get you prepared.'

'Prepared for what?'

'For the assessment centre. I'll coach you.'

'You'll coach… You're coming to England with me?'

'Of course, you're mine now.'

And that was it. Elsa found us a rented flat outside London and we moved in together. My mum was delighted that I had finally found a nice girl to settle down with. I didn't have the heart to tell her it wasn't quite like that.

Elsa was right. I breezed through the assessment centre and joined Warren and Partners. The other firm was not happy when I told them. When I mentioned their displeasure to Elsa she said, 'Did you tell them to go fuck themselves?'

'Good heavens no,' I replied.

'Shame, you should have.'

One morning, over breakfast, she turned to me and said, 'call your mum and ask her if she's free on this date.' She slid a piece of paper in front of me.

'Why? Are we inviting her over for dinner?'

'No, we're getting married.' And in true Elsa form, we did. It was a small ceremony in a registry office where Mum cried and Mark shook my hand. It was all over by lunchtime.

Despite Elsa graduating with first class honours she was adamant she didn't need a job.

'My career is managing your career,' she would say. And manage it she did. She ensured we were members of all the right clubs and societies and attended the most prestigious soirées. Soon, I was rocketing up the corporate ladder and became the youngest person to make equity partner in the firm. An achievement I bettered some years later when I became the youngest member of their

Executive Board at the age of thirty-six. A stratospheric progression which was all down to Elsa.

It was a period in my life when I would often look back at killing my first Pretty in Madrid. In my quieter moments I would drift off and watch Antonio spinning through the air, hurtling to the ground; his blood-red dressing gown flapping around his body. I still can't believe he made the entire journey down to the lobby in total silence. It was nothing like you see in the movies, that long drawn out scream until the impact. He was completely mute.

The combination of my high-octane job coupled with keeping up with my high-octane wife produced an adrenaline rush that had switched off my desire to kill Pretties. I still hated them, but my compulsion to terminate their lives had been dulled. Though as time went by I could feel that beginning to wear off. I could also sense Elsa was becoming restless. In the same way as my work had switched off my need to kill, so managing my career had negated Elsa's need to indulge herself in promiscuous sex. But now that I was at the top of my game, I knew her mind was wandering. So was mine.

One night we were sitting in the kitchen, having dinner at home when Elsa said, 'I have something to tell you.'

'Oh, what is it?'

'I need to fuck other people, is that alright?'

I reached over and took her hand.

'That's fine. I need to kill Pretties, is that alright?'

'Sounds like fun. What are Pretties?'

Chapter 16

My assault on the credibility of Abigale Greening had proved too much for Tracey Bairstow, who dissolved into floods of tears and had some sort of panic attack. Medical staff had dashed to her assistance as she crumpled to the floor. It was a magnificent performance. Mine, not hers.

The judge called a halt to proceedings and sent us home. He must have had a lunch appointment at his club or a date with his latest hooker. Either way, I'm now on the train home. The carriage is relatively empty so I have a seat. I want to surprise Elsa with a bunch of flowers that I bought at the station. It's a mix of lilies and chrysanthemums, her favourite.

My phone buzzes, it's Elsa.

'Hey, how are you? … that's good … cancelled … what today? … Oh, okay … are you alright with that? … Ha, that's a silly question … I'm on my way home, we had an incident in court … that's fine, I'll see you then … bye.'

I stare at the flowers wrapped in cellophane sitting on the table. Not sure they are going to have the same impact now. Despite this unexpected disappointment, I'm gripped with excitement.

I pass the rest of the journey answering emails and making calls. Soon the train pulls up at my station and I get off carrying my bags and the bouquet. I get into the car and travel the ten miles to my house.

'Hi!' I call out as I open the front door.

'I'm upstairs.'

I put my bags in the corner and carry the flowers up to the bedroom. Elsa is getting undressed.

'Hey honey, nice you're home early,' she struggles out of her jeans and hops across the bedroom planting a kiss on my lips.

'I brought you these.' I offer up the flowers.

'Oh, they're gorgeous. How lovely.' She kisses me again. 'Leave them on the dressing table and I'll put them in water later.' I knew they wouldn't illicit the same degree of appreciation — not now. 'I need to take a shower.'

Elsa strips naked and wanders into the en-suite. I hear the shower strike the cubicle wall. I sit on the bed and contemplate the contents of my pottery shed.

'I'm popping out for a while, won't be long,' I call out.

'Okay, see you when you get back.'

I change out of my suit and pull on jeans and a sweatshirt. I go downstairs, through the garden and into my workshop. The smell of smoke hangs in the air. I go into the drying room and examine the pieces of moulded clay, none have cracks or splits so the firing should go to plan. I pick up the Tupperware box and head out to the car.

It is a short drive to the disused quarry which is situated about a mile and a half from where we live. The wire fence that surrounds it is plastered with restricted access signs but we are so out in the wilds that no one polices it. I open up the chainmail gate and drive inside the compound.

A company used to quarry rock at the site, but that was more than twenty-five years ago and now the place has been taken over by wilderness and trees. The quarrying activity has left a gigantic hole in the ground, probably measuring four hundred yards across which over time has filled with water. I read in a geological report that it is two hundred and fifty metres at its deepest point. Not sure how they knew that, but I know it is deep enough to submerge a car.

I walk to the edge of the rim and look down the steep embankment to the water below. It is a long way down. The cars must be reaching thirty miles an hour when they crash into the water, making an almighty splash. Sometimes the windscreen shatters under the force of the impact – those ones sink the fastest.

I take the top off the Tupperware box and grab a handful of ash. I like standing in this position because no matter what the time of year, the wind is always at my back. I unfurl my fingers and Belinda Garrett takes off, sailing on the breeze across the open space. I grab another handful and release it. She floats like a cloud twisting and turning on the air currents.

I swing my arm in an arc. The entire contents of the container launches into the air. Belinda drifts and twirls on the breeze, soaring away from me to eventually land on the lake below to join the others. She was so lovely.

I take a deep breath, head back to the car and drive home where I find Elsa is still upstairs. The smell of her perfume greets me as I walk into the bedroom. She has one foot on the bed smoothing sheer stockings over her shapely legs, then stepping into black high heeled shoes. I can remember buying them for her when we were in Paris. She shimmies into a lace basque.

'Can you do me up?'

Elsa turns and I fasten the clasps at the back. She flattens it into place and sits at the dressing table, touching up her make-up. A silk dressing gown completes the look, wrapping it loosely across her body and holding it in place with a tie.

'How do I look?' she asks. The black and red lace is clearly visible above the dressing gown, the matching thong still in the drawer.

I lean in and kiss her on the cheek.

'Fucking gorgeous.' Her bright red lipstick and smoky eyes look sensational against her pale skin.

Outside I hear the sound of gravel crunching under the wheels of a car. Elsa hurries past me and down the stairs. I follow behind, breathing in the scent of her perfume.

There is a knock at the door. Elsa is standing in the lounge, waiting.

I open the door to find Callum on the doorstep.

'Hi Damien, my meetings were cancelled and I have to stick around for a couple more days, so I thought…'

'Hi, come in. Elsa told me your plans had changed.'

This is a very different Callum to the one I had let into my house eighteen hours earlier. There's no bottle of wine, only a luke-warm handshake and half a smile. He breezes past me into the living room with a hungry look in his eyes. I watch as Elsa tugs on the silk tie around her waist and her gown opens up.

Callum has none of the playful demeanour of last night. He grabs her, his hands caressing her breasts. He tries to kiss her but she shoves him back onto the sofa. Elsa straddles his lap and discards the robe. His hands are all over her.

She reaches for the buckle on his belt and looks over her shoulder. Our eyes meet and she shakes her head and mouths to me, 'See you later.'

I gaze at my wife as she is about to ride another man's cock and close the door.

One day she will say 'Yes'.

One day.

Chapter 17

Pietersen was sitting in the car outside the front of the police station, drumming her fingers on the steering wheel when Malice burst through the double doors and jumped in.

'Sorry about that. I wanted to check something before we left,' he said.

'What is it?'

'Garrett's credit card transactions—' The force of the car pulling away threw him back into his seat.

'You gotta bloody pump these service cars to get anything out of them,' she said. Malice was still trying to locate his seat belt as they flew out of the main gate onto the main drag.

'You like your cars?'

'I do,' Pietersen said shifting through the gears.

'What have you got?'

'A Porsche Boxster.'

'Nice.'

'It's second-hand but it goes well. I got it instead of a husband.'

'Oh, sorry to hear that.'

'I broke off the engagement and we split the money we'd saved. I'm happier with the car. What do you drive?'

'A Mustang.'

'That's nice.'

'I got mine instead of a wife too.'

Pietersen glanced across at him.

'Don't tell me… it's complicated…'

'Yeah, something like that. Take the next left.'

Pietersen did as she was told. Malice watched as the parade of battered houses and boarded up shops flew by the side-window.

Christ knows what she'd drive like if we had the blue lights on?

'Fine arts,' Pietersen said.

'What?'

'You asked what degree I did at Sheffield… fine arts.'

'Not what I was expecting.'

'I did a law conversion course afterwards but bailed out after the first term. It wasn't for me.'

'Why did you do it in the first place?'

'My dad persuaded me it was what I wanted to do, in truth it was always what he wanted me to do.'

'Is that when you joined the police?'

'Yup, spent three years in uniform then moved over to CID.'

'Which part of South Africa are you from?'

'Is it still that noticeable?'

'Yeah. Now and then. Plus the way you spell your surname?'

'My dad is from Durban and my mum is a Yorkshire lass. He works for the Foreign Office which took us all over the world. That's why I'm never sure where my accent is from. We spent many years in London then his last posting took him back to Pretoria where he still works.'

'And you didn't fancy it?'

'I already had a place in university, so decided to stay put. Do you know there are more foreign embassies in Pretoria than anywhere else in the world?'

'Can't say that I did.'

'Talk to my dad for more than two minutes and he'll tell you.'

Malice gave Pietersen further directions as they drove along the back roads, his eyes raking the side streets.

'This can't be the fastest route to the motorway? Where are we?' Pietersen asked, craning her neck, looking for road signs.

'I smacked it on the turnbuckle in the ring,' Malice said ignoring the question.

'What?'

'You asked me how I cut my eye. I caught it on the turnbuckle.'

'You box?'

'Yeah, since I was a kid.'

'Which gym do you use?'

'A place called Jim's Gym.'

'Not that shithole. Wouldn't catch me in there.'

'Hey, that's my mate's place,' Malice said.

'Sorry.'

Malice flashed a sideways glance.

'Do you box?'

'Yeah, since I was a kid.' She mimicked his response. 'My dad had a bee in his bonnet about girls needing to be able to look after themselves. I did karate and taekwondo but enjoyed boxing the most, so I stuck with it.'

'Which gym do you use?'

'Crosley's.'

'That's more like a dance class than a proper gym,' Malice laughed.

'Hey, I like it.'

'It's still a dance class... but you're right, Jim's place is a right shithole.'

Pietersen pulled up at a set of traffic lights.

'We have more in common than you thought.'

'Maybe. Though I'm not sure I can compete in the fine arts department.'

Malice flicked his head to the left, something catching his eye.

'I'll be back in a mo,' he said, before leaping from the car and running across the road, leaving the passenger door open.

'Where are you going?' Pietersen called after him, but he'd legged it. The lights turned green and the driver in the car behind honked. 'Shit,' she muttered under her breath while leaning across the front seat to pull the door shut. The guy behind hit his horn again. She held her hand up and shot across the junction, parking against the kerb on the other side.

Pietersen could see Malice chasing a man dressed in a yellow bomber jacket about fifty yards away. They darted down an alleyway out of view.

'What the hell are you doing?' She shook her head.

In the alleyway the man with the yellow bomber jacket was tiring. Malice grabbed him by the collar and slammed him into a roller shutter door. The man's slight frame bounced off the metalwork with a clang.

'Fucking hell, Swivel, don't do that,' Malice panted.

'I didn't know it was you Mr Malice, honest.'

'You sure about that, cos I reckon you've been avoiding me.'

'Honest Mr Malice. I've been busy that's all. New territories and all that.'

Malice forced his forearm under Swivel's chin. 'If I thought you were giving me the run around, you and I would fall out. You know that, right?'

Swivel's head was forced back into the corrugated metal. His eyes rotated wildly in their sockets. 'I know that, Mr Malice. I know that.'

'I've been meaning to bump into you because I have information that might be of interest.' Malice released his grip. Swivel's facial tick was going berserk, an affliction that made his eyes roll around in his head when he was under stress. Which, when Malice was within arm's reach, happened most of the time.

Swivel dug into his coat pocket and pulled out a bundle of notes. He thumbed five twenties from the roll and handed it over. Malice put the money in the front trouser pocket.

'It's good to see you, Mr Malice,' Swivel lied.

'You might want to give Fitchmore Place a miss, it's gonna get a little busy over the next week or so.'

'Thank you, Mr Malice. I'll do that.' Swivel was calming down and so were his eyes.

'If I thought for one minute you were pissing me about, Swivel.' Malice grabbed a handful of the yellow jacket and pinned him against the door. Swivel's eyes did a loop-the-loop. Malice released his grasp. 'Be lucky.' Malice slapped Swivel on the cheek and walked away. 'And next time... don't run.'

Malice made his way back to the car and slid into the passenger seat.

'Let's go.'

'Are we heading for the M4 now?'

'Head back the way we came.'

'You going to tell me what that was about?' Pietersen said, spinning the car around in the road.

'A spot of business, that's all.'

'Do all your business associates run away from you?'

'Only the ones who need to.'

Pietersen nosed the car into the tree-lined driveway of The Mexborough Hotel. It was a grand stone building located in its own grounds five miles outside of Maidenhead. The lawns had been manicured to death and a set of steps led from the car park to the entrance.

'Belinda Garrett lives in a rented house-share. A bit different to this place,' said Malice raising his eyebrows.

'Do you think someone else was paying?'

'I don't know, let's find out. Hey before we go...' Malice opened the door then stopped. 'I just wanted to say, I hope we didn't get off on the wrong foot earlier?'

'We? I'm pretty sure I didn't,' she replied, before getting out of the car and marching inside.

A huge crystal chandelier hung from the vaulted ceiling in reception and a red carpeted stairway curved majestically to the first floor. Lavish furnishings of polished oak and red push-button velvet gave the place the feel of an auction room before the sale. A young man was standing behind a desk sporting his best smile.

A sharply dressed couple walked by; the man with his arm around his partner's waist, whispering in her ear. The woman reeled away, slapped him on the shoulder and giggled.

'Bet they're not married,' Malice said as the couple skipped upstairs hand in hand.

'They're both wearing wedding rings.'

'Not married to each other, then.'

'Can I help you?' the lad behind the desk asked, still beaming. His name badge read David Merchant.

Malice flashed his warrant card.

'DS Malice and DC Pietersen, I wonder if you could answer a few questions.'

'Oh, err, I'll try.'

It was obviously not the response he was expecting.

'We believe this woman may have stayed here about three weeks ago. Do you recognise her?' Malice slid the photograph of Belinda Garrett across the counter. Merchant looked at the picture and screwed his face up.

'No, I've not seen her. I can ask my manager if you'd like?'

Malice nodded and Merchant disappeared through a door to the side. Pietersen pointed to the list of room tariffs displayed on the wall behind the desk. The top one read: Standard Double £250 — excluding breakfast. The remaining rooms progressively more expensive.

'Bloody hell,' Malice said.

There was the sound of a muted conversation taking place in the other room, then a woman came out.

'I'm Anna Robbins, the duty manager. David said you had a question?'

'Do you recognise this woman, she might have stayed with you three weeks ago?'

'Yes, that's Chelsea Campbell. She and her parents stay with us from time to time, they're a lovely family.'

Chapter 18

It was the day I asked a stranger to screw my wife ...

'Sounds like fun.' Elsa had said. Three words that brought music to my ears and set my heart racing.

We spent the next hour sitting at our kitchen table and drinking red wine while I poured out the dark recesses of my soul. I told her about my dad and the body parts hidden in the house; about my pathological hatred of Pretties and how I'd killed Antonio while on the lecture tour. I told her about my need to kill others and how I was struggling to keep it under control. It was bubbling to the top.

She listened, her eyes burning with excitement. When I finished, I waited for the howls of sickening protest. None came.

Elsa squeezed my hand and said, 'It's alright, you're mine now. We can fix this.' I nodded but had no idea what that meant.

Then it was her turn.

In typical Elsa style, she described her hierarchy of needs in clinical fashion. It was a starkly different list to the one developed by Maslow and a damned sight shorter: at the number one spot was wealth followed in close second by power. Her rationale being if you have those two in place, the rest would follow. I asked her how she satisfied her need for power when she had no job. Her answer was simple: 'I have power over you.'

I was expecting her to say that her third driving force was sex. 'It isn't,' she said shaking her head. 'Sex is an enabler. It enables me to get what I want — though I have to admit, it feeds my soul. That's what's lacking in our relationship and I need to get that back. I need to fuck other people.'

'I'm not enough for you?'

'Oh, honey, you never were. But the question you need to ask yourself is 'Am I enough for you?''

'Of course you are, in every way.'

'And you want to make me happy, don't you?'

'Yes.'

'Then let me sort this out.'

'But how?'

Elsa got up, came around to my side of the table and kissed me hard.

'As you Brits are fond of saying – we can eat our cake and have it.'

It was almost right – I knew what she meant.

The first guy's name was Patrick — a thirty something ex-rugby player who worked as a marketing manager for a soft drinks company. Elsa had chosen well. He had a beautiful smile, a well-honed physique and a wicked twinkle in his eye.

I arrived home one day from a pottery exhibition to be greeted by Elsa on the doorstep and an unknown car parked in the drive. She was dressed in a short summer dress, stockings and high heels. The lace around her stocking tops flashed when she walked.

A cascade of thoughts rattled around in my brain.

Had I missed something? Was I to be treated to Elsa's latest bedroom fantasy. And what the hell is that car doing there?

'I've been waiting for you to get home.' She tottered over and kissed me. The smell of her perfume set my head in a spin.

'Sorry, we finished later than expected.'

'Come inside, I have a treat for you.' Elsa took me by the hand and led me into the house. She paused in the hallway and planted a kiss on my cheek. 'I hope you like it,' she said, ushering me into the lounge.

'This is Patrick,' she announced.

'Oh, hi Patrick,' the look on my face must have said it all.

He rose from the sofa and shook my hand.

'Hello Damien, Elsa has told me so much about you.'

'She has?' I asked.

'I wanted to surprise you,' Elsa wrapped her arm around Patrick's waist. 'Don't you think he's pretty?'

'I'd prefer the word handsome,' Patrick said, giving us the benefit of his pearl white teeth.

I looked at Elsa's beaming face. The penny dropped.

Patrick was indeed handsome. He was a glorious specimen but he was not a true Pretty. He carried the air of a man who was blessed with good looks but one who had worked hard for his position in life. His gold wedding ring suggested Patrick was an upstanding family man who just happened to enjoy screwing other men's wives. Well... I couldn't hold that against him. Nobody's perfect.

I had to give my wife ten out of ten for effort, but a Pretty he was not.

Elsa coiled herself around him as they sat together on the sofa. Her stocking tops were now generously on display and, with me still in the room, it was obvious Patrick wasn't sure what to do next.

Elsa peeled herself off him and came over to me. She whispered in my ear.

I baulked.

'You want me to say what?' I asked.

'You heard me.' Elsa returned to the sofa, squeezing herself against our guest. I cleared my throat.

'Patrick,' I said. 'I want you to fuck my wife.'

He looked at me, then at Elsa, and then back at me. Elsa took his hand and slid it up her leg until it was buried beneath the hem of her dress.

'Off you go,' she said to me, making a shooing motion with her hand.

Patrick was our first, a good start but he was a long way short of being a Pretty.

That heralded a procession of men eager to screw my wife. Elsa had enrolled in a Swingers website designed to facilitate introductions between likeminded people. It was an exclusive club which prided itself on quality of service and ultimate discretion. I had to admit the blokes who walked through our door were indeed top quality, but then the fifteen hundred pounds a year subscription fee did have the effect of keeping the riff-raff at bay.

Elsa threw herself into her new hobby with a passion. Her infidelity had been re-awakened and she was making up for lost time. She had created a profile on the site which showed her in all her glory and under the section titled: 'Things I enjoy', was every item in the drop-down menu plus a number of things that weren't. We were listed in the couple's section and under my profile, all it said was 'Successful professional, does not participate.' Which summed up my position perfectly.

We met men and women in hotels as well as at our house. We never visited their homes because these were 'clients' who preferred to fly solo rather than get their other halves involved.

This immediately had the advantage that the 'clients' were screwing Elsa in secret. A perfect cover for what was to come next. The problem was, while she was happily getting laid every which way, none of them qualified as Pretties.

That was until Christian came along ... by accident.

I was working in London and Elsa had decided to join me to update her wardrobe along Oxford Street. A complex case was coming to an end and I'd chosen to stay over rather than face the tedious commute.

The hotel where we were staying was hosting an event — for the life of me I still can't remember what it was — all I know was the place was rammed with well-heeled people of both sexes, each one trying to outdo the other on the glamour scale. I'd arranged to meet Elsa for a drink in the hotel bar after work. As usual I over-ran and by the time I arrived, she was half way down a bottle of Chablis.

The bar was more like a speak-easy with high winged back chairs and comfy sofas arranged in intimate clusters around the room. The bar was decked out in oak panelling and Tiffany lamps, and the heavy dark wood bar stools should have come with a portable step to allow people to take a seat. A man in a white shirt and bow tie patrolled the optics and the crystal glasses. The room smelled of furniture polish and cologne.

I joined Elsa who was perched on a bar stool sipping her wine. A man in his thirties was the only other guest in the bar, sitting on his own in a red leather armchair. He was dressed in a dinner suit, twirling his beer glass round and round on the table in front of him.

Elsa kissed me on the cheek and I helped myself to the bottle in the ice bucket.

'Cheers,' she said holding up her glass.

'Sorry I'm late.'

'That's fine. I've been having fun.'

'Oh?'

'I think I've made a friend.' Elsa stared past my shoulder at the young man in the dinner suit.

'How come?'

'We've been keeping each other amused.'

I glanced back and he held my gaze.

'Really?'

'His eyes have been all over me.'

'Can't blame him.'

Elsa leaned into me and said, 'you're blocking his view.'

It was then I noticed Elsa was sitting with one foot on her bar stool and the other on the stool next to it. She was wearing her favourite 'little black number' which fitted where it touched, drop earrings and pearls. From his seated position the young man was being treated to a generous view up her skirt. I moved and sat on the stool to her left. We both stared at the young man and he shuffled in his seat. Elsa hitched her skirt a little higher. I sank my glass and refilled it.

The man downed his beer and smiled back. His floppy hair was swept casually across his forehead and his square jaw and dimpled chin gave him the look of a Hollywood leading man. He exuded the casual elegance of a man used to wearing expensive clothes and being admired for doing so.

I recognised the smile immediately. It was the smile of entitlement. The smile of self-satisfaction that said, 'I don't have to chase life, life comes to me.' The smile that told me everything I needed to know.

Elsa slid from the stool, straightened her skirt and sashayed over to him. He sank back into his chair and puffed out his chest. She bent over, putting both her hands on the arm of the chair, and whispered in his ear. There was a brief exchange and they glanced over in my direction. I took my cue and picked the ice bucked and glasses from the bar and joined them.

'Christian, let me introduce my husband, Damien,' said Elsa, taking the seat next to him.

'Hello,' I said.

'Hi Damien.'

'I asked Christian if he's been enjoying the view,' Elsa said.

'What did you say, Christian?' I asked.

'You're a very lucky man,' he replied, straightening his jacket and raking his fingers through his hair.

'I also asked him if he'd like to fuck me?' Elsa said reclining back and crossing her legs. Christian flashed me a look, not too sure how to respond.

'I… umm…' he stuttered.

'Oh,' I said putting the ice bucket and glasses on the table. 'Would you like some wine?'

'Umm, yes, thank you,' Christian seemed pleased with the distraction.

Elsa sipped her drink and turned to me.

'He doesn't look sure, why don't you ask him, Damien?'

I handed Christian a glass.

'Would you like to fuck my wife?'

'Yes… yes, I would. That is, if you're…'

The look in his eyes was unmistakeable.

It was the same as Antonio.

This was a true Pretty.

Game on.

Chapter 19

I'm sitting in the kitchen trying to work while Callum is banging away at Elsa like a jackhammer on steroids; the headboard is bouncing off the bedroom wall. I look at the clock. In five minutes they will have been at it for two hours.

Earlier, when I closed the door to the lounge, it wasn't long before the sound of Elsa panting and moaning filled the house. I sat on the floor outside the door and listened to Callum's athletic abilities whip my wife into a frenzy. After a while, it stopped and I could hear Elsa talking. She mentioned the word bedroom and I scarpered into the kitchen. Sure enough the pair of them came into the hallway, Elsa leading him by the hand. She was still dressed in her stockings and basque while he was naked from the waist down, the tail of his white shirt covering his arse.

He only had eyes for her as they walked up the stairs but Elsa looked over the banister in my direction and sucked on her finger. My cock almost burst in my pants.

Now I'm trying to focus on writing my closing arguments for the Bairstow case and it's not going well. I get up from the table to make myself a coffee and it all goes quiet. The bang, bang, bang is replaced with the sound of birds outside. I switch on the kettle and allow it to boil.

Elsa appears next to me.

'Wasn't expecting you?' I say.

'I wasn't expecting it either.' Elsa is dressed in the silk gown which she had discarded in the lounge. 'You making coffee?'

'Yeah, you want some?'

'No.' Elsa hugs me from behind, her arms wrapped around my chest. 'He's asleep.'

'Sorry, who?'

'Callum, he's fallen asleep. I guess the exertions of last night must have caught up with him.'

I turn on the spot to face her, still in her embrace.

'You okay?'

'No, not really.'

I kiss her on the forehead.

'What's the matter?'

'Are you busy?'

'I'm doing some work but it can wait. Why?'

'Callum might have finished but I haven't.' She drops her hand and rubs the front of my trousers, kissing me hard. I can taste him on her lips.

'What do you…?'

Elsa pulls away, turns the chair around and sits down, facing me. She slips the gown from her shoulders to reveal her naked breasts and opens her legs. I fumble with the button on my trousers.

'No, no, no,' she leans forward and grasps my hands, pulling me to the floor. I sink to my knees.

'That's better,' she whispers. 'And when we're done, he's all yours.'

Chapter 20

Malice kept his face dead-pan despite the fact that his brain was screaming the word, *Campbell?* 'When was the last time the Campbell family stayed with you?' he asked.

'I'll take a look,' said Robins as she settled herself behind the computer screen. 'They were here three weeks ago; arrived on Saturday twenty-third of March and checked out on Sunday. It was the usual arrangements — two double rooms with an adjoining door.'

'What do they do when they're with you?' asked Pietersen.

'They pretty much keep themselves to themselves. They order room service of oysters and champagne and also have dinner taken to their rooms. I think they run a family business and this is their way of getting together.'

'How often have they stayed here?' asked Malice.

'I can check back in our records but I reckon it would be around half a dozen times in the last six months.'

'Can we have a printout of the bill for their last stay?'

'Sure.' Robbins shuffled the mouse around and a printer under the desk spewed out three sheets of paper. 'Mr Campbell settles the account for both rooms.' She tapped the papers on the desk to straighten the edges and handed them to Pietersen.

'How would you describe them?' asked Malice.

A man wheeling a suitcase came into reception and leaned against the reception desk.

'Do you mind if we continue this discussion in the library?' Robbins glanced over at the new arrival. 'Someone will be with your shortly, sir.' The man with the suitcase nodded and pulled out his wallet. David Merchant appeared with his customary smile.

Robbins led the way across reception through a well-appointed bar area into a wood-panelled room crammed to the ceiling with books. The other two following behind her.

'A library!' Malice mouthed to Pietersen.

'How much?' she mouthed back pointing to the figure in the bottom right hand corner of the bill. Malice's eyes widened.

'Sorry about that. This is more private,' Robbins settled herself into a comfortable chair and the other two sat opposite.

'I asked you what the Campbell family are like?' repeated Malice.

'All three are lovely, very personable. They always take time to speak with the staff, you would never believe how rude some people can be. They think that just because—'

'Can you tell us more about them, Anna?' Pietersen did the necessary.

'The daughter is slim and attractive, maybe mid to late twenties. She tends to arrive first. She always has room 12 and her parents are in their late forties I would guess. She is very glamorous and he is...'

'He's what Anna?' Pietersen asked.

'Well... not glamorous.'

'How do you mean?'

'I suppose you would call him plain.'

'I don't understand.'

'What I mean is you would never put them together as a couple.'

Bloody hell Anna, put your claws away.

'And you think that's odd?' Malice asked.

'I've been in this game a long time and couples tend to complement each other in the looks department. But these two are poles apart.'

'What else can you tell us about them?' Malice was keen to move things along.

'I don't know what else to say. They are lovely guests.'

'How does Mr Campbell settle the bill?'

'He always pays cash.'

'Cash? Isn't that a little unusual?'

'Yes it is, but we cater for everyone here. When we have foreign guests, they often pay with cash.'

'How do they make a booking? I mean if it's over the internet you would need to guarantee the booking with a credit card, similarly if you ring up.'

'Mr Campbell calls the hotel and I make the booking for him.'

'How does he secure the room?'

'There is no need for that. I know Mr Campbell.'

'How did he make the first booking with you... presumably at that time you didn't know him?'

'He came into the hotel and made the booking there and then. He paid for his stay in advance.'

'In cash?'

'Yes, that's right.'

'How do they arrive at the hotel,' asked Pietersen looking at the bill.

'The daughter arrives by cab.'

'There is a room charge here for a taxi. What was that for?' Pietersen asked.

'Let me see,' Robbins reached over and took the bill. 'Ah, yes, this is to take her back to the train station. Mr Campbell always insists on everything being charged to the room.'

'But under normal circumstances you would take a swipe of someone's card to allow them to charge items to their room, in case they do a runner,' Malice said.

'That is a practice in other hotels but we don't have guests who would do *a runner*,' Robbins shifted in her chair.

'Do you have CCTV on site,' asked Pietersen.

'Yes we have it in the grounds but only in certain areas inside the hotel.'

'Why is that?'

'We like to maintain a certain... how shall I say, level of privacy.'

'Do you have it in reception?'

'No, we don't.'

'Can we get a copy of your CCTV footage for the Saturday and Sunday when the Campbells were staying here?'

'Erm, yes. I can organise that.'

'How do the parents arrive?'

'I'm not sure,' Robbins was rubbing her hands together in her lap.

'You're not sure?' asked Pietersen.

'That's right. I'm not sure.'

'Please excuse me for being blunt,' Pietersen leaned forwards. 'But you know the food they order from room service; how they like to have dinner served; the fact that the daughter travels to and from the hotel in a taxi and that they always settle their bill with cash. So, it seems a little odd to me that you don't know how they arrive at your hotel.'

'I don't know,' Robbins kept looking at the door.

'Anna, on the bill there is a space marked vehicle registration. It's blank, which would suggest Mr and Mrs Campbell don't arrive by car. Do they arrive by taxi as well?'

'I don't know. Now if you don't mind I—'

'If they did, there would be a second item on the bill for another taxi. You said yourself Mr Campbell charges everything to his room. So, where is it?'

'You look uncomfortable with my colleague's line of questioning, Anna,' Malice said, sitting back in his chair.

'I really must get on.' Robbins got to her feet.

'Do you run them back and forth to the station? Do you pick them up and bring them to the hotel and take them back on the Sunday?' said Malice.

'That's… that's…'

'What will we see when we look at the CCTV, Anna?'

'Nothing, you'll see nothing,' Robbins said with a quiver in her voice.

'That's right because you know where the cameras are, don't you?' Malice could smell blood. Robbins was rooted to the spot.

'If we dust the inside of your car, are we going to find the prints of Mr and Mrs Campbell?' Pietersen asked. Malice flashed her a sideways glance.

'I could get into trouble. I could lose my job.' Robbins flopped into the chair and put her head in her hands.

'That depends, Anna. All we want to know is how do Mr and Mrs Campbell arrive and depart from the hotel?'

'I pick them up from the train station. Mrs Campbell has a phobia about taxis and they asked me if I could provide the service. At first I said no, but Mr Campbell was very persuasive.'

'How much does he pay you?'

'One hundred pounds.'

'For the round trip?'

'Yes.'

'One hundred pounds for a twenty quid taxi ride. Doesn't that strike you as unusual?' asked Malice.

Robbins said nothing.

'Did he make that arrangement with you when he first made a booking?' asked Pietersen.

Robbins stared at the floor.

'Did he slip you a goodwill payment upfront for you to play chauffeur?' asked Malice.

'Yes, he did. He said his wife couldn't ride in a cab and he wanted me to help. They are generous guests and we like having them to stay,' Robbins was red in the face.

'I bet you do, Anna, I bet you do.'

Chapter 21

It was the day Christian came to visit…

If killing my first Pretty was an opportunistic affair, then the months leading up to killing my second were like waiting for Christmas. I had taken time off work to make good the preparations and after five weeks of hard graft, I was ready. My pottery workshop now boasted a hidden extension with new drains in the floor that ran directly to the cesspit, as well as a much bigger walk-in kiln. The freezer was in place and we were all systems go.

Christian had availed himself of Elsa's charms on four occasions; each time we met at the same hotel, each time we went through the same roleplay in the bar. Elsa would sit on the bar stool while Christian sat in the armchair getting an eyeful of what was to come.

Elsa was brazen. On two occasions, even though there were other people around, it made no difference. She gave Christian and anyone else who cared to look a floorshow. It reminded me of our times in Amsterdam. She said it heightened the anticipation.

When it was time for me to arrive at the bar, we went through the same routine of me offering him a drink and Elsa insisted that I utter the words, 'Will you fuck my wife, Christian.' To which he would answer, 'Gladly.'

When I wasn't working or listening to my wife have sex with other men, I could be found in my workshop, creating masterpieces in clay. I had entered a regional pottery competition with high hopes of winning. I'd made a Victorian-style jug and wash basin and was delighted with the results. The winners were going to be announced at a special event which was held in Bath and I was determined to go. Elsa had made other plans so I went on my own.

The event took place in the great hall of a civic building. It was a spectacular venue with high, decorative ceilings and ornate chandeliers. I mingled with the other competitors and judges, exchanging pottery anecdotes and discussing the latest techniques. I was in my element.

When the time came to judge the submissions, us competitors had to retire to another room to drink more fizz and talk about all things pottery.

We were called back into the room once their deliberations were complete to find rosettes placed next to the winning pieces. I was stunned to find my masterpiece had been unplaced.

How could that be?

I convinced myself that the judges had somehow missed my work and made a beeline for one of the panel judges who I knew from a previous competition.

'Sorry,' I said. 'Are you sure you've viewed every piece in the Victorian category?'

'Yes, pretty sure.'

'So you're not completely sure.'

'No that's not what I meant. We've looked at every piece in the category.'

'Have you looked at this one?' I pointed mine out to her.

'Yes, we have.'

'Can you tell me why it hasn't placed?'

'It is a nice enough design and the production is excellent but…'

'But what?'

'It's a little on the plain side.'

'Pardon?'

'It's a bit… dull.'

'I don't understand.'

'To put it bluntly, it's not pretty.'

I picked up my jug and basin and left. The disappointment was all consuming. What the hell did they mean by '*not pretty*'. By the time I arrived home my frustration had turned to rage. Elsa opened the front door when she heard my car crunching the gravel on the driveway.

'Well, how did you get on?' she chirped.

I got out of the car, yanked the jug from the back seat and hurled it to the floor. Shards of pottery burst into the air. The basin closely followed.

'They said they weren't fucking pretty enough.'

Elsa screamed and hid from the flying debris. I kicked a large piece of pot off the drive onto the lawn and stamped around, trying to obliterate what was left. Elsa ran out and grabbed hold of me.

'Stop it, Damien. Stop it.'

The drive was covered in fragments of glazed pottery. I hung onto her shoulders and wept.

'I thought that was my best work and… and…'

'Come inside and we can talk about it.'

I allowed myself to be taken into the house. I was distraught. Elsa sat me down in the kitchen and poured a large whiskey into a glass, setting it in front of me.

'Drink this.'

'Are they fucking blind?' I yelled at no one.

'There, there.' Elsa sat beside me and cradled my head against her chest.

'Don't they recognise talent when they see it?' I pulled myself away.

'Drink.'

Elsa held up the glass and I sank it in one.

'Fucking idiots!'

Elsa patted and smoothed my back like a child recovering from a tantrum. After a while I could feel the warming effects of the liquor easing my anger.

'Do you feel better now?' she asked.

'Yeah, a little. I'm sorry.'

'It's okay,' she replenished my glass and kissed me on the cheek

'I had such high hopes for that competition.'

'Next time. You'll nail it next time.'

'Fucking idiots.'

'Yes they are,' Elsa rocked me back and forth, my head buried in her chest.

'Wait a minute,' I said pulling myself away from her embrace. 'I know how I can make my work prettier. It's been staring me in the face all along.'

'How are you going to do that?'

'I need to think. It could work.'

'That's great, honey. I have good news if you'd like to hear it?'

'What is it?'

'I've been thinking.'

'About what?'

'I'm bored with him. He's all yours.'

The next time I saw Christian, he arrived at our home with a bottle of wine for me and bunch of flowers for Elsa. She was giddy with excitement, delighted we were moving on to the next phase. I had made a new Victorian water jug and wash basin to mark the occasion and they were resting in the proving room.

The planning had to be precise. Elsa had wrapped Christian up in an elaborate cobweb of intrigue and lies designed to keep him off balance and compliant. She'd weaved a narrative that convinced him I was getting paranoid at the prospect of their relationship being discovered. I was a public figure and a revelation that my wife was shagging another man would ruin my reputation. She told him I was thinking of calling a halt to their affair.

Elsa told him that was the last thing she wanted. It turned out — unsurprisingly — he felt the same. Unless he complied with her demands, it was all over. I watched her manipulate him over the phone, a performance worthy of an Oscar. He was putty in her hands. He didn't stand a chance.

The arrangements were simple: She swore him to secrecy and told him that on their next visit he must switch off his mobile phone to avoid the possibility of being tracked. He had to travel on A-roads to avoid motorway cameras and only use cash if he purchased anything.

The date was set and Christian duly arrived.

We went into the lounge. I remember the roaring log fire in the hearth and the smell of cedar wood. Elsa made it clear she was in a hurry. As soon as they sat down on the sofa she started pawing him and by the time I came back from the kitchen with a tray of drinks they were already upstairs. The sound of Elsa coming like a steam train filled the house. The prospect of killing a Pretty was proving a massive turn on — for both of us.

I sipped my wine and tried to keep calm. Christian's jacket was draped over the arm of the chair. I fished around in his pockets and found his car keys and phone. Sure enough, it was switched off. I paced around the house trying not to get too pissed.

The sound of the hectic bedroom activities continued for the best part of an hour, then it all went quiet. Elsa came downstairs wearing her towelling dressing gown. She went to the kitchen to get a glass and poured herself some wine.

'What's up?' I asked.

'I've had my fill. I'm going for a bath.'

'But I thought we were—'

'Don't worry, he's all yours. I persuaded him to try something a little different – you might find it amusing. Give me a shout if you need a hand.' She disappeared back upstairs into the main bathroom. I could hear water running and the sound of her favourite playlist.

I put down my glass, went up to our bedroom and pushed open the door to find Christian laying naked on the bedroom carpet. He was facedown with his arms tied tightly behind his back with rope; his wrists and ankles secured together. A second length of rope was wound around his neck, it too attached to his ankles, forcing his back into an arch. He rocked back and forth trying to relieve the pressure on his windpipe. He was trussed up like a turkey awaiting the Christmas oven. And I had just the thing.

The sound of Elsa singing to herself, as she sloshed the water to make the bubble bath foam, wafted towards me. Christian heard the door and tried to turn his head. I was standing directly behind him so he couldn't see me. Another rope was secured around the back of his head and by the grunts and moans it was obviously holding a gag in place.

I walked around and dropped down onto my haunches to face him. He craned his neck and his eyes popped from his face. Then he began to struggle against the ropes, twisting and turning to no avail. The grunting and moaning turned into a muffled scream.

I left the bedroom and went into the bathroom where Elsa was lounging beneath a blanket of bubbles. I leaned down and kissed her.

'I love you,' I said.

'I know you do,' she replied. 'Have fun.'

I went downstairs to collect what I needed. Because of the unexpected predicament of Christian, I would have to improvise. Plan A was no longer an option.

I stuffed my pockets, gathered the remaining items in my arms and headed back to the bedroom. Christian had managed to roll onto his side and was trying to pull down the tie holding the gag in place by running the side of his face on the floor. His cheek was red raw from the carpet fibres.

'Don't do that. You'll hurt yourself,' I said, rolling him back onto his front. 'And besides I don't want you to spoil that lovely complexion.'

He yelled and coughed behind the gag. Tears ran down his face.

I laid out the black plastic body bag on the floor and unzipped it. The buzzing sound sent him into a frenzy of activity. He jerked and writhed from side to side. But with each movement the noose around his throat tightened. His face went from red to purple. I leaned over and loosened it.

'Don't kill yourself,' I said but my advice seemed to make little difference, Christian thrashed around even more. I rolled him over so he was lying on his side in the bag.

I sat on the floor facing him for several minutes, then produced a clear polythene bag from my pocket and tugged it over his head. He went rigid as it covered his face. I wound the bag tight under his chin and it inflated like a balloon as his exhaled breath hissed from his mouth. I could see his eyes staring at me through opaque plastic. He sucked air into his lungs and the bag shrank to his face as if he'd been wrapped in clingfilm. His chest heaved and the bag inflated again.

The inside of the plastic fogged up with condensation. I wound it another turn around his neck. It shrank back to his face, then out again. His whole body juddered as oxygen deprivation assaulted his brain and his muscles. I unwound the bag, allowing air to rush in. Christian snorted through his nose, snot and mucus lining the inside. I twisted it around his neck again.

I wonder how many times I can make this Pretty boy dance?

I lost count.

He passed out half-a-dozen times and on one occasion I thought he was gone, only for him to resuscitate himself much to my delight. One unfortunate by-product of the game was that Christian had pissed and shat himself, but at least he did it in the confines of the heavy plastic body bag, otherwise Elsa would not be best pleased.

The capillaries in his eyes had burst, giving them a horror-movie look and veins in his cheeks had ruptured into purple tramlines. This was not the best method of preserving his Pretty looks, but as the saying goes: *I've started so I'll finish.*

I was having so much fun... then I misjudged it... and he was dead.

The noise of him choking was replaced with the sweet sound of Elsa singing *Over the Rainbow* by Eva Cassidy. One of her favourites.

It was time to make my latest work look pretty.

Chapter 22

E lsa wasn't kidding when she said she hadn't finished. By the time she pushed me away, my knees hurt and my neck ached.

'I needed that,' she said lying back in the chair, her face flushed pink.

'Was that okay?'

'It was more than okay.' She flopped forward, kissed me. 'I'll go wake him.'

'I'll be up shortly. Remember — yellow. It's always yellow.'

Elsa nods, gathering the robe around her and walking from the kitchen up the stairs.

I stand up, rub the feeling back into my legs and go to the fridge to remove a box of chocolates from the top shelf. Neither of us eat them but it's useful to keep a box handy. The top flips open to reveal the tray of sweet delicacies. I lift out the plastic tray, set it to one side on the worktop and switch on the kettle.

Under the tray are six glass vials containing clear liquid and a syringe. I swill out the Cafetiere and spoon in two scoops of ground coffee, then I fish two mugs from the cupboard and arrange them on a tray.

I take one of the vials from the box and pierce the rubber membrane with the needle, drawing the liquid into the barrel of the syringe. I picture Callum in my mind's eye — he's tall with broad shoulders and a slim waist. I reckon he weighs around fourteen stones, which roughly equates to one hundred kilograms. I tend to work on a dosage of 1.4ml / Kg so I squirt the entire contents of the syringe onto the coffee and repeat the process, only using half a vial the second time. It is notoriously difficult to gauge the correct amount and getting it wrong can have devastating consequences. And that would never do.

The kettle comes to the boil and I pour water into the Cafetiere and make a separate drink using instant coffee.

As I venture up the stairs, carrying the tray, I can hear whispered voices coming from the bedroom. I tap on the door.

'You can come in,' Elsa says.

I shoulder open the door to find Callum sat up in bed, Elsa nestling into his naked chest.

'Elsa said she fancied coffee,' I say holding up the tray for him to see. 'I made enough for two.'

'That's great,' Callum says, straightening himself up. The quilt cover slides down to his hips. Elsa peels herself away and props herself up against the pillows.

With my back to Callum I depress the plunger and fill the empty cup.

'Here you go,' I take the tray around to Elsa and she takes the red mug. I lean across and Callum takes the yellow one.

'Is this the same coffee we had last night?' he asks, taking a slurp.

'No, it's a different brand,' I reply. 'It's stronger and more bitter. I really like it and it's Elsa's favourite.'

'Wow! That *is* strong.'

I hover at the side of the bed. Elsa runs her free hand under the covers, it's obvious what she's going for. Callum's face freezes.

'Good, I don't want you falling asleep on me again,' she says, sipping at her drink. 'You can go now.' I nod and walk away like an obedient butler. 'Leave the door open, there's a good husband.'

My heart is thumping out of my chest. I get half way down the stairs and sit on the step. Murmured voices drift down to me along with the sound of Elsa giggling. I look at my watch. It says, four p.m.

By 4.10 p.m a different sound drifts down the stairs to me. Elsa is softly moaning. Fifteen minutes later she appears naked at the top of the stairs.

'I'm going to take a bath. Have fun.' She pads across the landing to the bathroom and closes the door. I hear water flooding into the bath and the familiar voice of Eva Cassidy. I get up and go into the bedroom.

Callum is lying on top of the duvet like a starfish. His eyes are as wide as saucers, his mouth gaping open.

'Fucking hell, the colours,' he dribbles the words from the corner of his mouth. I lift his hand into the air and drop it. It flops back with zero resistance. Looks like one and a half vials was spot on. He's fallen through the K-hole. A state that induces paralysis and hallucinations.

I watch his eyes scan around the room, wild with amazement. His face twitches.

There's been an explosion of different coffee types available on the high street — skinny late, macchiato, flat white, Mochaccino to name but a few. My coffee of choice is Americano $C_{13}H_{16}ClNO$, or coffee laced with Ketamine to give it its street name. Strong with a bitter after-taste. And in Callum's case, it has a *very* bitter after-taste.

I go downstairs and pull the body bag from under the stairs. The heavy plastic crackles as I roll it up under my arm. Back in the bedroom I run the zip down and lay it next to the bed. I lean over and roll Callum towards me. He tips over the edge of the bed and flops into the bag. He lets out a low groan as the fall knocks the wind out of him. I zip up the bag and pull him across the bedroom, down the stairs, through the kitchen, out into the garden to the shed. By the time I get there I'm out of breath.

I open up the concealed room and heave Callum into place. The butcher's hooks pierce deep into his back as I stab them through the muscle and out the other side. The chain on the hoist runs smoothly through my hands. Slowly he leaves the floor to an upright position, his feet brushing against the metal grating. Two rivulets of blood run down his back.

I tie his hands behind his back with a leather strap and do the same with his ankles. He begins to move against the bonds. His head lolls forwards and drool runs from his lips. It's a look that doesn't suit him, so I ram a towel into his mouth.

I make a noose in a length of string, tug his cock and balls through the loop, and tie it off. Elsa always said Callum had a magnificent penis and looking at the evidence in front of me she had a point. I pick up the scalpel, make a few tentative incisions and imagine how my glaze will look with such a handsome addition. I make

sure the noose is tight, I don't want him to bleed to death...
there are other impressive parts that need to make it into
the freezer.

I flash the blade and the first packet of joy lands in
my hand. Next is his tongue. Apparently, that was pretty
special as well.

Chapter 23

Malice and Pietersen had spent the past few hours trawling through CCTV from the Mexborough Hotel along with the footage supplied by British Transport Police. Both were losing the will to live.

'Have you found anything else on the Von Trapp family?' Malice asked sliding a cup of coffee in front of her.

She leaned back, stretching her arms up to the ceiling. 'Nope. But I got bloody square eyes.'

'Tell me about it. Let's take stock of what we have.'

'Okay.' Pietersen slumped forwards, minimised the current window and opened another. 'This screen grab shows Belinda Garrett purchasing a train ticket at Paddington. It looks like she's feeding notes into the machine which would explain why the purchase didn't show up on her credit card statement. This one shows her arriving at the hotel.' Another picture flashed up on the screen. 'She picked up a cab from the rank at the station.

The taxi firm that collected her from the hotel for the return journey on Sunday was called AA Cabs.'

'Have you managed to find that on the hotel CCTV?' Malice knew as soon as he asked the question he was not going to get a polite response. Pietersen gave him a glare. 'Okay, what else?'

'I have nothing which shows Mr and Mrs Campbell arriving at the hotel.'

'I reckon Robbins would have got them in through a side door to avoid the cameras.' Malice slurped his coffee and rolled up his sleeves. 'That's a great start, move over let me take over for a bit.'

Pietersen slid from her chair and arched her back, groaning as her spine complained.

'Mally!' Waite yelled from the corridor as she marched past. 'My office, now!'

Pietersen closed her eyes and allowed her head to drop in mock surrender. 'I'll trawl through the rest of it,' she said.

'Sorry.'

Malice stepped into Waite's office to find her changing out of a pair of high heels and into her work shoes.

'What bloody difference the height of my heels make to neighbourhood policing I don't fucking know,' she said through her teeth.

'Sorry, boss?'

'I've been in a joint neighbourhood policing strategy workshop.'

'Sounds like fun.'

'I wish. There were three other forces there and we had to *share* our approach and results.'

'Oh dear.'

'The invitation said, *smart, business, casual* – whatever the fuck that is?'

'Not sure I have clothes that fit that description.'

Waite stopped what she was doing and looked Malice up and down. 'I'm not sure you do either.'

'Thanks …'

'Apparently, me showing up in my work boots was not the done thing,' she finished tying the laces and stamped both feet on the floor. She pushed and slid her chair over to her desk.

'Must have been pretty tough on the male officers attending.'

'Very funny. How is Kelly doing?'

'Just fine.'

'Is that it?'

'Is it time for her appraisal?'

'No.'

'Then… she's doing just fine.'

Malice took a seat.

'Don't sit down, you're not staying.' He got to his feet. 'There's been a suspicious death on the Claxton Estate. A couple of uniform are at the scene and I want you to attend.'

'Oh come on boss. We are up to our bollocks analysing CCTV.'

'I'm not sure Kelly would agree with your assessment.'

'You know what I mean.'

'I do. I also know that everyone else is tied up chasing down leads after the raid. Which leaves you.'

'How come I get the odds and sods jobs?'

Waite fixed his with a stare and leaned forward with her elbows on the desk. A stance that Malice knew signalled the conversation was coming to an end.

'Firstly, attending a suspicious death is not an odds and sods job and, secondly, you were late for my briefing. Now piss off.'

Malice skulked out of Waite's office back to Pietersen whose eyes were getting squarer by the minute.

'There's been a suspicious death and the boss wants me to attend.'

'I'll come along too. It will be a welcome break from this.'

'I need you to stick with it. Cracking the CCTV is our best chance of getting a break.'

'Can't you give this to a junior?' she shrugged her shoulders and waved her hand at the screen. 'We've got a good photograph of Belinda, so identifying her wouldn't be a problem.'

'Unless something dramatic happened in the time I've been with Waite, you are the office junior.'

'Oh, bollocks.'

'The body was found on the Claxton Estate, a regular hang-out for druggies and homeless people. I'll be back as soon as I can.'

'Bring more coffee.'

'Deal.'

Malice left the station and drove to the estate. Memories of the previous night burst into his head and he thumbed the cut above his eye. He could see a police van parked in a street and pulled up behind it. A uniformed officer approached the car, he got out to meet him.

'Alright, Mally,' said the officer.

'Yeah. What have we got, Steve?'

'A woman called 999 saying she'd found a body and refused to give her name. It's male. That's all I can tell you. A CSI team are on their way.'

'Any sign of a struggle?' Malice popped open the boot and climbed into a paper boiler suit and overshoes.

'I couldn't tell without moving the body.'

'Have you sealed off the area?'

'Yeah, and we've marked the path to take.'

'Good.' Malice followed behind the officer, cutting across a cul-de-sac and walking between two end-terrace houses. To the right was a property boarded up with metal plates, to the left two people sitting in their back garden on fold up chairs enjoying the show.

'Fuck me there's another one,' the man said as Malice came into view. He was dressed in tracksuit bottoms and a vest, swigging from a can of lager.

'See, I told you something was going on,' said the woman sitting next to him sipping her tea.

Malice tipped his head to the side.

'We got an audience?'

'Yeah, they appeared shortly after we arrived and set up their chairs to eyeball what was going on.'

'Have you told them to move inside?'

'I did and she told me to piss off and reminded me they were on private property.'

'Charming.'

'Morning!' the man in the vest called out as they walked past. 'Nice day for it.'

The woman giggled.

Malice resisted the temptation to walk over and ram the can down his throat. Instead, they made their way past the gardens to the boundary of the estate. Against the overgrown hedge was a shallow embankment leading down to a dried-up stream. The place was littered with cans, bottles and plastic bags. The body of a man was lying at the bottom. He was face down, his arms by his sides.

Malice picked his way down the banking and arrived at the man's feet. The man's face was buried into the ground with only the back of his head showing. He skirted around him to get a better view. The CSI team showed up.

'You'd better take some pictures,' Malice said. He was beginning to get a bad feeling about this. The team clicked away and after what felt like an age said, 'We can move him now.'

Malice knelt down and tilted the body to one side. The CSI next to him rolled the man's head to expose his face. Malice held his breath as he stared down at the split lip and bruised cheek.

Then he held his eyes closed and mouthed a silent 'Fuck it' to himself.

Chapter 24

It was the day I came second and figured out how to win
...

Christian produced the most beautiful glaze. It dazzled and glinted, changing from green to blue to purple as the light reflected off the surface. A triumph.

I had entered a national competition to be held in Birmingham. My disappointment with the last competition was behind me and I was fizzing with excitement.

I'd chosen to mark the occasion by making something different. I entered an abstract sculpture standing twelve inches high on a brass base depicting a man and woman dancing. This was way out of my comfort zone of jugs, cups and bowls. Functional, stylish and beautiful was my usual stock in trade, this was — to say the least — unusual. When I showed it to Elsa she said,

'What is it?' which told me it was abstract enough. I asked her if she would care to join me at the event. She smiled and said, 'Not this time, honey.' I reckon what she really meant was 'Not anytime, honey.'

The venue was one of the smaller exhibition halls at the NEC. The great and the good of the UK potting world were there. Some I recognised, some I didn't. The gallery was sectioned off into various categories; mine was in the one called La Belle d'Amateur Abstract, which described me down to a tee.

I mooched around admiring the work of the other competitors, shaking their hands and exchanging pleasantries. All the while thinking: *mine's better than that!* After each walkabout I returned to my piece to find a small gaggle of people surveying it. I introduced myself and enjoyed the attention. On the table in front of the piece was a cardboard place-name sporting the title of the sculpture: *Simply Pretty*. A fitting tribute to the vacuous shit-bag who'd been banging my wife.

When Christian was hanging from the meat hooks embedded in his back, it hadn't been difficult to select my 'packets of joy'. Elsa had always said he was the most beautiful man she had ever seen. That made it easy. His face *had* to come off. Nose, lips, eyelids, eyes, cheeks: the works. However, the part that caused me the most inconvenience was his teeth.

I knew they could prove to be tricky so I'd practised on a pig's head. I told our local butcher that I was doing a sculpture of a pig and wanted to get the details of the head right. For a tenner he obliged and the following week he handed me a pig's head in a bag.

Pigs' teeth are bloody hard to dig out. I tried a number of tools and found a pair of electrician's pliers worked best. But when I used them on Christian they were useless. I think it was because the aperture of his dead gaping mouth was smaller than that of the pig and I couldn't get the same grip. I reverted to a pair of long nosed pliers which were less than ideal. Even when I sliced through his gums, in an attempt to make it easier, some of the teeth broke off. Never mind, they were still usable.

In life, his teeth beamed a smile that made people love him. In death they lay in my pestle and mortar while I bashed and ground them into calcified grit. But it was worth it. People commented about the glaze, quizzing me about how I'd achieved such a unique look.

'Was it cobalt?' one woman asked. 'Did you use copper oxide in the slip?' asked another. I shook my head and shrugged my shoulders. After all, even if I told them they wouldn't have believed me.

The time came for the judging panel to make their rounds. We all filed out into a separate room to enjoy the drinks and nibbles on offer.

After a considerable amount of wine, the MC announced that we could return to the hall. I tried to act nonchalant but couldn't help scurrying back. Next to my piece was a red, white and blue rosette with second Place written in the centre. I was ecstatic.

Other competitors came over to shake my hand and congratulate me. This was a big deal and I was soaking up the adoration. One of the judges took me to one side to ask about my glazing process. I made up some rubbish and he went away happy.

I was hooked.

Pretties were the way to go.

The celebrations continued well into the night and I can remember lying on my hotel bed staring up at the rotating ceiling trying not to be sick.

Why the fug didn't I come first?

The words buzzed around in my head as I drifted off into a drunken sleep. When I woke in the morning, the answer hit me harder than my hangover.

I need to take my 'packets of joy' when they're still alive.

Chapter 25

Callum is looking decidedly unwell. The packets of joy are wrapped in greaseproof paper and sitting on the table. He's turning grey. I put my fingers to the side of his neck and can feel the blip of a pulse. The tourniquet around his genitals has done the trick but the blood loss from removing his tongue has proved a challenge.

His pectoral muscles are missing along with his collar bones. Why Elsa should have made particular reference to them is beyond me, but mention them she did. The metal grid beneath our feet is washed a deep crimson.

I watch as the life drains from his body. I can see why Elsa was so keen to have him to herself. He's a classic Pretty.

I place each of the packets onto a tray and lay them in the freezer. I have a competition coming up and they'll play a starring role in my winning creation. It's another figurine depicting a woman dancing with a partner. I'm confident the packets of joy will make the glaze sing to the judges.

I strip off my apron and make my way out into the drying room. The warm air hits my face and dries my eyes. I lock the door, push the shelving into place and wander back to the house.

Elsa is busying herself in the kitchen.

'How did it go?'

'Fine, I reckon I'll be ready ahead of time.'

'Thanks for being patient,' she says, kissing me. 'What do you fancy for dinner? How about I make a curry?'

'That would be great. Do you have raita?'

Elsa opens the fridge and scans the contents.

'I can make some — just the way you like it. You know, I was thinking…'

'Oh, what?' I turn on the tap and squeeze a dab of washing up liquid into my palm.

'We should give the pub in the village a go. I hear it's under new management and the food is really good.'

'Sound good to me. I'll check my diary.' I rub my hands together to make a lather and wash my forearms, the white, foamy suds turn pink.

'We've not been out for ages,' she says.

'Who do you know that's been there?'

I pick up the nail brush and scrub the congealed blood and skin from under my fingernails.

'Jean was talking about it.' Elsa collects yogurt and cucumber from the fridge and reaches for the chopping board. 'You know her, the woman who goes to the same gym as me. She was impressed, we should give it a go.'

'Jean?'

'The woman with the dogs.' Elsa slits the plastic covering off the cucumber and starts chopping.

'Oh, yes, I know. The frizzy haired woman.' I look at my hands, turning them over. My fingernails are stained a stubborn shade of red.

'That's the one. She's ever so chatty.'

'Maybe we could go as a foursome?' I open the cupboard under the sink to grab the bleach. I squeeze the thick liquid into my hand.

'Nar, her husband is boring. Besides, it would be nice to go out just the two of us.' Elsa spoons yogurt into a bowl and adds the diced cucumber.

'Yeah, you're right. That would be nice.' I scrub away at my nails before rinsing under the tap, a spiral of rust-coloured water washes down the plughole. I swill my hand around the sink to dislodge the bits of cartilage sticking to the stainless steel.

Elsa adds mint sauce and a twist of salt and stirs. She dusts the top with chilli powder, covers with clingfilm and pops it into the fridge for later.

I towel my hands dry and wrap my arms around her. She melts into me.

'Fancy a coffee?' she asks.

'Nah.'

'Do you fancy sex?'

'I have things to do.'

'Not even a quickie? You're normally up for it when you've been working in your shed.'

'It's not a shed, it's a workshop. And besides, his car is parked on the drive and it needs to be at the bottom of the reservoir.'

'Okay, you sort that out and I'll get cracking with dinner. Maybe you'll change your mind when you get back.'

'Maybe.'

I kiss her neck and breathe in her perfume.

I go into the lounge and rummage around in Callum's jacket for his car keys and phone. His BMW is bright and shiny like it's just been washed.

'Won't be long!' I call out as I close the door.

I can already taste the raita.

Chapter 26

Malice was sitting in Waite's office putting two and two together and coming up with 'fuck knows'. He couldn't get the image of Burko's lifeless body out of his head.

Ninety minutes earlier the doctor had pronounced Burko dead at the scene; a necessary declaration from a police procedure point of view but entirely unnecessary as he looked as though he'd been run over by a petrol tanker.

Malice had a bad feeling: First Burko gets his face re-arranged, then two clowns with baseball bats try to put Wrigley out of action and now this.

What the hell's happening?

Waite clicked away at her mouse and a variety of windows and documents leapt onto the screen in front of her. As usual her office was a tip, littered with files and mounds of paper. Malice sipped his coffee.

'Okay, I got him,' Waite said leaning back in her chair. 'What's the score?'

'His name was Gerald Burke, AKA Burko. A low-level dealer who operated a handful of runners out of the Claxton Estate. I arrested him a couple of times but the CPS went soft and he got off with a kick in the shins and nothing more.'

'It says here you couldn't make the dealer charges stick.'

'That's right, so he walked. He's a long-standing operator who tends to stick to what he knows — mainly dealing in Class C with a few Class B — he doesn't shift the hard stuff in any volume.'

'What was he like?' asked Waite.

'I know this is going to sound stupid, but he was kind of a nice guy.'

'What! He sold drugs to kids, Mally!'

'No, what I mean is he wasn't a gangster. He didn't go around roughing people up or causing trouble. He bought shit and sold it on — that was it.'

'You make him sound like a candidate for *The Apprentice*.'

'You know what I mean.'

'If that's the case how come someone murdered him?'

'I don't know. Whoever it was worked him over pretty good. We'll get more information when they do the post-mortem. But he wasn't killed where we found him.'

'No?'

'Given the extent of his injuries we would have been walking through blood trails in the grass, but there was nothing.'

'Why dump his body there?'

'Maybe this was all about sending a message. After all, the estate was his patch. Whoever did this, wanted him to be found and the word to get around. This could be signalling a changing of the guard.'

'A turf war?'

'Could be.'

'Did he have anything on him? A phone or wallet?'

'No nothing. We've started house to house. The couple who phoned it in said they saw jack shit. The cheeky bastards then asked if there was a reward.'

'Any CCTV?'

'On the Claxton Estate? Come on boss, the cameras would be on eBay within hours of being installed.'

'Okay, smart arse.'

'I'm drawing up a list of known associates.'

'That's good. Keep me posted.'

'Erm, if it's alright with you, boss I'd like to keep hold of this one?'

'I thought you said you were up to your bollocks—'

'I know, I know. But as I've nicked him before and you said everyone was tied up with the fallout from the immigration…'

Waite shuffled a wad of papers into a neat stack and shoved them to the corner of her desk. 'Okay, you run with it and keep me in the loop. The minute the investigation gets too big you need to shout. If you don't, it will be me kicking you in the shins.'

'Understood.'

Pietersen stuck her head around the door.

'Sorry to interrupt, ma'am. Mally, I went through the CCTV from the train station.'

'And?'

'I found the Von Trapps.'

'The Von…what?' Waite waved her hand in the air like the queen waving to a crowd. 'Go… go!'

Pietersen pressed the doorbell and shuffled on the spot. Malice was standing behind her, his warrant card at the ready. There was no answer. She pressed again.

The door opened and a woman with a blonde pixie cut stood before them.

'Can I help you?' she said with a slight European accent.

'Are you Elsa Kaplan?'

'Yes.'

'Good evening. I'm Detective Pietersen and this is DS Malice, I wonder if we could ask you a few questions, please?'

'Oh, err, yes I suppose so.' She looked over her shoulder. 'Damien! Damien! The police are here!'

'Your husband is at home?'

'Yes that's right.'

'The police?' Damien appeared in the hallway. 'What do you want?'

'Sorry to disturb you, we wondered if we could ask you some questions regarding a missing person.'

Damien looked at the warrant cards on display in front of him. 'You're a little off your regular patch, aren't you officers?'

'We are, Mr Kaplan. Do you think we could come in?'

'Of course, we've just finished dinner. Come into the lounge.'

The smell of curry hit Malice and he realised he hadn't eaten anything since breakfast. His stomach rumbled.

'Thank you.' They both followed into the living room

'Please make yourselves comfortable,' said Elsa.

'We are looking into the whereabouts of this woman.' Malice handed her a photograph. 'Her name is Belinda Garrett.'

Pietersen lifted a jacket from the seat of the armchair and perched on the edge.

'Oh my God!' Elsa yelped.

'What is it?' Damien squeezed alongside her on the sofa.

'It's Belle.'

'You know this woman?' Pietersen asked.

'Yes we know her, but we... don't *know* her,' replied Elsa, her voice shaking.

'What does that mean, Mrs Kaplan?' said Malice.

'Well it means that...'

'What my wife is trying to say is that we are acquaintances of hers, but we don't know her on a personal level,' Damien put his hand on his wife's leg.

'How long has she been missing?' Elsa asked.

'When was the last time you saw her?' Malice asked, ignoring the question.

Elsa looked at Damien.

'Umm, it must have been a few weeks ago. Maybe last month.' Damien nodded.

'How did you come to know Belinda?' asked Malice.

'We see her socially.'

Elsa looked at the carpet and clasped her hands in her lap.

'Socially?' said Pietersen.

'Yes we... erm.' Elsa stumbled over her words.

'Officers, to spare my wife further anxiety, would you like me to explain?'

Damien took his wife's hand in his.

'Go on,' said Malice.

'You would know us as swingers,' Damien nodded at Malice. 'You would know us as having an open relationship,' he gestured at Pietersen. 'I find it fascinating how the descriptions of what folk do in the privacy of their own home changes over time. Anyway, whatever you want to call it, we have sex with other people — for fun.'

'Swingers,' said Malice.

'Yes officer, that's right. We hook-up with people for the purpose of having no strings attached sex. That could be with couples or singles, we're open to both.'

'And that's how you met Belinda Garrett?' said Malice.

'That's right. We got chatting in a bar and things progressed from there.'

'It would be helpful for us to have the details,' said Pietersen.

'That's fine, no problem.'

'Talk to me about the Mexborough hotel,' Malice asked.

'That's where we met. I would book two adjoining rooms and we shared the weekend together. There was nothing improper. She was not under age, nor was she coerced. There was never any exchange of money and what she did, she did of her own volition. I would go as far as to say she was more than a willing participant. Wouldn't you agree, Elsa?'

'Stop it Damien. Don't make light of it. They said she was missing. That's terrible. Poor Belle.'

Elsa began to cry, she wiped the tears from her cheeks.

'I know love, I know,' Damien wrapped his arm around her shoulders and pulled her into him. 'They'll find her.'

'How many times did you see her?' asked Malice, taking out his notebook.

'I don't know... five or six times. I lost count. We always saw her at the Mexborough. They will have records, you can check with them.'

'You use false names at the hotel. Why was that?'

'I'm a senior partner in a law firm. It pays to be discreet — and besides, it adds to the excitement.'

'Did she ever come here?' asked Pietersen.

'No, never. That would be too close to home, so to speak.'

Elsa sobbed against Damien's shoulder, then straightened up.

'You don't think something has happened to her, do you?'

'I'm sure she's fine, love,' Damien said, hugging his wife.

'Would you mind if we took a brief statement from each of you?' asked Malice. '*Separately.*'

Elsa looked at Damien. 'I'm not sure... I want you with me,' she said.

'It will be fine. Tell the officers what you know, it might help them find Belle. I'll put the kettle on while you talk to the officers. We'll have a cup of tea, okay?'

Elsa nodded and wiped her eyes with her sleeve.

'Yes, okay.'

Damien left the room followed by Pietersen. She scanned the hallway and dipped her head into the dining room.

'You like your art, Mr Kaplan,' she said as he filled the kettle.

'Yes, it is a passion of mine.'

'Nice pieces.'

Pietersen walked over to study a burnished gold and orange vase on the window ledge.

'I make them myself. That one won first prize in a competition.'

'Wow, that's impressive.'

'Do you like art?'

'I do. Do you mind?

'No by all means.'

Pietersen picked the vase off the shelf and turned it in her hands.

'How did you get that glaze effect?'

'You know about pottery?'

'A little.'

'It's a special recipe. I built my own kiln… would you like to see it?'

One hour and two cups of tea later, Elsa closed the door on the officers who were getting into their car. Damien was next to her. He slipped his hand into hers.

'That went well,' he whispered.

'Practise makes perfect.'

'You were brilliant. What a performance.'

'You were pretty good yourself.'

'What do you think?'

'I think I rather like him,' Elsa pursed her lips.

'No, seriously. What do you think?'

'They're going away happy. But they'll be back.'

Damien kissed his wife on the cheek.

'I was wondering... the offer you made earlier... does it still stand?'

'And what offer might that be?' Elsa pushed her body into his and allowed her hand to slide down to his crotch. 'This one, perhaps?'

Chapter 27

'That's a first for me,' Malice said as grey and black outlines of the countryside flew by the car window. Pietersen gunned the engine, sending them hurtling around the country lanes towards the motorway.

'Me too. It takes all sorts I suppose.'

'I loved it when he said we don't know her on a personal level... sounded pretty fucking personal to me.'

'There's something not right.'

'Swingers,' Malice repeated for the umpteenth time since they'd left the house. 'Swingers.'

'Saying it over and over won't help us find Garrett.'

'Yeah, I know. But... *swingers.*'

'Okay, apart from the obvious, what did you think?' she asked shifting down a gear.

'I mean, did they look like swingers to you?'

Pietersen shook her head.

'I don't bloody know. How many swinging couples have you met?'

'To my knowledge — none. But now I'm wondering.'

'Wondering what?'

'Well I never thought they would look like that, so now I'm thinking I might have done.'

'Can we talk about something else?'

'Like what?'

'Like… what did you think?'

'Oh, erm, it didn't feel right to me either,' Malice furrowed his brow and stroked the stubble on his chin.

'In what way?'

'They were too helpful, too open, too…'

'Prepared? It felt like they were expecting us and the whole thing was scripted.'

'Scripted — that's the word. Scripted.'

Pietersen glanced across at her partner.

'Not swingers… now the word is scripted.'

'Keep your eyes on the road or we'll end up in a ditch.'

'Yes, boss. Anything else?' She turned her head to look at him.

'We'll need to follow up on their statements. They gave us a lot of information which we need to corroborate.'

'One thing we know for sure… Belinda Garrett was alive after their last meeting at the Mexborough. We have her on CCTV catching a train back to Paddington.'

'And we have the Kaplans going in the opposite direction in their car which they'd left at the station car park.'

'So why do I get the feeling we've missed something,' she drummed her fingers across the steering wheel.

'Me too.'

'He has a real passion for pottery.'

'Who does?'

'Damien Kaplan. He's made some amazing stuff.'

The country lanes gave way to a duel carriageway and Pietersen relaxed back into her seat.

'Really,' replied Malice, in as bored a tone as he could muster.

'Yeah, really. He built his own kiln.'

'Fascinating,' he brought his hand up to his mouth and faked a yawn.

'Just thought I'd mention it.'

'Putting that fine arts degree to good use?' Malice said, stifling a laugh.

'Piss off.'

'Just saying.'

'By the way, what size jacket do you wear?'

'What?'

'Your jacket, what size is it?' she reached across and pulled at his lapel.

'I don't know – extra large.'

'What's that in inches?'

'What is this? An episode of the *Sewing Bee*.'

'I'm serious.'

'I don't know, it varies. I think I take a forty-six inch chest, long.'

'Mmm,' she mused.

'What, are you going to buy me a new suit?'

'No, the jacket I picked up off the chair was a forty-eight inch, long. And there is no way Damien Kaplan is anything like that. It would swamp him.'

The clock on the dashboard read 19.45 as they entered the outskirts of town.

'Stop!' Malice shouted.

'What?

'Stop the car.'

'But we are miles from the station.'

'Just pull over.'

'Okay, okay. Are you alright?'

Malice yanked his overcoat from the back seat and leapt from the car as it drew into the kerb.

'Give me ten minutes.' He banged the door shut and left Pietersen staring out the windscreen with her mouth open. Up ahead, four men were loitering on a street corner. Malice pulled his coat on and strode towards them.

Pietersen watched as he slapped one guy on the back and another on the shoulder.

What the hell's he doing?

She waited and watched.

'Anyone would think you've been avoiding me, Wrigley,' Malice said, letting his hand drop from Bullseye's shoulder. The other two men dressed in matching back tracksuits and hoodies grunted before making a sharp exit. Closely followed by Bullseye.

'Now why would I do that?' replied Wrigley.

'Have you heard?'

'About Burko? Everyone's talking about it.'

'Any ideas on who might have topped him?'

'No. There's a lot of chatter but nothing concrete,' Wrigley unwrapped another piece of gum and popped it into his mouth – to join the others.

'And what about the other night? What happened to the idiots with the bats?'

'You don't want to know.'

'I do.'

'Let's just say they went to a better place.'

'Shit. That wasn't a smart thing to do.'

'Maybe not, but that's what happened.'

'What did they say?'

'They said a lot but we couldn't understand them. They were eastern European and spoke very little English. Bullseye thought they were taking the piss and got a little over enthusiastic.'

'Why were they trying to bash your head in?' Malice shifted his position and glanced up the road to ensure Pietersen was still sitting in the car.

'No idea.'

'You need to give me more than that.'

'They kept saying the same thing over and over — Lubos Vasko.'

'What the hell is a Lubos Vasko?'

'I reckon it's a name... a Slovakian name.'

'I'll keep my ear to the ground,' Malice said, turning to leave.

'Hey, Mally. Thanks for the other night, man. I owe you.'

'Yeah, you do.'

Malice trotted back to Pietersen. He found her drumming her fingers against the steering wheel.

'Thanks,' he said, piling himself into the front seat.

'I suppose that was another *spot of business*.'

'Yeah it was.'

'You going to tell me?'

'Nope.'

'Does it help us find Garrett?'

'Nope.'

Pietersen slammed into first gear and screeched away. She glanced across at Malice.

'At least this one didn't run away.'

'He didn't need to.'

Chapter 28

Malice crunched his fist into the speed ball. It bounced off the platform above and he missed the rebound by a country mile. The gym was hot and smelled of poor personal hygiene.

Fuck it!

He tried again and managed to achieve the rolling rhythm that told him his hand-eye coordination was working well. Then he missed again and the suspended ball boggled around in front of him. He tore away the fastenings around his wrists and yanked off the lightweight gloves.

Bollocks to this.

He punched the ball hard, sending it thudding into the suspended platform and walked away.

'That little ball too fast for you,' Jim sneered as Malice passed by on his way to the changing room.

'Something like that.'

'You ain't gonna hit that thing proper until you fix whatever's going on in your head.'

Malice ignored the home-spun wisdom and slammed the heel of his hand into the door. That was the trouble with Jim. Not only was he a great trainer, he was a psychologist, a counsellor and all round clever git when it came to working out what was going on in people's heads.

'When Mohammad Ali beat Sonny Liston he didn't win because he was stronger,' he used to say. 'He didn't win cos he could punch harder, nor because he was fitter. He won because he got inside his head. If your head ain't right… nothing's right.'

And annoyingly the miserable bastard was right. Malice hadn't slept a wink. His thoughts were awash with visions of Burko's beaten body, the two men wielding baseball bats and a man named Lubos Vasco. Whoever the hell he was. Punctuated with the occasional light relief of drifting into the world of swingers.

He put his kit into his locker and made his way out.

'Get rid of what's in your head and then maybe… just *maybe*… you'll be able to do some good around here.'

Malice held his middle finger up and exited into the car park. The early morning sun was still below the horizon, tucked up in bed where most normal people were at this time. He got into his car and the roar of the engine woke up the birds.

Malice opened the door to the office to find Pietersen sticking photographs to a whiteboard with magnets. He'd spent the last twenty minutes shaving and taking a shower in the police station changing facilities and had used up the last of his deodorant. He was wearing a clean shirt and tie that didn't have food on it. He figured that if he was going to be working with a woman, it was unfair for him to turn up looking like he'd spent the night sleeping in a cardboard box underneath a bridge.

'Hey,' she said over her shoulder.

'You're early,' Malice looked at his watch. 6.50 a.m.

'Yeah, not through choice.'

'Oh?' he removed his jacket and dumped his bag on the desk.

'My car is on the blink. I wasn't sure if I needed to catch a bus to get to work.'

'What's up with it?'

'I don't fucking know,' Pietersen spun around and flapped her arms to her sides. 'What I do know is it's running rougher than a badger's arse and it will probably cost me a ton of money to get it fixed. A ton of money that I haven't got.' She flushed red in the face.

'That sounds shit.'

'Yes, it is. I only had the damned thing serviced a couple of months ago.' She turned to face the board, picked up a pen and began scrawling names under the pictures and connecting them with arrows.

Malice disappeared and came back with two coffees, handing one over.

'Sorry,' Pietersen said. 'I'm pissed off.'

'That's okay, your motor running rougher than a badger's arse will do that to you.'

She looked at him and half-smiled.

'I've been thinking,' they both said in unison.

'Ha, you first,' said Pietersen.

'What if they're lying?'

'My thoughts exactly.'

'What if the Kaplans are letting us see what's under the rug so we don't look under the carpet. It's a well-worn tactic to avoid further scrutiny. They've given us a lot of detail around Garrett's disappearance which really doesn't put them in a good light. The implication being *look how honest we are, so honest we're making ourselves look bad.* But what if they're lying?'

'There is no way that jacket was his.'

'Perhaps their latest conquest was lying in bed all the time we were there,' Malice took a sip and recoiled from the heat.

'They were acting pretty cool if he was.'

'And that's part of my problem with the Von Trapps, they're too cool.'

'These are the hotel bills from the Mexborough.' Pietersen pulled a wad of paper from the board. 'They got together on six occasions; each time checking in on a Saturday and leaving on the Sunday. The duration of time between visits is either two or three weeks.'

'Belinda's house mate said that she was going to see friends on this weekend.' Malice took the papers from her hand and pointed to a date on the wall calendar. 'Which is three weeks after they were last together at the hotel.'

'And the housemate is pretty sure a red suitcase is missing.'

'Exactly. Then there's the phone. I found it plugged into the wall at the side of her bed. Now who goes away for the weekend and forgets their phone? You might forget it when you go to the pub, or pop out to the shops. But for a weekend? You leave the house thinking — keys, wallet, phone.'

'Maybe she left it so her movements couldn't be traced. If she turns it on it will ping off the phone masts and give away her location. Now why would she not want others to know where she was?'

'If someone told her to?'

'The Kaplans,' Pietersen stabbed her finger into the board, just below their mugshots.

'What was it Damien said? They wouldn't meet her at the house because it's too close to home,' Malice slid into his chair and unpacked his bag, taking a moment to admire his handiwork with his freshly laundered shirt.

'We know she doesn't drive, and we also know that she bought her train ticket on the morning of travel when they were last together at the Mexborough. How about I get hold of the CCTV from Paddington train station on the Saturday morning of the weekend she went missing? See if I can spot her — it's worth a shot.'

'Good idea. Though Paddington is bloody massive, what about getting our hands on the CCTV at the nearest station to the Kaplans' place. That would be a narrower search. We can always circle back around to Paddington if that draws a blank.'

'Okay hold on,' Pietersen tapped away on her keyboard. 'The nearest is Fallgate Station. I'm on it.'

'I have a couple of things to follow up on with regards to the murder on the Claxton Estate. Can I leave you with that?'

'Yes, we might need to bring in some help,' Pietersen didn't look up from the screen.

'I'll have a word with Waite, see what she says.'

'Let's pay the Kaplans another visit later.'

'Good idea.'

Malice picked up the car keys from the desk with the Porsche badge on the keyring.

'Do you need this today?' he asked.

'What?' The jangle of the keys broke her concentration.

'Do you need your car? I'll take a look at it if you like.'

'There's no need. I mean … we have a stack of work—'

'I'll be back later. Oh, one more thing.'

'What?'

'I've never been very good at this relationship lark, so you might want to help me out.'

'Go on.'

'I would have thought Belinda Garrett is a good-looking woman.'

'Agreed.'

'So why would she spend her time screwing Damien Kaplan? Who, let's be fair, is no oil painting.'

'You're right he isn't, but his wife is. Didn't you say that Garrett likes boys and girls?'

'Yeah, her house mate said that.'

'And that's your answer. Unless Damien Kaplan is hung like Dapple the pony then my money would be on Elsa being the focus of Garrett's affections.'

Malice shook his head and walked away. The image his partner had just planted in his head would stay with him the rest of the day.

Malice shoved open the door and was immediately enveloped in an atmosphere of grease and oil. The source of the fumes emerged from a side office dressed in a set of overalls that constituted a fire hazard.

'Alright, Mally?'

'Here you go, Wazzer,' Malice said, handing over the keys. 'Pick it up later.'

Wazzer slid a second set of keys across the filthy counter top.

'It's got fuel in it,' he said.

'I owe you one.'

'No you don't.'

Malice went back outside and sucked fresh air into his lungs. He pressed the key fob and the indicator lights flashed on a white van. Or more accurately, a van that was once white. He climbed into the driver's seat and shoved the burger cartons, cans and newspapers off the dashboard. The interior smelled like the inside of the garage. He wound down the window and set off.

There was one distinct advantage of driving around in the stinking van. Swivel didn't give it a second glance as Malice pulled into a side street and parked. Minutes later he reached around the corner and grabbed a fistful of yellow puffer jacket. Swivel's eyes went into orbit and both his feet left the floor with fright. Malice frog-marched him into the alleyway and jammed him against the wall.

'Oh... err... Mr Malice. How nice to... it isn't that time already, is it?'

'Shut up Swivel. I don't want money, I want information.'

'Okay, about what?' Malice released his grip and Swivel smoothed the wrinkles out of his pride and joy.

'What do you know about Burko?'

'He's dead.'

'Don't fuck me about.' Malice was almost standing on Swivel's toes, glaring down at him.

'No, sorry, what I mean is. I heard he'd been murdered. Found him in a ditch on the Claxton, nasty business by all accounts.'

'Any word on who did it?'

'Noooo!' Malice shifted position and was now standing on Swivel's toes.

'Are you sure?'

'I'm positive, Mr Malice. No one knows nothing.'

Malice disregarded the double negative.

'I want you to keep your eyes peeled and your ears open. Is that clear?' Malice immediately regretted the 'eyes peeled' suggestion as they were going round and round faster than the whirligig in a kid's playground.

'Of course, Mr Malice, of course.'

'One last thing. Have you heard the name Lubos Vasco?'

'Umm… let me think… Lubos — what did you say?'

'Vasco, Lubos Vasco.'

Swivel shook his head frantically, sniffing up his nose.

'No, Mr Malice. Never heard of him.'

Malice checked his watch. This was going to take longer than expected. Swivel was lying. It was obvious — his eyes had stopped moving.

Chapter 29

Court room number one is rammed. I'm still buzzing from the coppers paying us a visit last night. When they left, the sex was amazing. Afterwards, I drifted into a deep sleep while Elsa went downstairs to watch TV. Well, when I say it was amazing... it was for me.

I snap back to the present and flip through my notes one last time. Today is a big day. The defence team have put Tracey Bairstow on the stand and I have the opportunity to cross-examine. Watch out Tracey; here comes the pain.

The clerk of the court brings us to order.

'All stand,' he crows.

Everyone gets to their feet. The cloaked figure of Judge Peregrine Mason creaks its way into view. He presided over my last case. It was a touch and go affair but I had my nose in front. He gave a summing up which was completely biased towards the accused and swung the jury to deliver a not guilty verdict. That's another rapist walking the streets.

Mason gathers his robes around him and sits in the big seat. He belongs in a mortuary rather than a courtroom.

Tracey Bairstow is led into the witness box. She's dressed in a demure cotton dress and no makeup, her face is the colour of uncooked pastry. A stark contrast to her flamboyant clothes, fake eyelashes and full war paint that she normally parades in front of her adoring public. She probably feels as dreadful as she looks.

We have the usual introductory remarks from the judge and then I'm on my feet.

'Ms Bairstow, can you tell the court the last time you saw your husband?'

'It was Friday the ninth of November last year.'

'Can you elaborate, please?'

'Yes, he was in the bedroom packing an overnight bag. He had a business meeting the next day with a prospective client. He was due to return on Sunday.'

'But the records show he left on Saturday morning?'

'Yes, that right.'

'Didn't you see him then?'

'No, we... umm... we slept apart that night and when I got up in the morning he was gone.'

'Why did you sleep in different beds?'

'We'd had a row.'

So far, so good. All of that is true.

'I'll come back to the argument later, if I may. Can you tell me where this client meeting took place?'

'In Birmingham.'

'Was it usual for your husband to go away on business over a weekend?'

'Yes, it happened from time to time.'

Yes, because he'd been balls deep in my wife on numerous occasions.

'How had he planned to travel to this meeting?'

'By car.'

'Surely catching a train would have been easier?'

'Brendan hates trains. He preferred to take the car.'

Not any more, it's at the bottom of the reservoir.

'Let me take you back to Sunday January fourteenth, 2018. I have here a paramedics report detailing the head injuries sustained by your husband. Do you remember the events leading up to this?'

'Yes, we argued and Brendan cut his head.'

'Cut his head? You make that sound like an accident, Ms Bairstow. Would you kindly tell the jury how Brendan was hurt?'

'We argued and he got violent. He grabbed me and I defended myself.'

'You struck your husband on the head with a heavy metal ashtray. That's right isn't it?'

'As I said he attacked me and I defended myself.'

'Brendan called an ambulance because he couldn't stop the bleeding.'

'I was defending myself.'

'The paramedic administered four steri-strips to hold the wound closed and Brendan refused to go to hospital or press charges.'

'I keep telling you. I was defending myself.'

'Is that in the same way that you were defending yourself when you smashed a bottle over his head while he was talking to Abigale Greening outside your gallery?'

'Umm… no… I mean.'

'Because we have already heard in her testimony that the CCTV footage at the time clearly shows you striking your husband when he is doing nothing more than standing in the street.'

'He was shouting at me.'

'Was he shouting at you the time you hit him with the ashtray?'

'He could have been. He was always shouting at me.'

'And you hit him to stop him shouting, is that right?'

'No, he attacked me.'

'He didn't attack you the evening outside your gallery but you still saw fit to strike him over the head with a bottle.'

'No it wasn't like that.'

'The jury have seen the footage and I put it to you it was exactly like that. You have a track record of attacking your husband and causing him serious physical harm. Don't you, Ms Bairstow?'

'No ... I mean ... he attacked me ... I was defending myself.'

'Did he shout at you on the evening when you last saw him?'

'I don't know.'

'Did you hit him over the head to stop him shouting?'

'No, no, I didn't hit him with anything!'

No, you didn't, Tracey, and neither did I. Though I did remove the pectoral muscles from his chest, his nose and his hands. There was a lot to choose from.

'Talk to me about this business meeting. Who was it with?

'I don't know. In his diary was an entry for *Spiral Design*.'

'This is an online diary.'

'That's correct.'

'Had you heard of this company before?'

'I had but, as I said, they would have been a new customer for us.'

'When your husband failed to return home, what did you do?'

'I called him on his mobile.'

'And what happened?'

'It went through to voicemail.'

'Did you report him missing?'

'No, no I didn't.'

'Why was that?'

'I just thought he was angry and was staying away to teach me a lesson.'

'Angry with you because of the row you'd had?'

'Yes, that's right.'

'Was it a serious argument?'

'Umm... I can't remember.'

'Serious enough for him to shout at you?'

'I don't remember.'

'Because we've already established that when Brendan shouts at you, you are inclined to hit him over the head with something heavy.'

'No, it wasn't like that.'

No, it wasn't like that. He drank a Ketamine Americano and was flying higher than a US drone over Kandahar.

'Tell the jury why your calls went unanswered?'

'Because he'd left his phone behind.'

'That's right. The police conducted a search of your property and found Brendan's mobile phone, switched off, in a drawer. Did he have a habit of going away on business and leaving his phone behind?'

'No.'

He'd been putty in Elsa's hands. She'd convinced him to leave his phone. After all, it was good to be on the safe side.

'What route would he have taken to drive to Birmingham?'

'I don't know; M25, M40 I suppose.'

'Do you know what ANPR is, Ms Bairstow?'

'Something to do with number plates?'

'Very good. It stands for Automated Number Plate Recognition, which is a system that records vehicles that are in transit on certain roads. There are a number of these on the route your husband would have taken to drive to Birmingham. Guess how many times it tracked your husband's car?'

'I don't know.'

'None. Not once. So, according to you, Brendan drove all the way to Birmingham to a business meeting with *Spiral Designs* and avoided every one of the ANPR cameras on the way.'

'Umm… I don't know…'

'When the police followed up with *Spiral Designs* they have no record of a meeting with Brendan. Why would that be?'

'I don't know.'

'Which hotel was he staying at?'

'What?'

'You said it was an overnight stay. Which hotel was he planning to use?'

'I don't know.'

'The police checked every hotel in Birmingham and none of them had a booking for Brendan Bairstow. Why would that be?'

'I…' her voice broke.

That's because he was at my house, enjoying the delights of my wife while I sat patiently in the kitchen awaiting my turn.

'So we are being asked to believe that your husband has a meeting with a company who have never heard of him, travels by car to Birmingham and takes a route that avoids all the ANPR cameras, has a non-existent hotel reservation and leaves his mobile phone in the house tucked away in a drawer. Is that what you're asking this court to believe?'

'No … I mean … yes … I mean …'

'I put it to you Ms Bairstow that you and your husband had an argument which spiralled out of control. You became violent and killed Brendan Bairstow. Then you panicked, concealed the body and fabricated this whole sorry story to cover your tracks. You even put an entry in his diary.'

'No, no, it didn't happen like that.'

'How did it happen, Ms Bairstow?'

'We fought, yes, but he left in his car and I didn't see him again.'

'You didn't even report him missing to the police, did you?' Tracey stared down at her shoes. 'His agent reported it to the police. You didn't do it because you knew precisely where your husband was.'

'No I thought he was doing it to teach me a lesson.'

'I think you were the one dishing out lessons that day, Ms Bairstow. A lesson that cost your husband his life.'

'God! For pity's sake… no.'

'Where did you dispose of the body and the car?'

'I didn't…'

'Where is Brendan now, Ms Bairstow? Where?'

'I don't know.'

I do. He's sitting on the window ledge in my kitchen, glinting in the sunshine.

Chapter 30

Malice burst into the office and tossed Pietersen's car keys onto the desk. She was hunched over her keyboard, scrolling through CCTV footage, surrounded by reams of paper.

'You were right. It ran like a badger's arse,' he said.

'Told you. Bloody thing,' Pietersen replied over her shoulder.

'It's a nice motor.'

'It's nice when it runs right.'

'A blocked fuel injector and a dodgy cable. It's a wonder it ran at all.'

'What?'

'That's what was wrong with it. My guy said you need to get it serviced by someone who knows what they're doing.'

'It's fixed?'

'Yep,' Malice slumped down in his chair and flipped open his laptop.

'Shit, thanks. I mean… how much do I owe you.'

'Nothing.'

'Come on I must owe something? That can't have been cheap?'

'How much cash do you have on you?'

'I don't know.' Pietersen found her bag and rummaged in her purse. 'Twenty-three quid and some change.'

Malice got up and wandered over, dipped his hand in and came away with the twenty-pound note. 'That'll do. You can buy me a coffee with the rest.'

'Twenty quid! It must have cost double that, and add a zero on the end?' Pietersen's eyebrows couldn't go any higher.

'Let's just say it's my way of saying sorry for getting off on the wrong foot the first time we met.'

'You don't have to—'

'It didn't cost *me* anything and this…' he held up the twenty-pound note, 'will buy my mate a few beers and a bag of chips.'

'I don't know what to say.'

'Talk to me about the Von Trapps,' Malice returned to his seat and folded his arms across his chest.

'I have the CCTV from their local train station as well as taxi records. I've also got a request in with the boss for the bank records of Damien and Elsa Kaplan.'

'That's good. Waite hasn't got back to me regarding us getting another body, I'll chase that up.'

Pietersen's phone buzzed on the desk.

'Excuse me, I need to take this,' she said, walking to the back of the room and staring out the window. When she disconnected the call, she spun around. 'Do you mind if I shoot off for a bit? Something's come up.'

'When you get back we'll take a run out to have another chat with the Kaplans.'

'Won't be long.'

Pietersen scampered down the stairs into the car park. She put the key in the ignition and fired up the Porsche. She listened to the familiar sound of the big engine idling inches behind her; a smile spreading across her face.

She pulled out of the car park and headed away from town onto the duel carriageway. The tuned exhaust growled with delight. She shifted through the gears and took her foot off when she ran out of road at one hundred and ten miles an hour.

Malice had been right — he'd certainly fixed it.

Pietersen cruised along a back road until she came to a public viewing area. The suspension bridge towered overhead. She got out and could hear the trucks and cars rumbling above her. She made her way along a narrow foot path which was overgrown. The wind was whipping through the valley making her eyes sting. She could hear footsteps behind her and so quickened her pace.

To the right was an underpass; a walkway that dipped under the road and led to nowhere. She glanced over her shoulder to see a man wearing a long black coat. She darted into the tunnel.

The place stank of stagnant water and piss. Streaks of green and brown mould ran down the walls from the water seeping through the roof. Cans and bottles were scattered across the ground. The sound of her heels reverberated off the concrete as the gloom quickly enveloped her. She could hear a second set of heels following. They were getting closer.

She made out, through squinting eyes, a cone of white light at the far end as the footsteps behind her were quickened.

Pietersen spun around.

'Where the hell were you last night?' a man said, catching up to her.

'I got tied up and couldn't get a message to you.'

'That's not acceptable.'

'I know, sorry.'

'Don't—'

'Don't what?'

'Don't fuck this up. You know what's at stake.'

'I said I was sorry.'

'Okay… how's it going?'

'He's difficult to keep tabs on.'

'How do you mean?' the man tapped a cigarette from a packet and lit it up.

'There's been two occasions where he ran off and had conversations with men where I wasn't included.'

'Ran off?'

'Yeah, he opened the car door and legged it. Twice.'

'Who were they?'

'Don't know. I didn't get a good look. The first was a man in a yellow jacket who Malice chased up the road. The second time he spoke with a tall lanky guy with a beard and a bald bloke who looked like a beachball in a tracksuit.'

'A lanky guy and a beach ball in a tracksuit? You gotta do better than that.' In the gloom Pietersen watched the red ring draw its way up the white tube. The man blew a plume of smoke into the air from the corner of his mouth, leaving the cigarette dangling from his bottom lip.

'Sorry. Like I said, they were too far away for me to get a proper look.'

'Did you get the feeling they were planned meetings?'

'No, I think it was pure chance. He saw them and jumped out.'

'Did any money change hands?'

'I was too far away.'

'Okay, what else?'

'We're working two cases. One involves a missing woman and the other is a murder. He's running point on both.'

'Shit, that's a lot of work.'

'Tell me about it.' Pietersen plunged her hands into her pockets and began shuffling her feet. She clucked her tongue against the roof of her mouth.

'What's he like?'

'A popular guy around the station, well regarded. He's pretty unambitious and has a prickly side. Though, he gets on well with his boss. She obviously trusts him. He's got a fractious relationship with his ex-wife and from what I can tell he doesn't over-indulge on booze.'

'Any other relationships on the scene?'

'Don't know. He hasn't mentioned anyone.'

'What else?'

'I checked the database and he doesn't have any informants listed. So, the men he met are off the grid as far as the department is concerned.'

'That fits. What else?'

'He fixed my car.'

'What?' the man removed the fag from his mouth and spat on the floor.

'My car was up the creek and he took it away and fixed it.'

'Very neighbourly of him.'

'That's what I thought.'

'What else?'

'Fuck me, Ryan, it's only been a couple of days,' Pietersen slapped her arms to her sides and turned on the spot.

'You need to get close to him.'

'Get close to him? It's not bloody *Love Island.*'

'I'm just–'

'D'you know what, Ryan, there is something else…' she stepped in close. 'If you're unhappy with the way I'm managing the job, then pull me out.'

'Sorry, there's a lot riding on this.'

'Yes there is, for all of us.'

Ryan paused and stared at his shoes. 'Do you need anything?'

'Yes, I need you to find another place for us to meet. I'm going to go back to the office stinking of piss.'

Back at the station Malice was surfing every database he could lay his hands on. Lubos Vasco was proving a difficult man to find; no mention of him anywhere.

When Malice had Swivel jammed up against the wall, he hadn't told him anything he'd not worked out for himself. Vasco was knocking over dealers and moving in on their patches. No one knew where he'd come from. He simply appeared and started shoving people out. Swivel had not had a visit, but he was expecting one. Which would account for him nearly shitting his pants when Malice grabbed him.

Malice's phone beeped in his pocket. It was a text message. On the screen was a picture of Amy and Hayley taken outside their house. Amy was dressed in her school uniform with her bag across her shoulder. Beneath the picture the text read:

Whistle and Flute, 7.30pm today, table 10.

Chapter 31

Malice was aware that Pietersen was talking, though his mind was elsewhere; occupied with the picture of his daughter and the Whistle and Flute pub. He balled his fists together in his lap.

'Are you okay?' Pietersen asked as she shifted through the gears having pulled away from the traffic lights. 'You seem distracted.'

'I got some family stuff going on.'

'Only I've been yakking away for the past twenty miles and you've not said a word.'

'Sorry.'

'Anything I can help with?'

'No. Me and my ex are going through a rough patch — again.'

'That can make life difficult.'

'Too right,' Malice stared straight ahead, his teeth clenched tightly together.

'I was thinking. I never got the chance to buy you a coffee to say thanks for fixing my motor.'

'There'll be other times.'

'I was wondering if you'd like a beer instead?'

'I don't know…'

'C'mon, it's the least I can do.'

'Maybe a quick one.'

'Or cocktails if you'd prefer. It might help to take your mind off things.'

'Erm, yeah, that would be good.'

'Which – beer or cocktails?'

'Beer. Beer would be good.'

Pietersen nosed the car into the driveway and the chippings crunched beneath the tyres. They got out and surveyed the house.

'Must have cost a packet,' Malice said.

'Sending people to jail must be a lucrative business.'

'It must be… on the rare occasions that happens.'

Pietersen pushed the button next to the door. A series of chimes echoed in the hallway beyond. Nothing happened. She tried again. Nothing.

'I'll check around the back.'

Pietersen left Malice on the doorstep and skirted around the side of the house. Malice tried the bell again.

She rounded the corner to find a huge garden at the back. The lawns were flanked by flower beds and hedges with the pottery shed in the far corner. An oval table and eight chairs took pride of place on the patio. She cupped her hands to the glass and looked through the kitchen window. Dishes were stacked on the draining board and a mug was sitting on the table.

'Detective Pietersen, isn't it?' Elsa called out as she emerged from behind a row of bushes.

'We rang the bell, but…'

'Sorry, I didn't hear you. I've been composting,' she was dressed in three-quarter length jeans and a baggy top with a pair of comedy sized gardening gloves.

'We wondered if you wouldn't mind answering a few more questions.'

'That's fine, though Damien is at work. Any news on Belle?'

'Our investigations are ongoing.'

'Are you on your own?'

'No, my colleague is at the front.'

'Shall we go inside for a coffee and leave him there?' Elsa shook her hands and the gloves fell to the ground.

'Erm, he'll not be impressed with that.'

'He might not be... but sometimes it's good to make them wait.'

Pietersen screwed her face up. 'I'm not sure that's going to work.'

'I'm only joking, come inside.' Elsa opened the back door and Pietersen followed her. 'Can you let your colleague in while I go upstairs to change?'

'There is no need for that.'

'Nonsense. I'm in my gardening gear.'

'You're fine, Mrs Kaplan, we only want to...' her words fell on deaf ears as Elsa disappeared. Pietersen made her way down the hallway and opened the front door to find Malice checking his phone.

'Bloody hell, you broke in?' he said.

'Hardly, she was in the garden. She said I should keep you waiting on the doorstep.'

'Why, what have I done?'

'Don't know. She's gone upstairs to change.'

'Into what?'

'Search me.' They loitered around waiting for Elsa to return. 'Perhaps we should—'

'Detective Inspector, how lovely to see you again. I hope your colleague didn't keep you waiting.' Elsa appeared at the top of the stairs dressed in a halter-neck maxi dress that floated open at the front as she walked. She glided down the stairs exposing a generous portion of leg.

Malice took a double take. Pietersen took a double dislike.

'I'll put the kettle on,' Elsa said. Her perfume wafted over them as she glided past.

'Put your tongue away,' Pietersen mouthed. Malice raised his eyebrows.

'So, what do you want to ask me?' Elsa posed as she pulled three mugs from the cupboard.

'The hotel records show that you saw Belinda Garrett five times over a twelve-week period. You got together every two to three weeks,' said Pietersen.

'That sounds about right,' Elsa removed the kettle from its stand and filled it with water.

'If we look at the pattern of your meetings,' Pietersen consulted her notebook. 'On the weekend of her disappearance she was due to see you and your husband. Had you arranged to see her?'

'No, our association with Belle had run its course. She told us she had met someone.'

'Who?' asked Malice

'She didn't say, and we didn't ask.'

'Is that the way it works?' he added.

'The way what works?'

'Couples who are into swinging.'

'Some folk swing when they are between relationships and others, like Damien and I, do it because … well, we just do it.'

'Did she say whether her new partner was a man or a woman?' asked Pietersen.

'Like I said, we didn't ask. She wanted to move on and that was fine with us.'

'Where were you the weekend Belle went missing?'

Elsa ignored the question.

'Can you help me with this?' Elsa said to Malice, looking up at the coffee pot sitting on the top shelf. 'I don't know why Damien insists on putting it up there. Would you mind?'

Malice sidled over and reached up.

'I mean, look…' Elsa squeezed herself against him with her arm in the air. 'He knows I can't reach.' She gazed up at Malice. He stepped away and handed over the pot. Elsa smiled, spooned in ground coffee and filled it with boiling water. 'Thank you.'

'Mrs Kaplan, where were you the weekend Belinda went missing?' Pietersen tried again.

'We were here all weekend. Damien was working and I pottered around the house.'

'Did you go anywhere? See anyone?'

'No. We decided it would be nice to have the weekend to ourselves. It's been a really busy time lately.'

'When was the last time you had any contact with Belinda?'

'At the Mexborough.'

'Is that when she told you about having met someone?'

'Now, if I remember correctly, yours is white with no sugar,' Elsa said, glancing across at Pietersen. 'And you... you're strong and black.' Elsa lasered Malice with her piercing blue eyes.

'Err, yea, that's fine,' Malice replied. If it wasn't for his Jamaican heritage they would have seen him blush.

'Mrs Kaplan, is that when she told you about having met someone?' Pietersen said with an edge in her voice. This was beginning to grate.

'Yes, it was. Obviously, we were disappointed but it was her choice and we respected that.'

'So, you had no contact with her after that date?'

'That's right.'

'Can I ask you a question of a more personal nature?' Pietersen said.

'Sure, fire away.'

'Did you and your husband both have a relationship with Belinda Garrett?'

'Ha, you really must be more direct. If by that you mean were we both having sex with her... the answer is no. *I* was screwing her, not Damien'

'What was he doing while you were having sex with her?' asked Pietersen.

'Come on — do I need to draw you a picture? You know what you boys are like.' She looked straight at Malice, who looked away.

'I don't think we have any more questions. Thank you for your time, Mrs Kaplan,' Malice had had enough.

'But you haven't finished your coffee.'

'We have to get back to the station,' he said, placing his cup on the worktop. Pietersen flashed him a look.

'Well, any time you want to talk more, just give me a call.' She plucked a used envelope from the letter rack and scribbled down a telephone number. 'Call me,' she handed it to Malice. He folded it in two and stuffed it in his jacket pocket.

'Thanks.'

Malice and Pietersen said their goodbyes and made their way out to the car. Elsa gave them a wave and closed the front door.

'Christ, that was like being in a lap dancing bar without the poles,' Malice said as he revved the engine and backed out of the driveway.

'I think she saw you as fresh meat,' Pietersen replied, giving him a sideways glance.

'It felt like it.'

'I got the feeling if I hadn't been there, you'd have been in trouble.'

'I got the feeling she's lying.'

Elsa's fingers danced across the screen of her mobile phone:

Elsa: The police were here. Same two as before.

Damien: What did they want?

Elsa: They asked more questions

Damien: Are you okay?

Elsa: Yes, fine. Talk when you get back later.

Damien: Do you want me to get you anything on my way home?

Elsa: Yes - him.

Chapter 32

Malice shouldered the door to the Whistle and Flute open, then walked into a wall of sound. Three televisions were blasting out a football game to the delight of a room full of people sitting at high tables that were covered with empty glasses. A young man and woman, both dressed in black, weaved their way around the room trying to collect them. It looked like a full-time job.

On the other side of the pub, people were trying to make themselves heard while enjoying dinner. Malice scanned the room and spotted an empty table in the corner with a Reserved sign on it. He wandered over and took a seat at table 10.

He'd spent the last ten minutes loitering outside pretending to be on his phone, stealing glances through the windows. There were two men that stood out like a pair of sore thumbs.

A big guy wearing a leather jacket that fitted him like a diver's wetsuit was standing at the bar staring straight ahead; either his beer was flat or the untouched pint in front of him had been there a while. A second man, tall and lean, was sitting at the opposite end reading a newspaper. In all the time Malice observed him, he hadn't turned the page once.

Earlier, Malice had spoken on the phone with Hayley on the pretext of arranging a visit to see Amy. She'd seemed fine. He wanted to say more but until he knew what he was dealing with it was best not to spook her.

Malice threaded his way through the morass of baying people and pulled up a chair. Out of the corner of his eye he saw the big guy pull out his phone. Malice could hear blood pulsing through his temples.

A man appeared from a side door. He was about the same age as Malice with a taut wiry frame. His hair was cropped and his pale blue eyes chilled his face. He dragged the chair opposite away from the table and sat down.

'I like a man who's early, Mr Malice.' He spoke with a thick accent. His open shirt showed a patchwork of DIY tattoos carved into his skin in black ink.

'If you go near my wife and daughter, I'll kill you.'

'Ex-wife, Mr Malice. And we have no intention of hurting them. That is not how we do business. I needed to grab your attention. Do I have your attention?'

'If you harm them…'

'I give you my word. You play ball and I have no interest in your family.'

'What do you want, Mr Vasco?'

'You know my name! Was that a lucky guess or have I come up on your police radar already? If it's the latter I would be surprised, so it must be the former. Which is it?'

'I know who you are.'

'I respectfully suggest you know my name but you have no idea who I am.'

'You have my attention, what do you want?'

'That is the trouble with you British, all business and no pleasure.'

Malice leaned forwards across the table.

'Don't piss about.'

Vasco didn't flinch.

'I like to conduct business in a civilised way,' he said, raising his hand without breaking eye contact. 'Some of the best deals I've ever done have involved good food, good wine and good entertainment. You Brits are all about getting to the bottom line as fast as possible. You need to enjoy the journey, my friend.'

He rolled up his sleeves to reveal more home-made tattoos. Malice noticed the top of Vasco's little finger on his left hand was missing; the same with the ring finger and little finger of his right.

The big bloke in the leather jacket lumbered towards them. He was carrying an ice bucket with a bottle of fizz and two glasses sticking out of the top in one hand and a paper carrier bag in the other. He placed the bucket in the centre of the table and arranged the champagne flutes. He handed the bag to Vasco who placed it on the floor. And with that, the big man sloped off back to the bar.

Vasco poured two drinks. Condensation fogged the outside of the glasses.

'I thought it would be good to get our new relationship off on the right foot. It's not the proper stuff I'm afraid, my man asked for champagne and the barman looked at him like he had two heads.'

'Not sure that's the only reason.'

'He's not pretty, I agree. But he's effective and fiercely loyal.'

'More effective than your other goons? I hear you're two men short.'

'That was unfortunate.'

'No, it was the work of amateurs.'

'You were there?'

'Have they run home to *matka* yet?'

Vasco's eyes flashed anger at the use of the Slovak word for *mother*.

'I asked if you were there?'

'And I asked if they'd run home to *matka*?'

Vasco raised his glass.

'We are the same, you and I, strong men who test each other out before making up our minds. I like that.'

'I've already made my mind up.' Malice left his glass on the table.

Vasco sipped his drink.

'It's not bad. Could do with being colder but then where I come from everything's colder. Apart from the women. That's another area where you Brits could learn some lessons.'

'What do you want?'

'Okay as you're insistent on conducting business — let's talk business.' Vasco drained his glass and topped it up, bubbles spilled over the rim onto the table. 'Are you sure?' he held the bottle up and Malice shook his head. 'I am, how you say, the new kid on the block and I'm currently in the acquisition stage of building my corporate enterprise. Sometimes that happens fast and at other times it's… let's say… problematic. But one thing I do know is it's important to have good market intelligence. Which I believe is what you provide.'

'Market intelligence? What the fuck is that?'

'How can I put it so you'll understand... it's important to know what's going on. And you are just the man to tell me.'

'I have no idea what you're talking about.'

'I think you do, Mr Malice. I think you're being modest.'

'I think you're being a dick.'

'Your friend Burko spoke highly of you. In fact, he spoke about you a lot. But then we were being rather persuasive at the time. So, you see, Mr Malice, I know exactly what you're able to provide. I'm intrigued to learn about the insights you can provide.'

'Go to hell.'

'Given my past, I might well do, but that's a long way in the future, and I prefer to live in the moment. We will of course recompense you for your efforts. Probably a lot more than you demanded from Burko.'

'I'm not—'

'There will be one big difference though, Mr Malice. You see, it would appear you were the organ grinder and Burko was the monkey. It's only fair to tell you that, going forward, I will be grinding the organ. You will find us straightforward to work with, I like to keep things simple.'

'I'm nobody's monkey,' Malice half got out of his chair and a fat hand clasped his shoulder.

'For a big man, you never see him coming.'

The man in the leather jacket eased Malice back into his seat and stood behind him.

'I'll fucking—' Malice gripped the table.

'No you won't. Because you're a sensible man who enjoys more than his police salary can afford. That's where we come in. I'll leave you now and we'll be in touch.'

Vasco rose from the table. 'Oh, I nearly forgot. I always like to leave my new business partners a gift to cement our relationship. Something to show you how committed we are to working in partnership,' he reached down, picked up the bag and placed it on the table. 'Please don't get up, Mr Malice. Enjoy the drink. It might be colder now.'

Vasco walked away flanked by the monster in the leather jacket.

Malice clenched and unclenched his fists and watched them leave. He peered inside the bag and fished out the contents.

In his hand was a big woollen hat. The type of hat that, if you wore it, would give your head the same profile as Marge Simpson.

Chapter 33

Malice bumped his near-side tyre into the kerb, his alloy wheel made a horrible grinding noise against the concrete. Normally that would have provoked a bout of swearing, but on this occasion, there were more important things to curse about.

He rapped his knuckles against the woodwork and a light came on in the hallway. The door opened.

'You gotta be kidding?'

Hayley was dressed in a towelling bathrobe and slippers.

'Hey, how are you?' Malice replied.

'What…?'

'Can I come in?'

'Mally, do you know what time it is?'

'I know, I just…'

'Just what?'

'I wanted a chat.'

'For Christ's sake.'

Hayley shuffled back into the lounge leaving the door open. Malice followed. She flicked the mute button on the TV.

'I… umm…' he said.

'What is it, Mally. What do you want?'

'Well—'

'Daddy!' There was the sound of scampering feet on the stairs and Amy flew into the lounge, her arms outstretched. 'I thought I could hear you.'

'Hiya, sweet pea,' he said, lifting her up.

'Amy, it's past your bedtime,' said Hayley folding her arms across her chest.

'I know, mummy, but daddy's here.'

'How was school today?' Mally asked.

'We did baking.'

'Wow! What like proper off-the-telly baking?'

'Yup. We made fairy cakes.' Amy fought against his grasp to get to the floor. 'Look.' She took his hand and led him into the kitchen where she prised the lid off a biscuit tin. 'They're lemon flavoured.'

Amy dug one out and gave it to Malice. He took a bite.

'Oh, wow! That is the bestest cake I have ever tasted.'

'Do you think so?'

'Do I think so? I know so!'

He munched away at the tasty morsel, rolling his eyes in mock ecstasy.

'Amy, it's time you were in bed,' Hayley called from the other room.

'Come on.' Malice took Amy back into the lounge, the remnants of the cake in his hand. 'Oh I nearly forgot,' he patted his pockets, 'you don't happen to know anyone who likes chocolate, do you?' He waved a Toblerone in the air.

'That's my favourite,' Amy squeaked.

'I don't believe you...' mumbled Hayley.

'Mummy, can I have some now?'

'No. Off to bed,' Hayley snatched the bar from Amy's hand. 'You can have this tomorrow. Go on — up the stairs.'

'Off you go.' Malice kissed Amy on the forehead and she scampered off.

'Really?' Hayley held up the chocolate. 'At nine o'clock on a school night. You are something else.' She slumped down onto the sofa, crossed her legs and began kicking her foot out.

'I saw it and thought—'

'Yeah and that's the problem, nothing good ever comes from you thinking. Are you going to tell me what the hell's going on?'

'How do you mean?'

'Oh come on, Mally. First I get a call from you on the pretext of making arrangements to see Amy—'

'Pretext? I wanted to know—'

'Then you show up with that look on your face.'

'What look?'

'For Christ's sake. I sometimes think you've forgotten I used to be your wife. The one who had to put up with a pile of shit every day that was dressed up as our marriage. The same look you had when you brought Al Capone to our door.'

'Al Capone?'

'He owned a pizza parlour, didn't he?'

'Well... yes... I suppose so.'

'I might not be married to you anymore but it hasn't gone away.' Her foot was pumping up and down.

'What hasn't?'

'My ability to know when there's a ton of trouble about to land in my lap.'

'You're such a drama queen.'

Malice collapsed into the chair opposite.

'Drama queen! You're fucking right there. Being with you, that shit comes for free. It's like an all-you-can-eat Khenan Malice buffet — where every plate is stacked full of shit.'

'It wasn't like that.'

'Oh, which part? The part when they kicked our front door in? Or the part when they trashed our house?'

'For Christ's sake, Hayley. I only—'

'Screwed up our lives. Yeah, you did that alright.'

'Mummy, I'm cold. Can daddy tuck me in with my blanket?'

Amy was peeking around the door.

'Of course I can, Sweet Pea.'

Malice jumped up and took his daughter back to bed. Hayley stomped into the kitchen to put the kettle on. Minutes later, Malice returned. One cup was next to the teapot on the worktop.

'We need a more formal arrangement. This isn't working.'

Hayley's knuckles were white as she gripped onto the worktop.

'Arrangement for what?'

'You seeing Amy. You can't just drop by whenever you feel like it. She needs routine and you swanning in and disrupting things is causing a problem. Not to mention the fact that whenever you do, I'm always the one who looks like the bad guy.'

'Sorry, Hayley. I just wanted to check you were okay.'

'I think it might be best if you don't come round until you get whatever it is sorted out.'

Malice stared into space as Hayley poured boiling water onto a teabag.

'I want you to stay with your sister for a while,' he blurted out.

'What?'

'It will only be for a few days. Tell her you're having some work done on the house.'

'Why would I want to do that?'

'And tell the school there's a family emergency and you have to take Amy out for a while.'

'Take Amy out of school?'

'A few days, that's all.'

'Mally, what the hell is going on?'

'Go to your sister's place.'

'Mally!'

'For a couple of days.'

'Couple of days for what?' Hayley pushed the cup away, slopping tea on her hand. She cursed and ran it under the tap.

'I have something that needs sorting and ...'

'And you need to know we are out of the way.'

'It's nothing serious, it won't take long.'

'Serious enough for us to have to do a disappearing act.' She pulled a towel from the hook on the side of the cabinet and dried her hand.

'It's for the best. A couple of days is all I need. Make some calls tomorrow and pack a bag, Amy will love an unexpected holiday.'

'Doesn't look as though I have a lot of choice.'

Malice nodded and walked through the lounge into the hallway.

'Call me when you get there,' he said.

The front door banged shut behind him.

Thirty minutes later the stench of burned out cars wafted through the air vents in the dashboard. Even if Malice was blindfolded, he would recognise the Claxton Estate in an instant. He parked up, popped open the boot and pulled the filthy coat around his shoulders. He glanced at his watch — still a little early for Wrigley and Bullseye. But he could wait.

'Mind your car, mister?' a shrill voice cut through the night air. A scruffy kid, about ten years of age, skidded to a halt on his bike. His face and clothes were the colour of the road.

'What?' said Malice.

'Mind your car for a fiver?'

Malice reached over and yanked on the handle bars. The front wheel twisted and the kid toppled to the ground.

'Fuckin' hell.' The kid sprawled on all fours, trying to free his leg from under the bike frame.

'Jonas!' another boy yelled. The back wheel of his bike skidding in an arc as he shuddered to a stop. 'What are you doing?'

'This wanker knocked me off. All I said was—'

'Jonas, don't.'

'He knocked me over.'

'I'm sorry, Mr Malice. He's my cousin and he's new around here.'

'He's going to get himself hurt.'

'Who the hell is this joker?' asked Jonas, tugging his bike upright and rubbing his knees.

'I'll have a word, Mr Malice.' The second lad was a couple of years older and at least a couple a shades cleaner.

'You do that Aaron,' replied Malice. 'And while you're at it, tell him that around here you mind cars for a tenner.' He tossed a note onto the ground and walked away.

'I'll sort it, Mr Malice. Don't worry about your car.'

'I won't, Aaron. I won't.'

Malice broke into a jog and was soon at the house. He grabbed the corrugated metal sheeting, slid it across and stepped through into the garden. The back of the house was in darkness. He stopped in his tracks.

It's too quiet.

He paced to the back door and stuck his head inside. The usual human jigsaw of bodies lying on the floor was absent. He edged his way to the foot of the stairs and stopped.

It's way too quiet.

After taking the stairs two at a time, he reached the landing. The room to his right was in darkness. He sniffed the air — it smelled of rusted iron. Then he stepped across the threshold and saw the silhouette of a man sitting in the armchair.

'Okay, Bullseye?' Malice hissed.

He flicked the button on his phone and a shaft of crystal white light cut through the gloom. Bullseye's head was tilted back, eyes staring up at the ceiling, his mouth gaping open. The front of his Demin jacket was stained brown with congealed blood. A six-inch gash ran along the side of his neck.

Malice scanned the beam around the room. The place was empty and the floor had been swept clean.

Shit.

He clicked a button and the station number came up on his phone. His thumb hovered over the button. He stared at it, glanced at Bullseye, then back to his phone. He switched it off.

Back at his car both kids were waiting for him on their bikes.

'Everything is in order, Mr Malice,' Aaron nodded towards the vehicle. 'And Jonas wants to say sorry.'

'Oh, then let him say it.'

Malice unlocked the doors.

'Sorry Mr Malice,' said Jonas.

'That's okay son. You learned a couple of lessons today. Rule 1: Know who's who; Rule 2: Know the price of everything.'

'Erm, Mr Malice,' Aaron sidled over to him. 'A man came round and gave us this. He wanted to stick it under your wiper blade.' He held an envelope in his hand.

'What did you tell him?'

'Jonas said if he did, he was gonna shoot him.'

'What did the man say to that?'

'He laughed.'

'What did he look like?'

'He was old and wearing a brown leather jacket.'

'By old do you mean… like me?'

'Yeah. He was a white guy with black hair and he spoke funny.'

'Funny how?'

'Like he was off *EastEnders*.'

Malice took the envelope and opened the flap. Inside was a picture of his daughter –the same one Vasco had shown him earlier — plus a note. On it was written:

Ryedale Park at 6am tomorrow. I'll be feeding the ducks.

Chapter 34

Malice strode across Ryedale Park trying to visualise the person the kids had described to him at the Claxton. But all he saw was a dead man.

The bottoms of his trousers were soaking up the early morning dew. The sun was trying to break through and the cold pricked at his face.

In a few hours Hayley and Amy would be safe and he could turn his attention to 'fixing' his little problem. Until then, he would have to play along. He had to play nicely.

Malice wound his way along a path and crested the top of a hill. A large expanse of water surrounded by trees stretched out in front of him. He deviated from the path collecting more dew as he went.

The lake was oval shaped with heavy stonework around the edges. Off to his right he could see a man with black hair, wearing a leather jacket, sitting on a park bench near the water, reading a newspaper. Malice marched over and sat beside him.

'You were early for the last meeting as well, so I hear,' the man said, not looking up.

'I like to be consistent.'

'Consistent or predictable? Both can get you into trouble.'

'That depends on who you're dealing with.'

'True.'

'How did you get my number?'

'We looked it up in the phone book — it was under 'Bent copper'. Oh and that reminds me…' the man removed a mobile phone from his inside pocket and threw it into the water. 'Don't bother trying to trace us.'

'Wasn't going to… pretty sloppy you held onto it this long.'

'Mr Vasco said he liked you. He said you and I would work well together — make a good team.'

'What do you want?'

'He also said you didn't do small talk. I see what he means.'

'Who are you? The third fucking Mitchell brother?' Malice said noting the guy's accent.

'Ha, very good. In fact, you can call me that. Mitchell… it does have a ring to it.'

'Why are we here?'

'Do you go grocery shopping, Mr Malice?'

'What the hell does that mean?'

'You see, on occasions I do the food shop. The problem is my wife doesn't trust me, so every time I go she gives me a list.'

'Fascinating.'

'And every time she puts romanesco and samphire on the list. Do you know what they are?'

'No.'

'Neither do I. And do you know what I do when she does that?' Mitchell turned sideways to face Malice.

'No.'

'I don't give a fuck. Because I know if we don't eat romanesco or samphire the sun will still come up in the morning. Do you know what I mean, Mr Malice? Life goes on.'

'I'm surprised you're married.'

'Oh?'

'You must have a really big dick, cos you're boring as fuck.'

'I'm only telling you the story because I have a shopping list for you — the difference is if you don't get everything on it, the sun won't come up for your family.'

'You go near my family and I'll kill you.'

'I wish I had a pound for every time someone said that. I'd be a rich man and wouldn't have to do this job. Actually, no, that's a lie. I'd do this job for fun.'

'Fun is going to be tearing you into strips.'

'That's not a smart move because if anything unfortunate should happen to me, Hayley and Amy will find themselves at the bottom of this pond. In pieces, wrapped in plastic.'

'You're bluffing.'

'Nope, afraid not. And we've chosen this pond because it's not too deep and they'll be easy to find. There's no point teaching you a lesson if you don't get to see how much trouble we've gone to.'

'I'll fucking—'

'No you won't, because you're a smart guy, and smart guys don't get their loved ones killed. You seem to believe you have a choice in this. Let me tell you — as your new best friend — you don't. We like to keep things simple.'

'When this is over—'

'And that's the best part — it's never over. It's the gift that just keeps on giving.'

'I'll—'

'You may have noticed a number of your unsavoury friends are no longer here and that provides us with a business opportunity. You see, I always think bad people behave a little like Mother Nature. The absence of your friends has created a vacuum, and Mother Nature hates a vacuum and will always try to fill it. That's where Mr Vasco comes in.' The newly christened Mitchell pulled an envelope from his inside pocket. 'To help that process along, this is your shopping list. We want an outline of your Neighbourhood Policing strategy and plans, a list of target estates, current drug operations and future hot-spots. That's enough to be going on with.'

'By when?'

'We're not unreasonable, Mr Malice. You have until seven o'clock tomorrow evening to tick off the shopping list. Or the sun doesn't come up. Have a nice day.'

Mitchell got up and walked away.

'How do I contact you?' Malice called after him.

'You don't.'

Chapter 35

I called Elsa a bitch last night. She laughed in my face. 'Of course I am,' she'd replied. 'That's why you married me.'

I'd tried to convince her that screwing Malice was not a good idea, besides, he didn't fit the profile.

'But he's not a Pretty!' I'd yelled.

'He looks pretty good to me.'

'You know what I mean.'

'It kills two birds with one stone. It was clear to see that me coming on to him put him off his game, which can only be a benefit. And it gets me laid. Where's the downside? Everyone's a winner.'

'I'm not a winner.'

'You're a winner every day — you have me.'

'But he's a copper!' I'd exploded and thumped my hand into the table. She laughed again.

'I've never knowingly had one. It'll be fun.'

'Fun? Listen to yourself. He's investigating us and you want to shag his brains out.'

'That's right. Both of those things are true.'

'But I don't want you to.'

'I don't care what you want. It's what I want that counts.'

The argument had continued into the evening but Elsa had made up her mind. I slept in the spare room and left for work this morning without saying goodbye. It's the first quarrel we've ever had, and I have to admit I'm still in a turmoil. I'm not sure what to do. He's not a Pretty and she's breaking our contract. The more I think about it, the angrier I get. And the angrier I get, the more I think about it.

I have to blank out the events of last night and get my head straight. The courtroom is packed and there's work to be done.

It looks like the mauling I gave Tracey Bairstow yesterday in my cross examination has taken its toll. She is a 'no-show' today on the basis of being ill. Maybe another panic attack. I can sympathise, given that she's sliding down the tubes faster than a fat kid at Centre Parks — and given the fact she's actually innocent, it's understandable she's feeling a little under the weather. Poor thing.

The judge has allowed proceedings to continue as Tracey is expected to join us later. The defence have called an expert witness; a woman named Dr Carol Glen, who knows everything there is to know about blood patterns. I've done my homework and she claims to be able to not only identify the type of weapon used, but also the sequence of blows carried out in the attack.

The defence barrister is on his feet, exalting her expertise and pedigree. To be honest I've tuned out. It would appear here is a woman who could tell me the last time I'd taken a shit by the blood on my Bic razor.

I glance up at the bench and it looks like Peregrine Mason has all but nodded off. My mind drifts to when I first clapped eyes on Brendan Bairstow, or more to the point, when Elsa did.

Elsa and I were attending a Law Society dinner. She was turning heads in a backless dress cut down to the small of her back and not much more covering the front. The event was winding up and most of the people had gone home. Elsa was attracting the usual attention from well-healed letches.

She gave me one of her 'Get me the fuck out of here' looks and I obliged, retrieving her coat and handing it over, much to the disappointment of the chap who'd just bought her a drink. I suppose he thought a bottle of Dom Perignon was a reasonable price to pay for ogling my wife. A little like pay for view, only more expensive.

We were heading out of the venue when Elsa spotted Brendan. He kind of fell out of the club next door, staggering around on the pavement. He was surrounded by a host of flunkies doling out damp handshakes and fake kisses to anyone who wanted them. The effects of a hefty snort of coke had made him break into a sweat. His eyes were the size of pool balls.

Tracey came out and tried to drag him back inside but he was having none of it. He yanked his arm from her grasp and she slapped his face — hard. The surrounding entourage made an 'Oooo-ing' noise and beat a hasty retreat. As did Tracey when it became clear he was not going to budge.

Elsa slipped her coat off her shoulders and handed it to me. She walked over to Brendan and struck up a conversation. Minutes later she brought him over.

'This is Brendan, he's had a row with his wife,' she announced. 'I said I would take care of him.'

And take care of him she did — for the next three nights. It had been a long time since I'd heard Elsa scream her pleasure like that. But there was something about Brendan that made her hit the high notes every time.

Brendan was a dyed-in-the-wool, 24 carat Pretty, and I couldn't wait.

It's all gone quiet in the courtroom.

'Mr Kaplan, do you wish to cross examine the witness?'

Shit, I'm on.

'Thank you, your Honour.' I flatten my tie and get to my feet. I'm going to enjoy this one. 'Dr Glen, you have an impressive resumé.'

'Thank you,' she says, her hands clasped behind her back, oozing confidence.

'Would you care to tell the court how many times you have appeared as an expert witness?'

'Erm, I don't know exactly. I would say it has to be approaching one hundred times.'

'Ninety-seven, to be precise. Quite a track record.'

'I have a specialist set of skills that are in demand.'

'Indeed they are, Dr Glen, indeed they are. You have told the court, in some detail, that the blood spatter found in the bathroom at the home of Brendan and Tracey Bairstow is not consistent with a blow powerful enough to cause death.'

'That's correct. The droplets were—'

'If I may be so bold as to interrupt. I am not interested in hearing your *expert* opinion again, Dr Glen. I take it as read that it is correct.'

Glen shifted position and clasped her hands at the front.

'Thank you.'

'I say that with a degree of confidence because you are usually correct, aren't you Dr Glen?'

'Yes.'

'Usually.'

'Yes.'

'Shall we be more specific for the benefit of the court? In the ninety-seven times you have been called to give expert testimony, how many times has your opinion been correct?'

I glance across at the jury and watch as most of them shift forwards in their seats .

'Umm, what I do is based upon science and logic—
'

'How many times, Dr Glen?'

'I'm not—'

'Let me help you. Do you recall the case of Edward Drummond? He was convicted of murder in 2011 when he was nineteen years old. A conviction secured partly on the basis of your testimony. Do you recall the case?'

'Yes… yes I remember the case.'

'How many years did Edward Drummond serve of his ten-year prison sentence?'

'I'm not sure.'

'Let me help you again, Dr Glen. He spent four years and nine months at Her Majesty's Pleasure in Wakefield prison. A prison that is dubbed the Monster Mansion because of the number of high profile sex offenders and murderers held there. A prison that houses six hundred of the country's most dangerous people. But Edward Drummond didn't fit in at Wakefield jail, did he, Dr Glen?'

'I don't know.'

'He was a model inmate and was due to be released having served half his sentence. Would you like to tell the court why he was therefore released after four years and nine months?'

'His conviction was quashed,' she mumbled into her chest.

'Sorry, could you speak up, Dr Glen?'

'His conviction was quashed.'

'That's right. Three months before he was due to be let out on license Edward Drummond was acquitted of murder. Why was that, Dr Glen?'

She's staring straight ahead, looking at nothing.

'Dr Glen, please answer the question,' the judge says, he too shifting forward in his chair.

'He was acquitted because new evidence came to light.'

'That's right, it did. Evidence that proved he was forty-seven miles away at the time the murder took place. A claim he made throughout his trial but your expert opinion placed him at the scene of the killing.

'Four years and nine months he spent in one of the most violent jails in the UK for a crime he did not commit. Edward Drummond didn't fit into Wakefield prison because he was an innocent man. He was three months short of serving his allotted sentence when he was released. I ask the jury to put themselves in his place and imagine how that must have felt? To know you've almost served a life sentence for murder when you weren't even there. I ask you, Dr Glen — how must that have felt?'

'Awful ...'

'A supreme understatement I would have thought. Your testimony put that young man at the scene of a murder when he wasn't even in the same town. So, when we look at your exemplary record, Dr Glen, it is worth bearing in mind that you don't have a full house. Do you?'

'Erm... no...'

'Maybe we should call Edward Drummond as an expert witness for the prosecution. I'm sure he would be more than happy to tell the court what it's like to be on the other end of your *expert* opinion. No more questions your Honour.'

I sit down and watch Glen dissolve in a puddle of her own incompetence. Members of the jury are scribbling furiously.

A clerk of the court rushes in and mutters something behind a cupped hand to the judge. I can tell from the expression on Mason's face that something serious must have happened. He only looks like that when we've over run and he's missing his lunch. He beckons us to approach the bench.

Ten minutes later I'm back in my chambers gathering my things together. Looks like I'm going to be home early this evening.

Tracey Bairstow tried to commit suicide in her custody cell.

Chapter 36

Fat rain dropped onto the windscreen and the automated wipers made a sweep. Mitchell fiddled with the controls, adjusting his seat position.

'This is nice,' he said rubbing his hands around the thick steering wheel. 'Never driven one before.'

'It's a car, it gets me from A to B,' Vasco stared out the side window.

'An expensive way of getting there, though.'

Vasco shrugged his shoulders.

'I liked the colour.'

A young face appeared wearing a baseball cap.

'Here's you order sir.' The lad leaned out of the window.

'Keep the change, son,' Mitchell said, handing over a tenner.

'Thank you. The sauces are inside' He took the cash with one hand and handed over three paper bags with the other. 'Have a nice day.'

Mitchell passed them across to Vasco who put them at his feet in the footwell. The engine growled and he pulled away into the main flow of traffic.

'Have a nice day? Whoever thought that up was a genius,' mused Mitchell. 'No matter where you go in the world they always end the transaction with 'have a nice day'. We should think of a catchphrase like that.'

'Maybe something like 'hope you don't die', though it doesn't have the same ring to it.'

'Ha, no it doesn't.'

'Tell me again, how did it go with Malice this morning?' Vasco shifted his position to look at Mitchell.

'Fine. He got a bit stroppy but nothing much. I told him what we wanted and when we wanted it and that was it.'

'That doesn't sound like the man I was sitting opposite in the pub.'

'I can only tell you what I saw. He asked a few questions and we did a bit of verbal jousting but that was all.'

'You say he was stroppy?'

'Yeah, like a toddler who didn't want to put his shoes on.'

Vasco shook his head and fingered the tattoos circling his neck. He reached between his feet and lifted up the bag; the car smelled of fast food. He delved his hand inside and came out with clutch of chips. He stuffed them in his mouth and rubbed the back of his hand across his mouth.

'We need to watch him.'

'I have it under control Lubos.'

'I don't trust him.'

'Lubos, he's a bent copper, you're not meant to trust him.'

'No I don't mean like that; his reaction doesn't feel right. I don't like it.'

'Why do you say that?'

'Because it is exactly how I would have reacted.'

'You would have stuck a knife in me.'

'Not if I had something else planned. We need to take extra care.'

They arrived at a patch of derelict land. In the centre lay an abandoned building with a high corrugated roofline and grey cladded walls. A chain-link fence ran around the perimeter, peppered with warning signs. Every window in the place was shattered. They stopped at the metal gate. Mitchell got out, snapped open the padlock and yanked the gate across. They drove across the yard and disappeared through a gap in the wall into the loading bay and stopped.

The vast building was empty apart from the girders supporting what was left of the external construction. Puddles of water filled the recesses in the floor and the place echoed with their footsteps as they marched across to the far corner. A set of metal steps led down into a basement corridor where the compressors and electrical switchgear used to be housed. The equipment had long since gone and the darkness wrapped around them. At the end of the corridor was a light and the silhouette of a man sitting on a chair.

The man got up when he heard them approach.

'Všetko v poriadku?' Vasco called out.

'Áno, všetko ticho.'

'Urobte si prestávku.' Vasco nodded and handed over one of the bags. The man took it and wandered back towards the stairs.

Mitchell slid a bolt across and swung a door open. The stench of human excrement hit them in the back of the throat.

He walked to the back of the room and switched on a camping light. The yellow glow slid around the walls and ceiling. There were no windows in the small room and the bare concrete walls did nothing to reflect the light.

Wrigley was standing in the centre of the room, arms out stretched like he was being crucified on an invisible crucifix. His wrists were secured to the ceiling by heavy metal chains. He jerked his head up when they walked in.

'Phew! Looks like you've shit yourself, Wrigley,' Vasco said, waving his hand in front of his face. Mitchell switched on another light. 'Funny isn't it? That despite everything, the body still has its natural rhythm. I'm a 'first thing in the morning' guy as well. Always makes me feel better. Like I've started the day right. Do you get that feeling, Mr Wrigley? Like you've started the day right?'

Wrigley groaned.

Vasco shoved his hand into the bag and brought out a chicken nugget.

'You know, I could never understand people's fixation with eating this crap. That was until I had my first Happy Meal at the airport when I arrived in UK. And then I got it. This stuff is as addictive as the merchandise we sell, don't you think?'

Wrigley stared straight ahead. His face was a mess. Purple bruises, cuts and swellings made him almost unrecognisable. A map of dried blood covered the front of his shirt. Vasco popped another morsel into his mouth.

'I need a drink.' Wrigley coughed the words.

'All in good time. Who'd have thought the simple act of standing could be so painful, eh, Mr Wrigley? If you crouch down to take the weight off your legs and back, your hands go numb; if you stand upright, the cramps set in. It's ingenious really. When they did it to me, I lasted three days and almost went insane. You can have water when you tell us what we want to know.'

'I told you, I don't know anything.'

'I have no idea why you are hell bent on protecting these people. They wouldn't give a toss about you. So why don't you answer our questions and all this unpleasantness will be over.'

'I can't say what I don't know.'

Vasco pushed his face into Wrigley's. 'And that's my problem. I don't believe you.' Vasco then paced around the room stuffing chips into his mouth. 'Where I come from Mr Wrigley this would constitute nothing more than a cosy chat. Okay, you have a few superficial injuries but a hot bath, a box of pain killers and some rest and you'll be good as new. This is nothing more than a friendly conversation.' He dropped the bag to the floor, stood in front of Wrigley and held his hands up with his fingers spread. 'They cut off the tops of my fingers with bolt cutters and made me eat them. To coin a phrase you British like to use: they tasted like chicken. Their intention was to remove them a joint at a time, but my men arrived and now I have these,' he waggled his fingers in the air. 'Pretty cool, eh? So, you see, we've not even got started yet.'

Vasco picked his bag from the floor and continued to munch away. Mitchell went outside into the corridor and returned wheeling a trolley. When Wrigley snapped his head to the side he saw three lorry batteries stacked on top of each other and wired together. Two thick black cables with clamps on the ends trailed on the floor.

'No, no, no. I don't know. I swear to you.' His speech was mangled due to his split and swollen lips.

'We are not interested in you Mr Wrigley. We want to know who the people are further up the chain. Who supplies the gear, where does the money go and who's the top man? It's really simple.'

Mitchell connected one end of a cable to a battery terminal and pushed a bath sponge into the jaws of the clamp. He did the same with the second cable.

'I can't tell you what I don't know!' Wrigley yelled. 'For Christ's sake, why don't you people listen?' he began to sob. 'Please, please don't...'

'We do listen, it's just that we don't like what you're saying.'

Mitchell snapped open the hooked blade of a knife and sliced through Wrigley's shirt. Three more cuts and the material lay in tatters around his shoulders. His torso shone creamy white apart from the angry patchwork of bruises covering his body. He twisted the top off a bottle of water and drenched the sponges, then emptied the remainder of the bottle over Wrigley. He handed the clamps to Vasco, who had donned a pair of heavy rubber gloves.

'Your fingers are fine, for now, Mr Wrigley. But you might find this stings a little.' He shoved the sponges into Wrigley's chest. Mitchell grabbed his Happy Meal and turned to shut the door.

Chapter 37

'I reckon someone shot it with an air rifle, so the quality isn't great,' Marjorie Cooper said as she froze the image on the screen. It was a cobweb of fractures radiating outwards from a small round indent in the centre. The picture was a kaleidoscope of colour. 'I think that's her.'

Malice and Pietersen peered over her shoulder.

'I can't make out anything?' said Pietersen inching closer.

Cooper pushed her thick rimmed spectacles to the end of her nose and sighed. 'Okay, so this is what we have.'

Waite had delivered on her promise to provide help with the CCTV footage. Marjorie Cooper was a one-woman surveillance analysis team. Give her a time window and a location and if it was there… she'd find it. At fifty-something years of age and thirty-two years in the force, she had a healthy disdain for anyone who wore a suit to work rather than a uniform. Malice and Pietersen were no exception.

'On the day in question there were four trains from Paddington to Fallgate Station,' said Cooper. 'Three were on time and the one was half an hour late. This is the footage taken at the exit at 11.05am. From your description and the photograph, Belinda Garrett is around five feet nine inches tall, slim build with blonde hair. I reckon that's her.'

They peered at the screen, the image distorted by the splintered glass.

'It could be, but it's hard to be sure. Are there any other cameras at the station?' Pietersen asked.

'Yeah, there are three altogether. The other two are broken or out of service,' Cooper said sitting back in her chair and removing her glasses. 'This is the best I could find.'

'Do you have anything to show where she went from here?' Malice asked.

'Nothing. I called the taxi firms in the area and no-one picked up a woman matching Garrett's description at or around her time of arrival,' Cooper replied.

'Shit.'

Malice stepped away, his fingers scratching under his chin in frustration.

'Can you run the footage again please, from the time when she comes into shot,' Pietersen asked, her nose almost touching the screen.

'Sure,' Cooper wound the thumbwheel in reverse and clicked play.

'Mally, look. There's a flash of red.' Malice joined Pietersen at the VDU. 'She's pulling a case behind her.'

'Her flatmate thought there was an overnight bag missing from her room.'

'The next step would be to get hold of the CCTV from Paddington station around the departure time and any footage from inside the train,' Cooper said replacing her glasses to the bridge of her nose.

'I've already put in a request, I can narrow down the time-window,' said Pietersen.

'Let me know when you have it,' said Cooper.

Superintendent Waite bustled into the office.

'Can I have everyone's attention please?' She strode up to the evidence board. 'Dennis Cane, AKA Bullseye, was found dead this morning,' she stuck his mugshot on the board next to Burko. 'A bunch of kids found him in a drug house with a knife wound to his neck. This is the second death in as many days, both violent, both bodies discovered on the Claxton Estate. I've handed both cases over to the Murder Squad to be headed up by DI Malcolm Wilson. He is at the scene now with the Crime Scene Manager and the Forensic Pathologist. Cane had defensive wounds on his hands and arms and we're treating his death as murder. Both men had known drug connections, if you have any intel please brief Malcolm's team accordingly. Any questions?' She scanned around the room. 'No... carry on.'

'Shit, another one,' said Pietersen, walking over to the board.

Malice ran his hand through his hair and went back to his desk. His phone buzzed in his pocket. He took it out and read the message.

'Ma'am!' he scurried after Waite. 'Can I have a word?'

'My office,' she barked over her shoulder. Malice skirted around the desks and followed her out. 'What is it?'

'Amy isn't well. Hayley took her to the doctors this morning and they've referred her to a specialist at the hospital.'

'Oh, sorry to hear that. Is she okay?'

'Yeah, she has an ear and throat infection and is running a sky-high temperature. She'll be fine, but we just need to get her checked out.'

'What do you need from me?' Waite was doing her best to sound compassionate.

'I might need a few hours off to help Hayley. I know we're busy, but things haven't been good between me and—'

'Tell me a time when we're not snowed under. That's fine, just make sure Kelly knows what she's doing.'

'Thank you, ma'am.'

'How's she getting on?'

'Well let's put it this way... one thing I don't need to do... is make sure she knows what she's doing.'

Forty-five minutes later Malice was pulling up outside a row of domestic garages on the outskirts of a housing estate. Every one of the doors could have done with a lick of paint.

He stepped out, fished a small key from his pocket and unlocked the one with No.44 scratched into the metal. He twisted the handle and heaved the up-and-over door open. The mechanism complained with a squeal.

He shimmied himself between the car and the inside wall before sliding into the driver's seat. The car smelled like old socks. The engine spluttered then cranked into life on the third attempt, black smoke belching from the exhaust.

Malice edged out of the garage and parked to one side. Then he got out, leaving it running, and backed his car into the vacated space. It was a tight fit. He gathered up his things and squeezed himself out.

The garage door banged shut.

Behind the wheel, Malice checked the controls were in working order — indicators, wipers, lights — and opened the windows to rid the interior of the smell. To his amazement they worked as well. It had been fifteen years since his father had passed away and the Rover 75 had been his dad's pride and joy. Maybe that's why every time Malice had come to sell it, he couldn't bear to part with it. Though, why the hell the vehicle held such a special place in his father's affections had always been beyond Malice. It was a shed of a car. But at least it was running.

He reached under the passenger seat and his fingers found their target; a man's brown leather toilet bag. He lifted it onto his lap and ran the zip down.

The smell of gun oil wafted towards him.

Game on.

Pietersen sipped her coffee. It was hot and bitter. A young couple were perched on bar stools in the window while a woman sitting at another table nursed a pot of tea. She was staring into space with shopping bags at her feet. A TV on the wall was tuned to the news channel. This was much better, not only did she have coffee, but she wasn't going to return to the office stinking of piss.

Ryan Anderson stepped up to the counter and ordered an Americano. He picked a newspaper from a rack and sat at the table next to Pietersen.

'This is more like it,' she whispered, sipping from her mug.

'I'm pushed for time and this is closer to the office. Too public for my liking.'

'I prefer this place.'

'Your message sounded urgent.'

'They discovered the body of a man on the Claxton this morning. They're treating it as murder. I reckon it's the guy I saw Malice speaking to when he bolted from the car.'

'On which occasion?'

'The second.'

'I thought you said you didn't get a good look at them?' Anderson flicked open the newspaper and held it up in front of himself.

'That's right, I didn't. But I reckon it's the man I said looked like a beachball. His name is Dennis Cane, AKA Bullseye. I ran him through the system. One of his known associates is a guy called Wrigley. I think he was the other bloke that Malice spoke to. I'm putting two and two together here, but I'm pretty confident it's him.'

'That's good work.'

'Bullseye was into drugs and so is Wrigley. Possession, supply, that type of thing.'

'Do you think Malice is involved in the murder?'

'I don't know. This is the second killing. Another man called Burko was also found dead on the Claxton. The Murder Squad have opened an investigation.'

'What do you want from me?' Anderson turned to the sports pages.

'See what you can find out about the three men. I'm sure Malice spoke to two of them and he might be connected to the third. I've got my hands full with the missing person case and it would help if you could do some digging.'

'Okay.' Anderson took a pen from his inside pocket, scribbled on the newspaper and tore off the corner. 'Are you getting closer to Malice?'

'I'm trying.'

'Good. There's no need to see each other tonight unless something else blows up. We'll meet at the same place same time tomorrow.'

'But the café will be shut.'

'Not the café, the underpass.'

Anderson got up from the table and left.

Tosser!

Pietersen took a slug of coffee instead of yelling out what was in her head. She glanced up at the TV to see a headline scrolling across the bottom of the screen.

Case halted when Catwalk Killer attempts suicide.

She picked up her drink and wandered over to the screen. The woman eyed her and pulled her bags closer.

'Sorry, I just want to listen to this,' Pietersen said by way of explanation. The woman looked unconvinced.

'There was pandemonium outside Southwark Crown Court today...' a reporter yelled into a big fluffy microphone, while being buffeted from all sides. 'When the trial of the so-called Catwalk Killer was halted after the accused tried to kill herself in her cell. The judge has called for a postponement pending psychiatric reports. There is no word on the condition of the fashion designer Tracey Bairstow — the woman accused of murdering her husband, the model and entrepreneur Brendan Bairstow.

This high-profile case continues to rock the fashion world…'

Pietersen wasn't listening. She was watching the figure of Damien Kaplan being jostled by the crowd. While all around him wore troubled faces, he was grinning like a Cheshire Cat.

Chapter 38

Malice returned to the station to find Pietersen, once again, drawing arrows on the white board. The place was quiet apart from the sound of Waite giving some poor individual the benefit of her experience at full volume.

'Did you get things sorted?' she asked, replacing the cap on the pen.

'What?'

'Your daughter… you said she was poorly.'

'Oh yes. She has to have more tests but they don't think it's anything serious. You know what it's like with kids, you worry about the smallest thing.'

'You know I have a car instead of a boyfriend, right? So, no, I don't know.'

'She'll be okay. Thanks for asking. I've been thinking…'

'About?'

'We need to split up.'

'I wasn't aware we were…' Pietersen pulled a face.

'Very funny. What I mean is, if we make the assumption that it is Garrett at Fallgate Station then she had to have had a lift to the Kaplans' place.'

'Because the taxi firms came up with nothing,' said Pietersen, tossing a marker pen into the air and catching it.

'Correct. So maybe one of the Kaplans was waiting for her... or...'

'Or maybe it was our friendly taxi driver, Anna Robbins, the duty manager at the Mexborough.'

'She was a taxi service before, why not use her again?'

'What are you proposing?'

'You pay Robbins a visit and I'll drop by the Kaplans ... see if I can rattle them.'

'Is that wise?' she cocked her head to one side. 'Would it be better if I went to talk to Elsa?'

'I can handle Elsa Kaplan.'

'I think a spot of handling is exactly what she had in mind.'

Malice rapped his knuckles against the woodwork and the sound echoed around the hallway beyond. He stepped back and whistled at the grandeur of the house.

I wonder if it helps to have a gaff like this if you plan on being a swinger?

After a long pause, he then tramped across the front of the house, around the corner to the back garden.

'Hello. Anyone at home!' he called out. Nothing.

He shrugged his shoulders and walked back, cursing his wasted visit, when a car pulled through the gates onto the driveway.

Elsa Kaplan jumped out.

'Detective Sergeant how lovely. I wasn't expecting you. You should have called ahead and I would have been here for you.'

'Mrs Kaplan, I wonder if you have time to answer a few more questions?'

'Of course, come inside. I've been to the gym.' She was dressed head to foot in black and green Lycra sportswear with sparkly trainers. 'Go through into the kitchen while I change.' Before Malice could say a word, she scampered up the stairs.

Malice did as he was told. He mooched and picked up the ornate vase on the window sill. He flipped it over to find the inscription 'DK 10 Nov 2018' etched into the clay on the bottom. The sound of an electric shower reverberated through the ceiling.

Pietersen's words barged into his head.

I'll be fine.

Minutes later, Elsa came downstairs wearing a short bathrobe, towelling her hair dry.

'Let me fix you a coffee.'

'No, that won't be necessary, if I could just—'

'I'm having one and it would be rude to drink it on my own. How often do you go to the gym?'

'Occasionally.'

'You look like you work out a lot, very impressive.'

'We want to check—'

'Damien is at work. So, if you don't mind just talking to me?'

'That's okay, I wanted to ask if—'

'He's done it again, he knows I can't reach,' Elsa said, pulling a chair away from the kitchen table and positioning it against the worktop. She stepped up onto the seat and reached up. The bathrobe rode up. She held the position, the cafetiere in her hand. 'You were saying?'

Malice pulled his notebook from his pocket and was determined to stare at that. Elsa stepped off the seat giving him a generous glimpse of her inner thigh. Malice's notebook ploy wasn't working.

'Tell me again, when was the last time you saw Belinda Garrett?' asked Malice.

'Divorced or separated?'

'What?'

'You come over to me like a man that is either divorced or separated. My money would be on divorced. Am I right?'

'Can we stick to the questions, Mrs Kaplan.'

'That *is* a question, Detective.'

'When was the last time you saw Belinda Garrett?'

'Spoil sport,' Elsa pouted. 'It was at the Mexborough. She came over for the weekend as usual and it was then she told us she'd met someone. We wished her well in her new relationship. Of course it was sad but that's what happens.'

Elsa busied herself with the kettle and brought two mugs from the cupboard.

'You met her six times over a twelve-week period — every two to three weeks. The pattern suggests that you were due to meet her again on or around the weekend she disappeared. Had you arranged to see her again?'

Elsa poured boiling water onto the ground coffee.

'We've been over this once, Detective Sergeant, when you were last here.' She turned to face him, leaning against the worktop, the top of the robe coming loose. 'Why do you want to go over this again?'

'We need to be thorough.'

'Was I not convincing the last time?'

'As I said, we need to be sure.'

'Did you come here for something else?'

'What do you mean?'

Elsa stroked her finger down the lapel of the robe. 'Oh come on, Detective. Don't be coy.'

'Mrs Kaplan—'

'You liked my coffee so much you wanted more.' Elsa straightened the robe and poured the drinks. 'Here's your coffee, please take a seat.'

Malice sat on one of the chairs with the drink in front of him while Elsa continued to lean back against the work surface.

'So you didn't see Belinda Garratt again after the Mexborough?' he asked.

'That's right.'

'We have reason to believe that she visited your house the weekend she went missing.'

'Really? That's interesting,' Elsa took the seat opposite, clutching her mug in both hands. 'Why do you think that?'

'Did you or your husband drive to Fallgate train station to pick Belinda up?'

'Good heavens, no. As I said we've not had contact with her since.'

'Did you pay Anna Robbins to pick her up?'

Elsa shifted her position and the gown gaped open. 'Mmm… no, we didn't do that either. We only used Anna when staying at the hotel.' Elsa played with the silver chain around her neck. 'So, let me get this straight. You believe Belinda was at the train station and she was on her way here?'

Malice was struggling to maintain eye contact. He took a hasty swig of coffee to distract himself.

'There's a strong possibility, yes.'

'I can assure you, if her plan was to pay us a surprise visit, she didn't turn up. How's your coffee?'

'Umm, it's fine. Thank you,' Malice allowed his eyes to drop to Elsa's cleavage.

'Are you okay, Detective? Would you be more comfortable sitting in the lounge?'

'No, no, I'm okay here.'

'You look a little… uncomfortable.'

'I'm fine,' Malice dragged his eyes back to his notebook. 'If you hadn't arranged to meet Belinda, why would she make the journey here?'

'Search me,' Elsa made the theatrical gesture of holding her arms out to the side. The robe gaped further. 'It certainly wasn't so we could have one last good-bye fuck, because we'd already had that.'

'Is it possible your husband had made arrangements and kept them from you?'

'It is possible I suppose, but highly unlikely. We are a very open couple, Detective, and have no need for secrets.'

Malice was beginning to think Pietersen had been right.

'That's all for now, Mrs Kaplan. Thank you for answering my questions.'

'Oh don't go, you haven't finished your drink,' Elsa got up from the table. The gown parted to reveal her naked underneath. 'Can't you stay a little longer, I'm sure you have more questions for me.'

There was the sound of a key in the front door.

'Elsa! I'm home.'

Chapter 39

I'm charging around my workshop with an axe in my hand yelling at Elsa. She's nowhere to be seen. She's in the house doing what-ever-the-fuck she does when I'm not there. I'm shouting at myself because the bloody woman will not listen.

I'd arrived in the hallway to find Elsa in the kitchen with her bathrobe gaping open and *Malice* sitting at the table taking it all in. I made some excuse to get rid of him and just about managed to keep my temper in check until I heard his car disappear off the drive.

'I told you *no*!' I'd yelled at her.

'And I said it's not about what you want. It's never about what you want,' she'd replied, peering through the side window.

'He's not a Pretty.'

'What does that matter? I've screwed people before who aren't Pretties and you've not minded in the least.'

'This one's different.'

'Why? Because he's a copper?'

'No it's because… because…

'He's investigating us?'

'No, it's not that.'

'I told you… I'm putting him off his game. He's definitely interested.'

'For Christ's sake Elsa, this is different. I don't want you to—'

'You're over reacting. Nothing happened.'

'Only because I came home.'

'I must admit, your timing wasn't great,' Elsa said, faking a pout.

'I'll report him for misconduct in a public office.'

'No you won't, Damien. He'll deny it and I'll deny it. You'll make yourself look foolish. And anyway, I'm not sure the members of your practice would look too kindly on you bringing scandal to their door. Relax and let me have some fun.'

I'd faced her and took her hands in mine. 'Let's log onto the website and find you someone new. They don't have to be a Pretty, you can choose anyone you want. How's that?'

'I want him.'

'But I don't want you to have him.'

'I don't care.' She'd planted a kiss on my cheek and breezed past me, making her way up the stairs.

And that was it — discussion over. I picked the axe from the wood pile and retreated to my workshop.

I swing the razored edge through the air.

'I don't want you to have him,' my snarling voice reverberates off the walls. 'I don't want you to…' I chop away at some imaginary demon in front of me. 'He's an ugly bastard, why would you want to fuck an ugly bastard?'

I'm screaming at the top of my voice. The floor is peppered with droplets of saliva, blown through clenched teeth.

He's fucking ugly, she's breaking the contract.

I stomp into the proving room, yank the rack away from the wall and throw open the door. Callum greets me. His bloodless body, hanging by the hooks in his back.

'Argghh!'

The axe head buries itself into his shoulder. I work the handle back and forth to free the blade and the next blow slices deep into his neck. One of the hooks tears through the dead flesh under the impact. He's left swinging at an angle.

I take a back-hand swing which severs his head. His carcass clatters to the floor as the other hook gives way.

I raise the axe high above my head and bring it down between his shoulder blades. The sound of cracking ribs fills the small room.

'I said no!' I scream. My boot slams onto his back and the bones tear through his skin as I tug the axe free. 'He's fucking ugly.'

The axe head buries itself deep in the body cavity.

'You're breaking the contract!'

I swing the axe like I'm chopping wood. Bone and skin shower the walls and my legs.

His torso cleaves wide open.

In my head I can see her riding him like a rodeo bull at a fairground. The razor-sharp edge severs Callum's arm at the shoulder.

'I said no, Elsa. Fucking no!'

Chapter 40

Pietersen thumped her hand into the door and breezed into the office, the image of Kaplan's smiling face loomed large in her mind. Malice was sitting at his desk. While his laptop was open he wasn't taking a blind bit of notice of what was on the screen, he was gazing into the middle distance.

'You hungry?' Pietersen asked, dumping her bag onto the desk.

Malice jumped, crashing out of his daydream. The one filled with Lobos Vasco, Hayley and Amy – oh, and Mitchell's head on a spike.

'Hi, I was just…'

'Booking a holiday in your head from the distant look on your face. Have you eaten?

'No, what's the time?'

'Way past lunchtime. Grab your coat, my treat.'

'Why do I need a coat?'

'There's a pub up the road. They do cracking food. If you won't let me buy you a drink for fixing my car, the least you can do is let me buy you a Panini and a coke.'

'Panini...·that's like eating stale bread.'

'Bloody hell you're hard work. C'mon.' Pietersen fished her purse from her bag and stuffed it in her pocket. Malice thought about the offer and all of a sudden, he was starving.

'You're on.' He followed her out.

The pub was a ten-minute walk. Malice sucked in the fresh air to clear his head. Hayley should be at her sister's place by now, that is if she'd heeded his pleas for her to go. He checked his phone for the umpteenth time — nothing.

They walked in silence, each one deep in their own thoughts.

The pub was a regular haunt for the older boys at the station, but not today. Today it was empty but for a few blokes sitting at the bar, sinking beers like they were in a rugby club boat-race. A jumble of dark wooden tables and chairs choked the place, making it difficult to navigate a path to the long bar. The carpet and wallpaper had seen better days — probably sometime back in the eighties.

'Grab a table and I'll get a couple of menus.' Pietersen wandered over the chap standing behind the bar and staring up at a golf match playing on the TV. 'What do you want to drink?' she called over her shoulder.

'A coke,' Malice said, siding into a seat facing the door.

'Cheap date.'

His phone buzzed. The tension left his shoulders when he read the message telling him that Hayley and Amy had arrived safely at her sister's house. With them out of the way he could get down to the serious business of dealing with Vasco and his crew.

His mind was racing when Pietersen came back to the table carrying a couple of drinks and two packets of crisps gripped between her teeth. She opened her mouth to let them fall onto the table.

'Salt and vinegar or prawn cocktail?' she said. Malice took his coke and looked at her with his brow furrowed. 'They stopped serving food at two o'clock so it's only fair you get first choice.

'I wasn't planning on being *this* cheap.' he picked up a packet, ripped it open and laid it on the table between them. 'We can share.'

Pietersen followed suit with the other packet.

'Thanks for fixing my car.' She held up her drink.

Malice chinked his glass against hers. 'You're welcome, thanks for a sumptuous lunch.' He took a swig and munched on a handful of crisps.

'It's the least I could do.'

'How did you get on with the taxi woman?' he asked.

'Robbins hadn't had any further contact with the Kaplans since they last visited the hotel. Over the weekend in question she'd been running a staff training session and I can't see her being able to pick Belinda up from the train station. I also got Garrett's phone records back and there were no calls from either of the Kaplans after their last meeting.'

'That's not helpful.'

'Anyway... I'm more interested to know how you got on with Elsa?' Pietersen stuffed more crisps in her mouth and leaned forwards across the table. Malice retreated, sitting back in his chair and wiping his mouth with the back of his hand. 'Well, what happened?'

'I was saved by the bell when her husband came home unexpectedly,' he replied.

'Oh shit! I was joking when I said—'

'Let's just say you were right.'

'Did she come on to you?'

'More or less laid it on a plate — literally.'

'What did you do?'

'Stuck to the questions and made a sharp exit when Damien got home. He didn't seem best pleased to see me,' Malice took a swig of coke and grabbed more crisps.

'Did you manage to rattle her cage?'

'Not that I could tell. She kept to her story and simply reflected our latest thoughts back to me; if Belinda Garrett was at Fallgate station, they were unaware of it and she didn't visit their house.'

Pietersen nodded and tapped the side of her head with the index finger of her right hand. 'Ah, that makes sense. I reckon Damien must have come home early because the trial he's working on got put on hold when the accused tried to commit suicide.'

'How the hell do you know that?' Malice almost spat his lunch out.

'I saw him on TV leaving the courthouse, smiling like a crazy person.'

'Smiling?'

'Yes, like his numbers had come up on the lottery. Never seen a bloke look so happy. Can't get his face out of my head,'

'They seem both as bad as one another.'

'Did you believe Elsa?'

'No, I didn't. She's lying.'

'Yessss, get in!' the man behind the bar punched the air with his fist. Then looked around sheepishly and started cleaning glasses with a towel.

Pietersen finished off the last of the crisps and ran her finger around the packet, picking up the crumbs. 'We need hard evidence that Garrett was on that train. Then the next time we speak to them will be in an interview room at the station.' Pietersen licked the salt from her finger and changed tack. 'The guy found murdered on the Claxton, he was the man you spoke to when you bolted from the car the other day,'

'Shit, Kelly, where did that come from?' Malice did a double take.

'I recognised his mugshot.'

'Yeah, it was him, or rather, it was the other guy I wanted to talk to. Bullseye never says a lot.'

'Have you told DI Wilson?'

'Not yet I haven't had chance. Too busy fending off Elsa Kaplan.'

'What did you speak to him about?'

'C'mon, Kelly, not this again.'

'We're working together and I want to help,' Pietersen tried to make the comment sound like a casual remark but deep down she knew it was a clumsy approach. What else could she do?

'Like I said, it wasn't Bullseye I spoke to.'

'What did you say to Wrigley?'

'Wow! How did you...?' he did a second double take.

'It says Detective on my warrant card, you know? What did you talk about?'

'Bloody hell, Kelly. If you must know it was mostly bollocks. But it's good to keep your ear to the ground.'

'Are they informants?'

'Not officially, but they know what's going on.'

'And they tell you?'

'Something like that.' Malice played with his phone, flipping it over and over on the table. He picked up the empty glasses. 'Do you fancy another?'

A man in his late twenties pulled up the chair and plonked himself next to Pietersen. 'So, you weren't able to come out for a cheeky one last night, and yet here you are – having a cheeky one.'

'Do you mind? This is work, Martin.' she huffed.

'Looks like a cheeky one to me,' the new arrival reached across with an open hand. 'My name's Martin, pleased to meet you.'

Malice shook it.

'My name's Mally, I work with Kelly.'

'Apparently so.' Martin replied breathing alcohol fumes across the table.

Pietersen squared herself to face him.

'Bugger off, Martin.'

'That's not very nice, I've only just got here.'

'Yeah, well you can 'only just' piss off and drink somewhere else,' she held his stare.

Martin straightened in his seat, swept his floppy fringe across his forehead and fingered the silver earring in his left ear. His denim jacket was stylishly threadbare and his beaming white smile would have lit up his face if it wasn't for his bloodshot eyes. 'But I've made a new friend,' he nodded towards Malice, 'and it would be rude of me not to buy a round of drinks.'

'Martin you're being a prick,' Pietersen said.

'Kelly do you want me to—' Malice got no further.

'I got this,' Pietersen held up her hand to cut him off.

'What were you two talking about? I love a nice chat,' Martin asked, resting his elbows on the table and looking from one to the other.

'Leave now,' she whispered.

'Fucking hell Kell, I only want a chat.'

'Do one,' Pietersen said, getting to her feet and leaning over him

Martin remained in his seat, staring at the table. He jumped up, his face inches from hers. 'And what happens if I don't want to?' He grabbed her shoulder. 'What if I—'

Pietersen clamped her hand over his and wound her right arm around his shoulder. She forced him over double, banging his face into the table. Malice snatched the glasses to stop them bouncing to the floor.

The barman tore himself away from his afternoon viewing and called out, 'No rough stuff inside, use the carpark around the back.'

'And I told you to go,' she grabbed a handful of hair at the back of his head and spat the words into his ear.

'Shit, Kell, I was only …' he whimpered, his fingers clawing at the varnish on the table.

'Now fuck off.' Pietersen released him and Martin staggered backwards, rubbing his cheek.

'Bitch,' he ricocheted off a couple of tables on his way to the door. 'You're a psycho.'

'Yeah, that's right Martin, I'm the psycho,' Pietersen remained standing.

'Bitch,' he snarled as he barged his way outside onto the pavement. The door clattered shut behind him.

Malice was still holding two empty glasses, one in each hand.

'You okay?' he asked.

'I told you - I got this.'

'Who the hell was that?'

'That … was what I swapped for a Porsche.'

'Do you want to leave?'

'Christ no, I want to know what Wrigley told you'

Chapter 41

Malice was finding it hard to concentrate. He glanced at his phone under the desk. The picture of Amy and Hayley taken outside their home was on the screen. Beneath it was a new message.

Whistle and Flute, 7pm today, table 10.

The text had come through shortly after the altercation between Kelly and her ex at the pub. Malice had made up some cock and bull story about needing to get back to the station and they'd left. Which was a blessing — because Pietersen's questioning about Wrigley was beginning to grate on him.

He checked his watch — not long to go now.

Pietersen had her eyes glued to the CCTV footage of Paddington station at the time Garrett caught the train, while Marjorie Cooper did the same. It was clear there was professional reputation at stake regarding who would find her first. Malice's money was on Cooper.

He pressed pause and zoomed in. The face of Damien Kaplan filled the screen.

Christ, I can see what she meant.

The picture showed Kaplan on the steps outside the courthouse and all around him were stunned and worried faces while he wore the broadest grin — like all his Christmases had come at once. Malice scrolled through the files gathered during the investigation.

Shit.

'Hey Kelly, come and take a look at this,' he called across the office.

'What is it?'

'Maybe nothing but…'

Pietersen pushed herself away from the laptop and stood up, stretching her arms above her head. Cooper glanced over and cracked half a smile. The advantage was hers.

'Kelly, could you step into my office please?' Waite poked her head around the door. A Superintendent trumps a Sergeant any day.

'I'll take a look at it later,' Pietersen said to Malice, who shrugged his shoulders. She followed her into her office.

'Please close the door,' Waite said, taking a seat behind her desk. 'This is Frank Crosley from the Professional Standards Department.'

'PSD? What's this about, ma'am?'

'Kelly, do you know a Martin Edwards?' Crosley asked.

'Yeah.'

'How do you know him?'

'He's an ex-boyfriend. We were engaged to be married but split up about seven months ago.'

'He's made a serious accusation that you assaulted him in the Riverboat Arms public house earlier today. He said it was an unprovoked attack.'

'That's nonsense.'

'You understand we have a duty to investigate all complaints?' he replied.

'I understand the role of PSD, and I can assure you he's making it up,' Pietersen shook her head and rolled her eyes.

'He walked into a police station to report the assault,' Crosley continued.

'But it wasn't like that, he put his hands on me and I defended myself.'

'He disputes that account and has a witness statement from the barman who also says you attacked him first.'

'Ma'am, I can assure you this is rubbish,' she held her hands out in front of her palms facing up.

'It's Mr Crosley you need to talk to Kelly, not me,' Waite replied.

'The CCTV from inside the bar will confirm my version of events,' Pietersen said.

'We spoke to the barman and the CCTV is out of action.'

'Bloody convenient. Just a second.' Pietersen left the room and came back with Malice. 'DS Malice was with me when Martin came into the pub.'

'What happened, Mally?' asked Waite.

'Umm,' Malice cleared his throat. 'We were sitting at a table, discussing the Garrett case and this guy barged his way into the conversation. He was reeking of booze and slurring his words. I didn't know who he was but it was obvious Kelly did. She asked him to leave on several occasions and he refused. It appeared to me that he wanted to provoke an argument, he was looking for a fight, but Kelly was having none of it. I asked if she needed assistance and she said 'no'. He got more and more aggressive and grabbed her by the shoulder. Kelly defended herself and placed him in a restraining arm lock. The force used was appropriate. When she released him, he did a lot of swearing and left. That was it. Why, what's this about?'

'Would you be willing to make a statement to that effect?' Crosley asked.

'Of course. Has this Martin guy made a complaint?' said Malice

'He said I attacked him,' said Pietersen.

'Is anyone taking into account this guy was pissed as a fart?' said Malice.

'I can assure you we know how to deal with this, DS Malice,' Crosley bristled.

Malice shook his head.

'And I can assure you that is not what happened,' Pietersen continued to protest.

'Okay, I'm satisfied for now but I'll need statements from both of you,' Crosley got up to leave.

Waite dismissed Malice and Pietersen with a wave of her hand and they returned to their desks.

'The little shit,' Kelly said under her breath.

'He seems a nasty piece of work, you're better off with the Porsche,' Malice replied.

'Thanks for doing that. I owe you again.'

'There's only so much coke and crisps a guy can take.'

'No seriously, thank you.'

'When you came to get me and mentioned PSD I knew what must have happened. You'll be fine, don't worry about it.'

'With everything we have on right now this is not what I need,' she slumped back in her seat.

'I thought at one point you were going to shove his head through the table.'

'Don't think it didn't cross my mind.'

'Good job you didn't.'

'You said you had something to show me.'

'Hey you two.' It was Cooper. 'Come and see what I've got.'

They scurried over to where she was sitting. She pushed her glasses onto the end of her nose and gestured at the screen in a 'ta-da!' kind of movement.

'This is Garrett boarding the train at Paddington at 10.35 from platform seven and this is her caught on the onboard camera leaving the train at 11.43. A journey time of an hour and eight minutes which would put her at Fallgate Station. It took me a while to locate her because the train had been delayed coming into Paddington and consequently had a platform change.' Cooper sat back, her record intact.

Malice and Pietersen stared at the two images on the screen.

'I think we need another chat with the Von Trapps,' said Pietersen.

'And a warrant. That's amazing, Marjorie, thank you.'

Cooper pushed her glasses to the bridge of her nose and gathered her things together.

'I am the eyes of this police force, DS Malice, I see everything.' She swept out of the room with an air of 'my work here is done'.

'You said you had something to show me,' Pietersen asked.

'It was what you said about Damien Kaplan leaving court.'

'Honestly, it was freaky. I can't get his face out of my head.'

'You mean this face,' Malice spun his laptop around to show the grinning features of Damien Kaplan.

'Given they'd just been told the accused had attempted suicide – that is weird.'

'I agree. So I did a spot of digging.'

'And?'

'The case involves a celebrity couple from the fashion business where the wife is accused of murdering her husband. They have a well-documented and turbulent relationship with a history of physical violence on both sides. He's reported missing by his agent and the wife knows nothing about his whereabouts. His blood has been found in the marital home but so far, they've not uncovered his body. She denies the charge but there is a ton of circumstantial which points the finger at her.'

'Why are you tell me this?'

'One of the reasons they've been unable to find the husband is he left his mobile phone at home on the day he went missing. Does that sound familiar?'

Chapter 42

I open the kiln and remove the metal trays. They are warm to the touch but not too hot to handle. One by one I tip the powdered ash into a plastic container and snap the lid shut. Callum's remains have filled it nicely.

My initial flush of rage has subsided and chopping his body into bite sized chunks definitely helped. But the anger remains.

He's ugly. She's breaking the contract.

If she wanted to screw someone ugly — she has me. She doesn't need to go elsewhere.

I've spent the whole day in my workshop and I'm parched and famished. I take the plastic container and head to the house. Elsa is in the kitchen.

'Oh hi, I was wondering when you'd surface,' she says, coming over to give me a kiss. I skirt around the other side of the table to avoid her.

'I'm going out.'

'You're not still annoyed, are you?'

'No I'm not annoyed.'

'That's good, because, as I said, nothing—'

'I'm fucking furious.'

'Oh, come on, Damien don't be like that. I'll make it up to you,' she says, reaching across and grabbing my hand. 'Do you fancy something special?'

'I'm not in the mood.'

'Maybe not now, but when you get back…'

'Are you going to give up chasing that copper into bed?'

'No.'

'Then I'm not interested.'

'For Christ's sake, Damien. What's got into you?'

'I'm off out.'

I storm out of the house and get into my car. The engine cranks over and I speed away. I can't get the vision of Elsa writhing around in our bed with that bastard out of my head. The picture stays with me all the way to the quarry.

I get out and weave my way through the fence to the rim of the overhang. The water at the bottom is black and still; it looks like crude oil. The lid snaps open and I bring out a heaped handful of Callum. My fingers unfurl and he takes off on the wind. It's not the last journey he's going to make. I have a competition coming up and the dear boy will be taking pride of place. He's coming to Leeds with me.

I try to visualise the design of the piece I intend to make, but Elsa barges into my head again. That bloody copper is stood in our kitchen with his trousers around his ankles, she's on her knees giving him the Dyson treatment.

I bury my hand in the ash and throw a fistful into the air.

Now she's on all fours and he's banging her from behind.

The next handful gets hurled.

The sweat on his back is glistening as he fucks my wife to a standstill. She's wailing like an alley-cat.

I throw the container and watch it clatter down the steep embankment to the water below; clouds of ash catching on the breeze.

Elsa's breaking the contract.
She wants to fuck an Ugly.

Chapter 43

Pietersen picked her way between the puddles of questionable origin to reach the mid-way point in the underpass. The acrid stink of piss rasped at the back of her throat. She checked her phone then tutted to herself. She was early.

She'd wanted to time her journey so she spent as little time in this cesspit as possible. Now all she could do was try not to gag as she was waiting. The mould covering the walls seemed to have spread since she was last here. The click-click-click of marching heels grew louder and Ryan Anderson appeared at the opposite entrance. He strode towards her, oblivious to the puddles.

'We met this morning, is there a problem?' he squawked when he was in earshot.

'No, I don't think so,' she shook her head and shrugged her shoulders.

'What does that mean?'

'I got into a scrape with an ex-boyfriend and he's lodged a formal complaint. PSD are involved. I don't think it jeopardises the operation but I thought you needed to know right away.'

'Fuck! What happened?' Standing beside her, he flicked a cigarette from the packet and lit up.

'He grabbed me in a pub and I restrained him. He's saying I attacked him first and the barman is supporting his version of events.'

'Any witnesses?'

'Malice was with me and will provide a statement saying it was self-defence and reasonable force was used.'

'What did the person from PSD say?'

'He said it was fine for now and he'd be in touch.'

'Shit, Kelly, what were you thinking?' Anderson walked around his small circles with his hands stuffed in his pockets, blowing smoke around.

'I was thinking of not getting beaten up — that's what I was thinking,' she shrieked back at him.

He stopped and shook his head, puffing away like he was about to chuck the habit forever. 'We can't get involved, it would compromise your position.'

'I don't want you involved. The purpose of this conversation is to keep you in the picture, that's all.'

'Let's hope your ex drops the complaint when he learns about the witness statement.'

'Yeah, he might not,' she shook her head.

'Okay, we'll cross that bridge when we come to it. How's it going with Malice?'

Pietersen coughed and waved her hands in front of her face as a cloud of smoke enveloped her.

'Fucking hell, Ryan, as if this place wasn't bad enough.'

'Sorry.' He tossed what was left of the fag onto the floor, not bothering to stub it out with his foot. The piss would take care of it.

'I think I'm getting somewhere. He started to open up about Bullseye and Wrigley but then it all kicked off at the pub and he went silent on me.'

'That's good. You seem to be gaining his trust. I'm sure this complaint will fizzle out. Apologies that I reacted the way I did. It's just–'

'I know, there a lot riding on this.'

'There is. Are we done?' he half-turned to walk away.

'I don't think it's him.'

'Who, Malice?'

'I know he fits the profile, but I think we're barking up the wrong tree.'

Anderson stepped in front of her and cocked his head to one side. She screwed up her face at his ashtray breath.

'Are you serious, Kelly? Operation Honeywell has been a huge success. We've recovered close on eight million pounds worth of assets and seized as much again in drugs. Everything Casper has given us has been absolute gold: warehouses, counting houses, trade routes – the full shebang. Not to mention a fistful of bad people who are now behind bars.'

Pietersen turned away and slapped her arms to her sides, it was her turn to walk in small circles. For once, ignoring the puddles.

'I've read the files so I know all that, but there's a nagging voice at the back of my head telling me it's not him.'

Anderson grabbed her arm, blocking her path.

'Now listen, Kelly, you need to stick with this. Casper went into witness protection and has been singing better than Susan Boyle ever since. He told us there was a bent copper in this division, so we ran the numbers and came up with Malice. You know the type: he has a prickly association with authority, he's been had up on multiple disciplinary charges, has a stalled career, a broken marriage, two houses to finance – the list goes on. You have to admit he fits the bill.'

Pietersen yanked her arm free and shoved herself into his personal space.

'You don't think I know all that?' she hissed the words through gritted teeth. 'But I can't help feeling we're looking in the wrong place.'

Anderson backed away.

'It's natural that you have doubts, you've formed a good relationship with him. You said yourself you're gaining his trust. It takes time.'

'Make up your mind! The other day you were pushing me for results!'

'I know, but that's my job. I need to know that every day you're moving things along. You're doing great – don't let yourself be knocked off course.'

She stared at the floor, grinding her teeth.

'Okay.'

'Same place, same time tomorrow?'

'For fuck's sake.'

Malice pounded his fist into the bag and the chains jolted against their fixings in the roof. He followed through with a left hook and a straight right. When the bag swung back, he gave it a savage right hook; heaving out a roar as he did so.

He needed to clear his head, to rid himself of the problems of the day. This was the best way he knew how.

Jim was dancing around the ring with a couple of youngsters, demonstrating some nifty footwork. He moved like someone forty years his junior.

'Balls of your feet, balls of your feet!' he chanted. 'Sideways step, balls of your feet.' The two men dancing next to him were gloved up and wearing head guards. 'Right, let's go again.' Jim stepped aside and the men squared up to each other.

Malice removed his gloves and towelled the sweat from his face. When he'd arrived over an hour ago his shoulders ached and his neck hurt — the occupational hazard of someone who spends their time sitting down and staring at a laptop for a living. He rolled his head from side to side and walked to the changing room.

That's better.

The place was empty. Malice showered and changed out of his kit into casual clothes. The only thing that wasn't casual were the steel toe-capped boots he pulled on and laced up tight. He reached up and brought down the medical kit from a shelf and opened it up. After fishing around, he found the pack of razor blades. He removed one, unwrapped it from the waxy paper and wound off a length of sticking plaster. He repeated the process twice more and put the box back where he found it.

Then he made his way across the gym to the door marked Exit.

'You didn't fancy taking on that little ball again then?' Jim yelled at him.

'Bollocks!'

'Yeah, that's what's in your head.'

Malice didn't turn around. He flipped Jim the middle finger and walked out into the night air. He flung his kitbag into the back and slid into the driver's seat.

The problem was, Malice needed to be in two places at once — preferably three. He drummed his fingers against the steering wheel and resorted to his favourite method of choosing:

If it was me, what would I do?

He turned the key and set off.

The petrified rubber on the wiper blades did nothing but smear the rain across the windscreen. He cursed and slowed down, unable to see. The headlights of the cars coming towards him dazzled through the thin film of water. It was a shit car, for sure, but it did have one redeeming feature — Vasco and his men had never seen it before.

After driving for fifteen minutes he pulled over against the kerb, flipped open the glove compartment and stuffed the gun down the back of his jeans.

If it was me, I'd go for Hayley.

He stepped out, wrapped the collar of his coat around his neck and tugged the peak of his cap over his eyes. The streetlights washed the road in an orange glow. He walked towards No.37, scanning left and right as he went. At the entrance to the drive he bent down to fiddle with his laces. One last check. Nothing.

Malice strolled up the front steps and pushed a key into the lock. The front door swung open and he went inside.

If Hayley knew I had a key she'd go ape-shit.

He unloaded his bulging pockets; several lengths of chord, two rolls of duct tape and a knife. He went through the house, drawing the curtains and switching on the lights.

Mitchell had seemed old school when Malice met him by the lake. He was gambling on his methods being old school as well.

This would be a two-man job. The first guy goes around the back of the house while the other knocks on the front door. When the home owner opens the door the second guy engages them in conversation: *'I wonder could you help me, I'm looking for a Mr Williamson, I think he lives around here?'* The guy at the back gains entry to the property and waits. When the conversation ends the homeowner goes back to watching *Casualty* or whatever and is over powered. Once secured, the first guy lets the second guy into the house. And then the fun begins. Tried and tested, works every time.

Malice left the kitchen light off and unlocked the back door. No need to have windows smashed when it wasn't necessary — Hayley would do her nut.

He settled down with his back against the cupboard and checked his watch. 7 p.m.

Game on.

His phone vibrated in his pocket. He pulled it out. It was a text message from an unknown number.

On the screen was a picture of Hayley and Amy standing next to a blue Ford Fiesta — *her* blue Ford Fiesta. Hayley was chatting to a woman standing in the doorway of a terraced house. The message on the bottom read:

Hope Hayley's having a nice time with her sister. Don't keep me waiting.

Chapter 44

Malice scrabbled to his feet and dashed about the house switching the lights off and opening the curtains. He slammed the back door shut, locked it, then sprinted out the front and down the steps. His heart banging against his ribcage.

The old diesel engine complained when he slammed his foot into the carpet in an attempt to race up the road. It managed a leisurely take-off until the revs got high enough to give it a kick in the arse. Malice's head was a turmoil of possibilities.

Did they have Hayley and Amy? Was there someone with them now? What if ...?

He shoved the thoughts to the back of his mind and concentrated on getting to the Whistle and Flute without killing himself or the car in the process.

Twenty minutes later he screeched to a halt in a side street, picked a buff coloured folder from his kit bag and legged it up the road. He reached the pub when a black van pulled alongside him and the tall, lean guy that Malice had seen before jumped out of the passenger seat and slid open the side door.

'You're late. There's been a change of venue, get in.' Malice glanced inside the cab to see the big guy with the bald head and leather jacket behind the wheel. 'Lubos is expecting you,' he said in mangled English. 'Gimme your phone.'

'What?'

'Your phone, give it to me.'

Malice reached into his pocket and handed it over. The Slovak dropped it onto the road and crunched it under the heel of his boot.

'Hey! What the hell?'

'Get in the van.'

Malice stepped up into the back and the door clattered shut behind him. The back windows were blacked out and the window into the driver's cab was boarded up, leaving the interior completely dark. The van pulled away and Malice fell to the floor, sliding into the back doors as the vehicle powered up the road.

'Fuck!' he yelled trying to get up. A sharp right turn sent him crashing against the side. He spread his arms and legs out like an upturned starfish to gain some stability. A left turn had him smacking into the other side.

Malice couldn't see a hand in front of his face. The van steadied and he was able to slide on his arse and jam himself into the corner, digging his heels into the corrugated floor. It was like being in a tumble dryer.

He tried to get his bearings but the constant turn-left, turn-right, had him disorientated. He braced his body and had no choice but to ride it out.

Half an hour later the van shuddered to a stop. Malice heard the cab doors open and the side door slid across. The two men walked away. He rubbed his elbows and knees trying to massage the bruises away, then shuffled forwards and peered outside. He was in a warehouse which, from the look of it, had long since been decommissioned. The place was bathed in semi-darkness with pools of water on the floor where the rain had come through the roof. He staggered out and arched his back, he could feel the vertebrae cracking into place.

In the centre of the vast space was a free-standing metal structure. A huge mezzanine platform supported high in the air by eight stanchions with a prefabricated office perched on top.

'Mr Malice!' It was Mitchell standing at the base of a staircase leading to the floor above. 'Please come and join us.' His voice reverberated around the cavernous interior.

Malice walked towards him carrying the file. Mitchell beckoned for him to follow up the steps to the office. 'Glad you could make it. We were worried about you.' The metal staircase creaked and groaned as the men climbed the stairs. The room was big with windows set in one side overlooking the warehouse floor below. There was a distinct smell of mouse droppings and dead rodents.

A large oval table took centre stage, surrounded by chairs and a chest freezer hummed in the corner. Fluorescent lights buzzed overhead. Malice said nothing and went inside to find Lubos Vasco flanked by the big bald guy sporting his leather jacket.

The lanky bloke made the universal gesture that said 'raise your arms'. Malice did as he was told and an expert pair of hands patted him down. In seconds he was relieved of his gun and his knife.

'This is where we hold our board meetings,' Vasco said, sitting at the head of the table, his hands folded on top of themselves.

'Bet you don't take minutes,' Malice said, dropping his arms while making a snap assessment of his situation — *Not good.*

'Ha, no we don't. Sorry about the transport. We could have put a bag over your head but that is so overdramatic. Danek is a terrible driver, I hope the ride wasn't too rough.'

'It was fine. Why the change of venue?' replied Malice.

'When I heard about the conversation you had with your new best friend, I think you've christened him Mitchell — which is very funny, I love the way you Brits give each other names that, how you say, 'take the piss'. Anyway, I took the precaution of not believing you and thought some additional security measures were in order.'

Mitchell picked up a briefcase which was sitting behind the door and took a seat at the table, he rolled up his sleeves.

'Maybe he gave you a skewed version of our chat,' Malice jerked his thumb at Mitchell, causing him to smile.

'No, no I don't think he did. Why is your ex-wife and daughter staying with her sister?' asked Vasco.

'No reason.' Malice yawned and moved across to the window with his back to Vasco. The lights inside the office made it impossible to see what the rest of the warehouse had to offer. 'She often goes there. Her sister is divorced as well so it's great opportunity to drink wine and bitch about their ex-husbands.'

'It is like that the world over, Mr Malice. Only in my country they do it with vodka. Why is it women choose to marry rubbish men and are then horrified to find they make rubbish husbands? I'm sure you were a little on the wayward side before she met you?'

'I was,' Malice turned and edged towards him. The big guy stepped forwards. 'It's like the saying goes: a man marries a woman hoping she won't change and she does, while a woman marries a man thinking she'll change him and he doesn't.'

'You're a philosopher, like me, Mr Malice. I said I liked you.'

'Can't say it's mutual.'

'My problem is I don't believe you: It is unusual to take your daughter out of school during term time, am I right?'

'What can I say, she's a terrible mother.'

'I hope you weren't thinking of doing anything stupid?' Mitchell chipped in.

'Like stealing sensitive operational information from my employers? That kind of stupid?' Malice said, pulling up the chair which was closest to the door. The lanky guy crabbed sideways and stood in the entrance.

'You came tooled up,' Mitchell said eyeing the weapons.

'Like I said – I'm not stupid,' said Malice, trying to keep the man by the door in his peripheral vision.

'Very wise, Mr Malice. Now let's try again; why were you late and why is your wife not at home?'

'Hayley has taken Amy to visit her sister. There's nothing unusual about that, and as for me being late …' Malice slid the folder across the table. 'This proved more difficult than I thought.'

'Is it all there?' Vasco picked it up and flipped open the front cover.

'Not quite. The force is taking part in a neighbourhood policing conference so I couldn't get my hands on some of the material. I'll have it next time.'

Vasco thumbed through the papers. 'This is good, you have been a busy boy.'

'Maybe I'll get a gold star?' Malice stole a sideways glance at Mitchell.

'Maybe. But I'm still perplexed by your ex-wife and daughter.'

'Why's that?'

'To be honest it's less to do with them and more to do with you.'

'I don't understand,' Malice pursed his lips and shook his head.

'I told Mitchell that I liked you, because I look at you and I see myself. I am the bleached version of course but inside we are the same.'

'I have all my fingers, so maybe not.'

'Ha, there you go again, with the ready joke. You and I are very much alike and if it were me I would have sent my ex-wife and child away. Then I would have abducted one of my men and sliced bits off him until he revealed as much about the organisation as possible. But most importantly I would want to know … where does Lubos Vasco hang out? Am I right?' Vasco leaned forward, placing his heavily tattooed forearms of the table and cracking his knuckles.

Malice leaned forward and did the same.

'It's an interesting theory,' Malice said as his joints popped under the pressure. 'But you've failed to consider what's in the file. If I was going to do that, why would I go to the trouble of lifting the intel?'

'That's easy …' replied Vasco. 'It's called *contingency*. I believe that like me you're a thinker, and I would be thinking – what if my plan goes, how you say, tits-up? I would need a fall-back position to keep everything on an even keel, while I wait my chance.'

'Chance to do what?'

'Kill us all.'

'Ha!' Malice flopped back in his chair and put both hands on his head, interlocking his fingers. 'Then it's a good job I have a stronger moral compass than you, Mr Vasco. Because that sounds convoluted and dangerous.'

'As am I, Mr Malice, and when I look at you I see myself staring back which means you're dangerous too.'

'As much as I appreciate the compliment I think you're forgetting two things. It is not *your* family that will end up at the bottom of the lake if things go wrong, now is it? And secondly, take a look around, the odds don't look good to me.'

'That's a fair point, I do agree you're in a predicament. Mitchell here, is always telling me to loosen up a little. He tells me my paranoia is hurting our business, stopping us making new and exciting deals.'

'Maybe you should listen to him.'

'I respect what he has to say but I cannot switch it off.'

'I can assure you, Mr Lubos, on this occasion the man from *Eastenders* is right.'

Vasco looked across at Mitchell, who nodded.

'This is for you,' Mitchell snapped open the catches on the case and opened it up. He removed an envelope and tossed it across the table.

'What is it?' asked Malice.

'This is a business, and we are business men. It is for you to enjoy,' said Vasco.

Malice slid his finger under the flap to find the envelope stuffed full of twenty-pound notes.

'Five grand. Don't go mad with it,' Mitchell said closing the case. 'I bet Burko and Wrigley weren't as generous.'

'Is it clean money? I don't want any nasty surprises when they check the serial numbers,' Malice waved the wad of notes in the air.

'Do we look like fucking amateurs?' Mitchell planted both hands on the desk and half got out of his seat. Malice balled his fists. The guy behind him stepped forwards.

'Now, now, gentlemen,' Vasco waved his hands to calm the situation. 'Let's play nicely. I think this calls for a drink, You wouldn't drink with me last time, Mr Malice, but I will be offended if you do the same again.'

'How can I refuse,' Malice relaxed when he saw Mitchell return to his seat.

'I told you we like our drinks cold. You will find vodka in the freezer, would you be so kind as to do the honours?' Vasco said, looking across to the other side of the room.

Malice rose from his chair, walked across and slid his fingertips under the rubber seal to lift the lid. The suction gave way with a hiss and the top flew up. Inside was Wrigley, his glassy eyes stared up at Malice and his tongue was protruding from his mouth. His face glistened with ice and frost.

Both hands were clasped across his chest holding a bottle of vodka.

Chapter 45

Malice knew all eyes were on him. He gazed down at Wrigley. Ice crystals hung from his lashes and eyebrows. The vodka bottle lay on his chest.

It was flat and rectangular in shape with the name Double Cross etched in black down the side. Malice grasped the bottle to prise it out of Wrigley's clutches. It was stuck.

The first bars of his daughter's favourite song rang out in his head – that annoying one from *Frozen*.

He tried to prise away one of Wrigley's fingers. It was solid. Malice twisted the bottle and Wrigley's arms moved. There was nothing else for it.

Sorry about this…

Malice wrenched the bottle and it came free with a snap. Two of Wrigley's fingers broke off, still welded to the glass. Malice closed the lid and placed the vodka on the table in front of Vasco — digits and all.

'Are you shocked?' Vasco asked.

'No. After you killed Bullseye, and Wrigley went missing, I knew he'd show up somewhere. It was only a matter of time.'

'He wasn't very cooperative to begin with, but in the end, we got what we wanted.'

'So why kill him? Wrigley was a smart operator, he could have been an asset.'

'It was an accident. I got carried away with the lorry batteries and his heart gave out. In hindsight he'd probably given us all he had, but I was having too much fun. You know how it is when you get a rush of blood to the head. I made it clear to him it was nothing personal.'

'I'm not sure he would see it that way.'

'You British are way too squeamish about this type of thing.'

'I'm not squeamish. I'm just surprised you didn't see how valuable he could have been to your organisation.'

Vasco took a knife from his pocket and flicked open the blade. He took the bottle and sliced through the red seal securing the ornate silver cap.

'It's good to celebrate our new working relationship with a proper drink. This is good shit, not the teenage stuff you sell in this country. It comes from the town of Stará Ľubovňa, located in the Tatra Mountains in north-eastern Slovakia. They boast that it is seven-times distilled and seven-times filtered – eighty percent proof. Even the bottle is made of high end French crystal.' Vasco snapped off the cap, held the bottle in the air and prodded one of the stray fingers. 'I do like my vodka with extra body. 'Do Dna! Mr Malice. Here's to galloping paranoia,' he took a mouthful, followed by another and handed it to Malice who took a tentative swig. The liquid burned as it made its way into his stomach. He passed it to the big guy who knocked the fingers off the bottle onto the floor and gulped down two mouthfuls, wiping his mouth on the back of his hand.

'I think we are done here,' Vasco announced. The other two men took turns swigging from the bottle. 'We will digest the information you've kindly provided and let you know how we want to proceed.'

The lanky guy stepped aside.

'What about my stuff?' Malice said.

'We'll drop it off at your home, in a box marked Amazon,' said Mitchell taking another slug from the bottle. 'Nice to see you again, Mr Malice, the gentlemen will take you back.'

Malice picked up the envelope containing the cash. 'Can I ride in the front this time?' He stood at the top of the mezzanine stairs. 'After you.'

The big man shook his head.

Malice took hold of the handrail and made his way down to the ground floor. He pushed his thumb under the waistband of his jeans, felt the edge of the sticking plaster and began picking at it with his nail.

At the bottom, Vasco's men strode across the warehouse to where the van was parked, chatting in Slovak and laughing. Something had tickled them.

Malice lagged behind, stuffed the envelope into his pocket and used both hands to peel away the sticking plaster, freeing the razor blade stuck to his skin. He did the same on the other side.

They reached the van and the lanky guy went around to the driver's side and opened the door. The fat bloke walked to the opposite side, tugged on the handle and slid open the side door. Malice went to step up into the back.

His arm swept upwards in an arc.

The razor blade sliced through the fat bloke's windpipe and he staggered backwards. A second downward slash severed the arteries on the side of his neck. The big man fell against the side of the van, clutching his throat with both hands. His eyes were bursting from his face and his mouth was flapping open but all that could be heard was the sound of his neck gargling. Arterial blood pumped through his fingers onto the paintwork. His legs gave way and he slumped to the floor.

Malice ran around the back of the van and approached the driver's door. He tugged the handle and it flew open. The lanky guy had the shock of his life being confronted by Malice but had an even bigger shock when the razor sliced the side of his neck open. He twisted to avoid the second blow and the blade carved through his scalp, leaving a pelt of flapping skin and a flash of exposed bone.

Malice slashed at him again and cleaved another gash in his neck. The man was clawing himself across to the passenger seat to get away. Malice grabbed his legs, upended him and shoved him head first into the footwell. Blood spurted onto the windscreen as the man lost his grip on his neck. The next beat of his heart sent blood spraying across the air-conditioning controls. Malice drove hard and crumpled the lanky guy into the small space, his arms and legs flailing against the force. All the while the red stuff was soaking into the carpet in the footwell. Then the struggling stopped.

Malice patted the man's pockets and found a knife. He dropped down from the van and hurried to the fat guy lying half-under the back wheel and came away with a handgun.

That will do nicely.

He returned to the driver's seat and turned the key. The sound of the diesel engine filled the warehouse. He buzzed down the window and altered the position of the side mirror. In the reflection he could see the lights from office windows and a person crossing in front of them. The lanky guy was still upended with his head buried under the dashboard and his knees on the passenger seat.

Malice slammed the van into reverse and gunned the engine. He picked his spot and let out the clutch.

The van hurtled backwards.

He kept his eyes glued to his side mirror.

A bit to the left, a little to the right.

The mezzanine floor got bigger in the mirror as he sped towards it. He could see a figure staring out of the window. It looked like Mitchell.

The back of the van crashed into one of the front stanchions holding up the structure. There was an almighty bang as the fixing bolts were torn from the concrete floor. Malice kept his right foot hard down and smashed into a second stanchion located directly behind, knocking it out of position. There was a squeal of sheering metal.

He selected first gear and rammed into the front steps, sending the structure flying from its fixings and onto the floor. The van spun around and Malice picked his next target. Two more support legs lay to his left, directly underneath the office. He revved the engine and reversed towards them.

Malice was aware of voices, screaming and shouting overhead. One in English, the other in Slovak.

The van thudded into the first girder and there was a moment when it looked like it was too strong. But the impact disintegrated the concrete and the metal buckled.

Malice shot the van forward, then came to a juddering stop, flinging him against the steering wheel. The back wheels spun on the concrete, sending smoke into the air. The metalwork was embedded in the back of the van, holding it firm.

There was a loud grating noise. Malice glanced across to see the remaining supports start to cave. He jumped from the cab and ran.

The groaning sound got louder as the mezzanine floor fell forwards. He could see Mitchell standing with both hands pressed against the window and Vasco was silhouetted in the doorway to the office.

Then everything went into slow motion.

The two remaining stanchions at the front crumpled under the weight and the back supports were torn from their mountings. The leading edge of the mezzanine tipped forward and crunched into the concrete.

This catapulted the office over the handrails, sending it crashing to the ground on its side. There was a cacophony of breaking glass and the walls of the office collapsed. Vasco was thrown clear, landing in a heap. Mitchell was still inside.

Malice ran over and clambered through the shattered wall panels.

Where is the bastard?

Mitchell was lying face down, the top half of his body framed by the window. The glass on which he was lying had splintered into a thousand pieces, most of which was imbedded in his flesh. The conference table was pinning him to the floor. A rapidly expanding pool of blood filled the recess of the frame.

The freezer had burst open and Wrigley was thawing out in a corner. Malice looked around for his gun and knife.

Where the hell are they?

He patted Mitchell's pockets and removed his mobile phone and wallet. Next to him was the briefcase and the folder containing the police intelligence. Malice snapped open the catches and lifted the lid.

There they are.

He put the file in the case and negotiated his way through the wreckage into the warehouse to where Vasco was lying; twitching and moaning.

Malice put two fingers to his neck. The pulse was strong. He patted Vasco's pockets and came away with another phone and wallet.

'You fucking shit,' Vasco croaked, his face a bloody mess.

'You should never have listened to Mitchell. Always trust your instincts. Galloping paranoia is your friend.'

'I will make you watch as I torture your family.'

Vasco coughed blood onto the floor.

'You were right all along,' Malice said, getting down to floor level to look directly into Vasco's face. 'You and me, we're the same. Except...' Malice removed the third razor blade stuck to his body. 'I'm alive. And you're dead.'

He slashed the blade across Vasco's neck and walked away.

There's one more thing to do.

Chapter 46

Pietersen was curled up on her sofa in her pyjamas watching back-to-back episodes of *Friends*. It was her go-to remedy whenever she'd had a shit day. And boy was she in need of Ross & Co. tonight. She absentmindedly dipped into a bag of popcorn and came up empty-handed.

Oh, yeah. I've eaten them.

She knew every episode off by heart, but despite her mouthing along to the words, half her head was still in work. The Garrett case was bugging her, Malice was bugging her. Martin bloody Edwards was bugging her. The popcorn running out wasn't helping.

She downed what was left of her drink and went to the fridge for a top-up. The wine swirled around in the oversized glass. She took a slug and returned to the sofa.

Oh, and Ryan sodding Anderson was bugging her as well.

Why the hell he insisted on meeting in an outdoor toilet was beyond her. When she'd got back home she'd stripped off in front of the washing machine and piled her clothes into it. She didn't want to wash them with anything else. The stink of stale piss was still lodged in her nose despite half a bottle of shower gel and a handful of scented moisturiser.

There was a bang at the door.

'Who the hell...' she checked her phone. 20:10. She padded into the hallway,

'Who is it?'

'Kelly, it's me.'

She sighed silently, held her eyes closed for a long second, then shouted through the door. 'What do you want, Martin?'

'I just want to talk.'

'After the stunt you pulled today, you can fuck off.'

'I only want to talk,' his voice had a childlike quality which Pietersen had heard too many times before.

'Like this afternoon?' she snapped.

'I'm sorry babe. I wanted to grab your attention, that's all.'

'That's all! Trying to cost me my job more like.'

'Open the door, Kell, this is stupid.'

'Okay, I need to put something on.'

'I've seen it all before.'

Pietersen returned to the door and opened it as wide as the security chain would allow.

'You got two minutes,' she said.

'Can't I come in?' he was shuffling from one foot to the other while staring at the floor.

'You're wasting time, Martin.'

'Oh Christ, Kell, I'm sorry about today. I didn't know what else to do.'

'How did you know where I was?'

'I was waiting outside the police station, and when I saw you leave I followed.'

'When we spoke in the pub you were drunk. How did you get like that if you were outside?'

'I had a bottle of gin in my pocket.'

'You don't drink gin.'

'I do since we split up,' he sidled up to the gap between the door and the frame. Pietersen wedged her foot against the bottom of the door.

'What the hell do you want, Martin?'

'I want you to give me another chance.'

'After what you did?'

'It was a moment of madness. I didn't mean to …'

'You didn't mean to fuck my best friend. Well, let me rephrase that, someone I thought was my best friend.'

'It was nothing, Kell. She meant nothing.'

'Oh great, so you screwed up our wedding day over a woman that meant nothing?' Months of anger and tears came bubbling to the surface. She swallowed them back down.

'I can't say sorry any more than I have done.'

'So you keep saying.'

'Come on, Kell. Let me in.' He was smiling his best 'this will win her over smile'.

'No, and stop calling me Kell.'

'What if I drop the charges?'

'I have a witness statement from the officer who was with me. Needless to say, it doesn't correlate with your version of events.'

'Oh come on Kell, I mean Kelly, it doesn't have to be like this.'

'Like what?'

'Give me another chance and I'll drop the complaint. I'm desperate Kelly, I didn't know what else to do. Let me in.' The smile made another appearance.

'You didn't know what else to do?'

'I needed to get your attention, that's all. I didn't mean you no harm.'

'So you made a complaint against me to get my attention?'

'I'm sorry. I was desperate.'

'And you'll drop the charges if I agree to give us another go?'

'Yes, I will. I promise

'I'm not sure.'

'Let me in and I'll show you how sorry I am.'

'Nope, I don't think that's necessary.' Pietersen held up her phone so he could see it through the gap. 'Say goodbye, Martin.' She pressed the red button to stop the recording and banged the door shut.

That was one less thing to bug her.

Malice was also shuffling from one foot to another on a doorstep. He glanced across the road at his Ford Mustang and thanked his lucky stars he'd ditched the Rover and managed to grab a change of clothes. Back at his flat, the washing machine was already getting rid of the blood stains and another hot-wash when he got back should do the trick.

He looked at his watch — he was pushing it. A light came on in the hallway and the door opened. It was Hayley.

'Hi,' he said, giving her a half-smile.

'Hi.'

'You look tired.'

'That's hardly a surprise. It's been stressful.' She had one hand on the door and the other on her hip. She leaned into the edge of the door.

'What have you been stressed about?'

'Are you for real? How about wondering whether or not I'll have a bloody home to come back to.' Now both hands were on her hips.

'Everything's sorted.'

'Are you sure?'

'I'm sure, you're safe.'

'Has someone been in my house while I've been away?'

'Not to my knowledge.'

'Well it looks like it, I'm going to get the locks changed just in case.'

That's fucked it.

'If that makes you feel better....'

Hayley moved onto the top step and pulled the door behind her, forcing Malice to take half a pace back.

'Will I hear about it on the news?' she hissed, her stare boring into his face.

'Depends,' he looked away.

'On what?'

'On what other news is around at the time.'

'I'll take that as a 'yes' then.'

'Is Amy still up?'

'Yes but she's tired from the journey.'

'Do you think I could...'

Hayley cast her eyes to the heavens and stepped back into the house. Malice ambled into the hallway.

'Daddy!' Amy came running and threw herself at him when he entered the lounge. 'I've missed you.'

Malice scooped her up in his arms and swung her around. 'I've missed you too, Sweet Pea. How were things with aunty what's-her-face?'

'It's Aunty Izzy, you know it is.'

Malice stroked his chin.

'Umm … Nope, I only know an aunty what's-her-face. Who's this Izzy woman?'

'She's mummy's sister, silly. We had a great time.'

'That's good.'

'But I have to go to school tomorrow.'

'Indeed you do young lady, school is important.' He dropped her onto the sofa and plonked himself next to her.

'I bought you a pressie.' She scampered down and ran to her bag on the table.

'For me! A pressie! I love pressies.' He rubbed his hands together.

'Aunty Izzy gave me pocket money and I spent some of it on you.'

'That's fab, what is it?'

'Shut your eyes and hold out your hands.' Malice did as he was told and felt an object drop into his palm. 'Okay, you can open them now.'

He opened his eyes to find a half-eaten bar of Toblerone. He held it in the air and inspected the ragged edges of the wrapping.

'Has a little mouse been at this?'

'Me and mummy ate some, but you can have the rest.'

'Half-eaten chocolate is my all-time favourite pressie. I love it.' He hugged her.

'Go get yourself ready for bed, Amy, and I'll be up in a second,' Hayley said appearing from the kitchen. 'Say goodnight to daddy, he was just leaving.'

'Nite, daddy,' she squeezed him hard and kissed him on the cheek'

'Nite, Sweet Pea.'

Amy dashed up the stairs.

'I'm tired too. You need to go,' Hayley said brushing her hair away from her eyes.

'Okay, I wanted to see you were both okay.'

'We're fine.'

Malice made his way to the front door. 'You ate my present.'

'Yes, I did.'

'That wasn't very nice.'

'We need to talk about access. I can't have you calling round whenever you want to. It's disruptive to Amy.'

'I remember.'

'Goodnight Mally,' she closed the door behind him.

Malice arrived home having made a detour to the corner shop. He set the briefcase on his coffee table and cracked open a beer. After collapsing onto the sofa, he flipped open the locks and removed the file, both guns, the knifes and the belongings he'd taken from Vasco and his men.

In the case were two envelopes. The one Mitchell had tossed to him across the desk, plus another. He opened the flap on the second envelope to find an even fatter bundle of notes.

Malice let out a long, slow, low whistle.

He stacked them on the table and rooted around inside the case. It was empty. He shoved his fingers deep into the pockets in the divider and could feel something hard. It was a memory stick.

He retrieved his laptop from the next room and slid the device into the USB port. The red LED flickered and an icon came up on his screen. He double clicked and took a gulp of beer.

Please enter the six-digit password

Fuck!

Malice took another swig and scratched at the label on the bottle. He thought about Vasco and Mitchell, what was it they kept saying? 'We like to keep things simple.'

He typed in 0,1,2,3,4,5 and hit return.

Incorrect password.

He tried again, this time with 1,2,3,4,5,6.

A window came up showing a single Excel file. He double clicked and a spreadsheet filled the screen.

I wonder which one of them created this?

Along the bottom were a series of tabs, each one labelled with some kind of shorthand. He scanned across and mumbled them under his breath: 'Humb, Mersey, Av&Som, Met, GMP, Suff, W York, Notts…' The list went on.

He opened one of the tabs which brought up a table. Down the left-hand side were three words: Vanilla, Suntan and Rolex. The column to the right had the heading: Date. And the next two columns read: Amount and Total.

Looks like a payment schedule.

Malice skipped through the tabs at the bottom.

What the hell is this?

Then the penny dropped.

The tabs are police forces: Humberside, Merseyside, Avon and Somerset, Metropolitan, Greater Manchester ...

Malice scrolled along until he found the one corresponding to his own force. He clicked on it. On the left-hand side were two words: The first was Komodo with seven payments alongside it totalling fifty-five thousand. The dates went back nine months and the last payment had been made two weeks ago.

The name below it read: The Jam. Yesterday's date was in the cell to the right and the figure of five thousand was written next to that. For the second time today, a song played in his head – *A Town Called Malice.*

This is my payment schedule.

His finger hovered over the delete button. Then he did a double take on the Komodo payment dates.

Shit!

Chapter 47

Malice was trying to come down after the events of the previous evening. He'd treated himself to an extra hour in bed along with a shop-bought coffee which was cooling on his desk.

When he'd arrived for work his first port of call had been to chat with those *helpful* people in Equipment and Supplies. You would swear the kit they issued was their own personal belongings the way they begrudgingly allocated stuff out. It was like Oliver taking his bowl to Mr Bumble and uttering the words 'Please sir, I want some more.' More often than not with the same response.

That being said, when Malice handed over what was left of his phone in a plastic bag, even he had to admit his explanation sounded a little flaky.

'Can I have a replacement phone, please?' he'd asked the bloke, sitting at a desk behind the counter.

'What happened to your last one?' came the bored reply, the man not even bothering to look up from his paperwork.

'It broke.'

'How?'

'I darted across the road and it bounced out of my pocket. A car ran over it.'

The man removed his glasses and ambled over. He took the bag and emptied the pieces onto the worktop.

'That's in a bit of a mess.'

'As I said, it got run over. I work in CID, I need a phone.'

The man glared at Malice, then looked at the splintered debris scattered on the counter. He stroked his brow. 'What the hell were they driving, a tank?'

'Just give me a bloody phone.'

After much form filling, the man handed over a new device and Malice inserted his SIM card.

There, that wasn't so difficult now was it?

He cracked the lid from the cardboard cup and inhaled the intense coffee aroma. This should have been a morning for easing himself back into work mode, and putting the troubles with Lubos Vasco behind him. However, there was a problem.

'It's like fucking Beirut out at the Matlock trading estate and I'm eager to hear what you have to say about it.' Samantha Waite was not a happy Superintendent, her voice thundered down the corridor from the briefing room. 'Do you have anything to tell me?'

There was a low-key response which Malice couldn't catch but there was nothing low-key about Waite's second salvo.

'I've got a warehouse that's been burned to the ground with traces of accelerant all over the place, a torched van, the charred remains of four bodies and another one who surprisingly hasn't been affected by the fire and looks as fresh as a daisy. And to top it all there's not a scrap of I.D. on any of them. What the hell's going on?'

Malice winced and took a slug of coffee. *That* was problem number one. The risk of being pulled into the investigation to help was running high.

Problem number two was the contents of the flash-drive.

Pietersen came into the office and gestured with her thumb over her shoulder.

'What's going on in there?' she said.

'Waite's giving Wilson and his team the hair dryer treatment. Apparently, we now have five more bodies and an arson attack on a warehouse.'

'Shit, are they connected to the other murders?' she shuffled out of her jacket and dumped her bag by the side of her chair.

'I think that's what Waite is trying to establish.'

There was a bang as the briefing room door slammed shut. A welcome silence filled the office.

'I've got good news,' said Pietersen, pushing her hair behind her ears and taking a seat. She looked like the cat who'd got the cream.

'Go on.'

'I had a visit last night from Martin.'

'I thought you said 'good news'.'

'He told me he would drop the complaint if I gave him another chance; and more or less said he'd made up the complaint solely to get my attention.'

'That's a turn up.'

'Yeah, and the best thing is … I recorded him saying it!' she flung her arms in the air like she'd scored a winning goal. 'I've been with PSD this morning and handed over the recording,'

'Boom! Let's hope that's the last you hear from him.'

'Unfortunately, I doubt it.'

'Any chance of you two ever …'

'After what he did, no chance. I've decided on a new dating plan.'

'Oh?' Malice wasn't sure he wanted to hear what was coming next.

'I'll never date a man who I could beat in a fair fight.'

'Not sure that's a wise choice, in your case it narrows down the field too much.'

Pietersen pulled a face at him. 'Very funny. How was *your* evening?'

'Pretty boring,' Malice forced a yawn.

'Sometimes boring is good.'

'Yeah, sometimes. My turn; I have bad news.'

'Oh?'

'The judge refused our application for a warrant to search Kaplan's place. He said we had insufficient evidence to support what we were looking for.'

'He's got a point. All we know is she caught a train and got off at Fallgate station.'

'Yeah, he said pretty much the same thing.'

'Do you think Garrett went to their house?'

'Not sure, all I know is every time I speak to the Von Trapps an alarm goes off in my head telling me they're lying.'

'This trial involving Damien is interesting,' Pietersen took a notebook from her bag and flipped over the pages. 'You were right about the husband leaving his phone at home but that's not the only similarity to Garrett's disappearance. They both left their homes on a Saturday; he was supposed to be visiting a company that didn't exist and she was visiting a friend who we've not been able to trace; and we've not found a single item of their personal effects anywhere. Not his car, nor her suitcase – nothing.'

'How long ago did he go missing?'

Pietersen turned the page.

'His wife last saw him on Friday the ninth November last year and he was reported missing by his agent sometime the following week.'

'But you said he left the house on Saturday?'

'They'd had a row and he'd slept in another room, when she got up the next morning he was gone.'

Malice fell silent.

Fuck.

Chapter 48

The problem with murdering my wife is I'd be killing the best part of myself. Everything I own and everything I am, I owe to her. It seems churlish to snuff her out over another man, especially given our marital arrangements. But I'm struggling to control the rage inside and whichever way I look at it, she's breaking the contract.

It's late morning and I'm back in my workshop, swinging the axe like a man possessed. Which I suppose I am. I've spent the last two hours trying to persuade Elsa that screwing Malice is not a good idea. I appealed to her sense of logic and her love for me. The first she discarded and the second she laughed at.

'Damien, this is not about you,' she'd said. 'It's about me and what I want. And I want him.' She repeated the mantra over and over as I twisted and turned my arguments, trying to make her change her mind. I might be king-pin in the courtroom, but in my own house I feel like the jester.

'You've never denied me anyone before, what's different with this one?' she'd said.

'He's ugly.'

'No, he isn't. He has a rugged charm and a sensational body. Have you seen the way his muscles ripple under his shirt and the way—'

'Look!' I'd yelled in desperation. 'I came up with these.' I showed her a parade of beautiful men and women from the swinging website. Each one eager to take Elsa to heaven and back. 'Pick one, pick two… or three,' I'd said scrolling through the profiles.

'I can have those any time. Right now I want him.'

'For pity sake, Elsa. Do it for me.'

'Oh Damien, you are funny. I'm going to have him. And that's that.'

The more she refused to change her mind, the angrier I became. In the end I called her a bitch which prompted her to shrug her shoulders and announce she was going for a bath. That's the second time this week I've called her that.

How I wish there was an exsanguinated corpse hanging in the drying room. Someone I could chop to pieces while thinking of my wife. But no such luck. I have to make do with my mind's eye images of Elsa and that bloody copper, hacking at them through the air.

Then a different thought enters my head.

I could make it look like a disappearance.

I could spin the story that Elsa had gone behind my back to meet Belinda and in a crazed sex session she'd died. Elsa must have disposed of the body and… and…

My head goes into overdrive.

This could work.

I practise my defence.

'I only went along with the story to protect her. I love Elsa and will do anything for her — including letting her bed other people. I'm a helpless, besotted husband.'

I'm liking this.

I'd need the police on my side to have any chance of them believing me… but I could do that. I need to play nicely the next time I see them. I could make myself out to be a victim of our wayward lifestyle.

'I'm under the spell of my promiscuous wife.'

I could make that sound convincing. After all, it's not far from the truth.

There would be a scandal but after things had died down I'd be in the clear. Maybe a temporary suspension from the partnership while the investigation was ongoing but then I could throw myself at their mercy to re-instate me afterwards. They'd go for that.

'The police investigation was getting too close and she's done a runner. There's a large quantity of cash missing from our account and she's taken off. Do you think you can find her? I have no idea where she is.'

But I'd know precisely where she was. Her beautiful parts would be baked in the glaze of my latest creation while what's left is floating on the wind down by the quarry

'Screw an Ugly over my dead body,' I rant to myself.

She can't do it. She won't do it.

I'll make sure of it.

Chapter 49

Malice drove down the tree-lined country lane and passed the entrance to the driveway. Pietersen craned her neck to get a better view.

'Yup, two cars. They're both at home,' she said, shifting in her seat.

'Good.' Malice kept on going, spun the car around in a side road and headed back to the house. 'Are you okay with this?'

'Will you stop asking that! I'm fine. The bigger question is… are you?' huffed Pietersen.

'We need to split them up.'

'From what I've seen she's gonna jump at the chance of having some *alone time* with you.'

Malice flashed her a sideways scowl.

'Are you being my bloody mother again?' he snapped.

'I only have your best interests at heart.'

'Concentrate on your own job.'

'Yes, sir.'

The gravel crunched under the wheels as they pulled up behind the cars.

'Let's keep this off the radar as far as Waite is concerned,' Malice said, killing the engine. 'I'm not sure she'd be too keen on two of her team chasing around the countryside on the basis of a hunch.'

'She doesn't need another reason to go ballistic, that's for sure. She was terrifying this morning.'

'Yup, she's one scary woman.'

'I'm being serious … you do know this is crazy, right?'

'I know.'

'Okay I just wanted to check. Let's hope Damien doesn't stick us with a harassment charge.'

'That's where you and your fine arts degree comes into play. Let's go.'

They got out of the car and approached the front door. Pietersen rang the bell. The blurred outline of a figure could be seen through the ornate glass, walking down the hallway. The door opened. Elsa's face lit up as soon as she clapped eyes on Malice.

'Detective Sergeant, what a lovely surprise,' she squeaked, immediately striking a pose. She was dressed in jeans and a baggy sweat shirt. Malice had never before been so relieved to see a woman fully clothed.

'I wonder if you have time to answer a few more questions, Mrs Kaplan,' Malice said.

'Of course, please come in.' Elsa moved to one side as they filed past. 'Hello my dear, it's nice to see you, too.'

'It's Detective Kelly Pietersen, Mrs Kaplan.'

'Yes, I remember. Please come through, Damien is in his workshop. I'll give him a shout.'

Elsa beetled off, through the back door and into the garden. Malice and Pietersen followed her as far as the kitchen.

'That one,' Malice mouthed the words and pointed to the vase on the window sill. Pietersen picked it up and turned it over. She nodded and put it back.

'Damien, the police are here!' Elsa's voice carried on the breeze. 'Something about more questions.'

He emerged from the workshop and the pair of them strolled back to the house.

'This is the third time. You must be bored by now?' Damien said as he entered the kitchen.

'I'm sorry, Mr Kaplan, but this is a fast-moving investigation and we need to check things out,' Pietersen said. 'We do appreciate your cooperation.'

'How can we help?' Damien asked.

'It's more Mrs Kaplan this time.' Malice leaned against the worktop. 'You've been very frank and open with us about your lifestyle and about your relationship with Belinda Garrett.'

'There is no point in being anything else. We have nothing to hide,' said Elsa.

'So we know that while you both knew Belinda, it was Mrs Kaplan who had the sexual relationship with her.'

'That's correct.'

'We need to understand more about that relationship,' said Pietersen looking at Elsa.

'Umm… okay… that's fine with me,' Elsa shrugged her shoulders.

'If you don't mind I'd like to talk to you privately, Mrs Kaplan,' Malice said.

Elsa beamed at the suggestion.

'Of course. Damien would you be a love and put the kettle on.'

'Umm, yeah I suppose so. You don't want me?' he asked.

'Not this time, Mr Kaplan. If that's okay?' replied Pietersen.

'Yeah, well, if Elsa says it's okay then I guess…'

Elsa turned to Malice. 'Let's go to the study, it's more private there.'

The two of them trooped down the hallway and disappeared through a door to the left.

'Thank you for being so helpful, Mr Kaplan. We do appreciate it,' Pietersen said.

Damien put the kettle on to boil and broke out mugs from the cupboard. His gaze landed on the yellow mug, paused, then snapped out of it.

'We're only too pleased to help. Elsa told me you have a new lead. She said Belle caught a train to Fallgate.'

'Yes that's one of our lines of enquiry.'

'You could have knocked me over with a feather. I can't think what she was doing here. Do you have her on CCTV leaving the station?'

'I can't discuss the precise details, Mr Kaplan.'

Damien added milk to the cups and smiled, recalling the time when he'd shot the camera with an air rifle. 'One black, one white and neither of you take sugar?'

'That's right, thanks,' Pietersen mooched around the kitchen. 'I have to say, Mr Kaplan, these are works of art. Very beautiful.' She motioned to the vase on the window ledge

'They are rather lovely if I do say so myself. I won a competition with that one — the North West finals. I beat off some tough competition.'

'The glaze is amazing.'

'It's what won me first prize.' Damien poured the hot steaming coffee and offered her a mug. 'I'll take these in to the study.' He shuffled off with a drink in both hands and came back.

'Would you mind showing me some of your other work?' I studied fine art at university and joined the pottery club. I was never very good at it, things kept cracking and exploding in the kiln.'

'It can be the most frustrating of pastimes. Many hours of work can come to nothing in an instant. I have some more through here.' Damien picked up his drink and wandered through into the lounge. Pietersen joined him. 'I won a prize for this one too.'

Pietersen looked at the figurine of a dancing woman which was sitting on the sideboard.

'Wow! You don't just do vases then?'

'No, I do all sorts; jugs, tea sets, modern sculpture — the lot.'

'That is impressive, people tend to stick to one thing. May I…?'

'Of course.'

Pietersen picked up the figurine and turned it over in her hands. '

This is stunning, Mr Kaplan.'

'Thank you. I have another over here which required a different set of skills,' he said, pointing to a water jug sitting on the hearth of the fireplace.

'Did you make that for a competition as well?'

'Yes, I think that one won first prize in its category.'

'I have to ask… may I?'

'Of course.'

Pietersen picked it up and went over to the window.

'This crackled effect on the glaze is mind blowing, how did you achieve that effect?'

'That's a trade secret. If I told you, I'd have to kill you… so to speak.'

Pietersen replaced the jug on the hearth.

'You have a real talent, Mr Kaplan.'

'You're very kind. It's not often I get to chat about my work with people outside of the competition world. There is a set here you might find interesting.'

He opened a glass cabinet and brought out a china teapot. On the shelf below were six cups and saucers. He handed the teapot to Pietersen.

'Oh my goodness, bone china. This is so delicate.'

'Yes I think I was lucky with that one. It could so easily have shattered in the firing.'

'Was this a competition piece?'

'I won first prize.'

'I'm in awe of these,' Pietersen handed it back. 'Do you sell them?'

'There is a gallery in London who exhibit some of my pieces and they tend to be purchased by collectors. But most of the competition pieces I keep myself. That sounds awful doesn't it?'

'Not at all. If I made something this beautiful I'd want to keep it as well.'

'There's another piece here…'

'Sorry, Mr Kaplan, do you mind if I use your loo? Too much coffee, I suspect.'

'No, not at all. There's one down the hallway or you can use the one on the landing upstairs.'

Pietersen chose the upstairs toilet. She pushed open the door and locked it behind her. Adorning the window ledge was another brightly glazed vase that sparkled in the sunlight. She sat on the edge of the bath and took out her notebook and pen and tried to write.

But she couldn't… her hand was shaking.

Chapter 50

The station was in chaos. Superintendent Waite had lit a sizeable fire under Wilson and his team and had them running around like a bunch of kids caught scrumping for apples. She was sitting in her office barking orders like a Hollywood three-star general. All that was missing was a pantomime dame and the chant of 'it's behind you!'.

Malice had things to do; things that were best kept off Waite's radar — at least for now. With so much frenetic activity going on he was still worried they would be dragged into the murders at the Matlock warehouse. He decided the best course of action was to give his boss an update, knowing full well she wouldn't have the time nor the inclination to listen.

He door-stepped her in her office and launched into his speech. She held up her hand for him to stop.

'That all sounds good, Mally,' she said, interrupting his flow. 'But can't this wait until a better time?'

'Erm, yes. Of course ma'am,' he tried to sound disappointed.

'I've got a shit load of plates spinning at the moment, can you handle this and keep me out of it?'

'Sure, I just wanted to—'

'I know and under normal circumstances I'd be — Malcolm! I need a word!' she half got out of her chair and yelled at Wilson as he ghosted past the open door.

'Ma'am, I was just on my way to—' Wilson looked frazzled.

'I've had the Chief on the blower,' she shooed Malice out with a wave of her hand. 'Fuck knows how but the press has got hold of…'

Malice heard no more as he closed the door and made his way back to his desk. That should buy them some time.

Pietersen clicked the cap onto the pen and studied the six dates she'd written on the board.

'Great job,' Malice said. 'Do all women have the ability to remember dates? Hayley used to drive me nuts with her 'It's so-and-so's birthday next week'. I struggle to remember my own bloody birthday.'

'That says more about you than your ex-wife,' Pietersen said, tossing the pen onto the desk. 'Are you sure nothing happened when you were with Elsa? She didn't come on to you or anything like that?'

'What are you, my mum?' Malice joined her at the board and surveyed the dates.

'No, I'm just checking.'

'I keep telling you, nothing happened. I stuck to the script and asked her questions about Garrett. She answered them and that was it. Sorry I'm not giving you your *Loose Women* fix.'

'Oh please!'

'You don't watch it?'

'No. I have a job.'

'And that's the only reason?'

'Pack it in. Let's feed the dates into the Central National Database for missing persons; see what the National Crime Agency has to offer.'

Malice went back to his desk and logged into the system.

'We need to be smart about this,' he said clicking away with his mouse. 'There are about two-hundred and fifty thousand people go missing every year, we can't simply put the dates in and hope for the best. Let's think this through and build a profile of who we're looking for.'

Pietersen tapped the side of her head with her finger. 'The majority of those who go missing are kids and teenagers. We need to rule them out. I think we're looking for people aged twenty and over. I reckon Elsa prefers her bed partners with a little more experience.' She picked up the pen and got the ball rolling by scribbling on the board.

'Agreed. We're also looking for individuals who've been missing for some time. Except for Garrett all the dates are old.'

'Yup. We're probably looking for professional people, where their disappearance has come as a surprise to their family and friends.'

'Which would also rule out those who have gone missing before,' Malice added.

'That's right. Their disappearance would be seen as out of character and unexplained.'

'Most likely they would have some kind of back story that doesn't ring true.'

Pietersen compiled a bullet point list of criteria under the dates.

'Anything else?' she asked.

'Nope, that's all I can think of for now.'

'Let's feed this in and see what comes up.'

Malice brought up the data base and started populating the fields. He hit the *Search* button and a blue circle spun around in the centre to the screen.

No matches found

He input in another date from the list.

No matches found

And the next.

No matches found

'Shit. This isn't working,' he said, putting his hands on top of his head and looking up to the ceiling.

'Perhaps we've narrowed down the search parameters too much. Maybe we should–'

'Or maybe … I'm an idiot.'

'How so?'

'I'm searching against the wrong date!' His hands flew to the keyboard and he began tapping away. Pietersen walked over to join him.

'How come?' she asked.

'There are two dates in the system: The first is when the missing person was last seen, or when they last had contact with someone, and the second is the date they were reported missing. In some cases that could be the same day or they could be days apart.'

'Okay so let's step through what we know about Brendan Bairstow.' Pietersen plunged her hands deep in her pockets and paced around the office, weaving her way in around the desks. 'He was last seen by his wife on Friday 9 November and left his home the next morning. He was reported missing the following week. If he follows the same pattern as the Garrett disappearance then Elsa had been screwing him for months and poor old Damien wasn't getting a look-in. By the time Brendan arrived at their house Damien Kaplan must have been chomping at the bit for some action. Let's suppose they killed Brendan on the day he arrived.'

'Which would make it Saturday 10 November,' said Malice.

'That would mean the dates on the pottery don't correspond to when the persons went missing–'

'They correspond to the dates they were killed,'

She was now looking over Malice's shoulder. He typed the new date into the system and hit *Search*.

1 match found

He clicked on the link and the screen filled with details and a picture.

'Christian Thompson, reported missing thirteenth of May, 2010. He fits all the criteria. The date on the vase corresponds to the day after he was last seen. Let's try another.'

1 match found

'Bingo!' Malice said. 'Same thing. Melissa Cromwell, reported missing twenty-fourth of June 2012.'

Ten minutes later he hit print and retrieved a ream of paper from the printer. He slid the documents across the desk to Pietersen. 'Six dates, six missing people, six reasons to have another chat with the Kaplans.'

'And while we're there, look for a piece of pottery with DK 13 April 19 carved into the clay. The date Belinda Garrett was murdered.'

Chapter 51

The rest of the day passed by in a slow-hand-clap of frustration for Malice and Pietersen; the process of checking dates and requesting CCTV footage almost grinding them to a halt.

'If this lot comes in we're going to be glued to our laptops for a month,' said Malice, hitting send on another request. It was late and his desk was a graveyard of coffee cups.

Pietersen's workspace looked no better.

'It might be wise to have a word with the boss to see if we can have Marjorie Cooper again,' she said massaging her temples with her fingers.

'Not sure I want to get that close to Waite at the moment.'

'You're not scared of her.'

'I'm not. But she might ask me a question I don't want to answer.'

'If we don't get Cooper, we're screwed.'

'I'll pay her a personal visit. She likes me.'

'Not sure she likes anyone.' Pietersen stretched her arms above her head and let out a sigh. 'That's me done.' She got up and pulled her jacket off the back of the chair.

'Any plans for tonight?' Malice asked.

'No, nothing I'm afraid. I might take a trip to the gym, but on the other hand the Chinese is a lot closer.'

'See you tomorrow, I want to finish this off.'

Pietersen picked up her bag.

'Don't stay too late.' She left the office and ran down the stairs to her car. She was late.

She piled into the driver's seat and burned rubber on her way out the car park.

The houses and shops sped by as she left the station in her rear-view mirror, her head buzzing with the revelations of the day. In no time she was getting out of the car and jogging towards the underpass. It was a couple of minutes past seven o'clock. Ryan Anderson was already there, cloaked in his usual shroud of cigarette smoke.

'Alright?' Pietersen said.

'Fine, how's your day gone?' he replied, leaning back with his foot braced against the brickwork.

'Busy and boring, in equal measure. This missing person case is growing arms and legs and turning into a monster.'

Pietersen got closer and her eyes adjusted to the gloom. She looked him up and down. Gone was the work attire, replaced instead with a black dinner jacket, a crisp dress shirt and red bow tie.

'Anything new on Malice?' he asked.

'Nothing. Though he did seem different today, more relaxed. What did you find out?'

'You were right. Wrigley and Bullseye are both involved in the drug scene. Wrigley is the brains of the outfit and is a mid-level dealer whose been around a long time.'

'I know at least one of them who isn't around anymore.'

'That's Bullseye. He worked as an enforcer for Wrigley who has a syndicate of runners and a tight operation,' Anderson kicked himself off the wall and polished off the last third of his cigarette. He tossed the burning ember onto the floor.

'We know that already,' she said, shrugging her shoulders.

'There was an interesting pattern when it came to Wrigley's charge sheet. He had a number of brushes with the law a few years back the most serious of which was when he got arrested for possession with intent to supply. There was a screw up with the warrant and the case was dropped. Since then he's managed to avoid any contact with the police.'

'Lucky I guess?'

'The arresting officer was … DS Malice,' Anderson said the words like he was delivering a punchline.

'Malice said he knew him.'

'Up to that point Wrigley had his collar felt on a regular basis, then he comes up against Malice and slips off the radar.'

'Do you think he's in Malice's pocket?'

'Malice could be feeding him intel in exchange for a cut of the profits.'

'It's possible I suppose,' her nose wrinkled as a new smell wafted towards her.

'The other name you gave me was Gerald Burke, AKA Burko,' said Anderson, ticking off the list in his head.

'What about him?'

'Same pattern. Malice arrests him a couple of times, can't make the charges stick and then Burko manages to avoid getting into bother with the police.'

'Are there any others?'

'I'm still digging.'

'Thanks, that's helpful.'

'I have another name for you,' said Anderson, edging towards her. The stink grew stronger.

'Oh?'

'Lubos Vasco. Does that ring any bells?'

'No.'

'Casper says he's a big fish who has his sights set on this patch.'

'Why is it only coming to light now? Casper's been in witness protection for months.'

'He or she likes to play games and drip feed us tit-bits of information to maintain their value. Knowledge is power and all that. By all accounts Vasco has some serious muscle behind him and is not afraid to use it to get what he wants. There's nothing on the system about him so he must either be new or very cautious, or both.'

'His name hasn't come up,' she pinched her nose.

'Given the murders of Burko and Bullseye it's worth bearing Vasco in mind.'

'I will. Is there anything else?' she glanced around trying to locate the source of the offending odour.

'Not from me. How are things going with PSD?'

'I've not heard anything from them. I think it's gone away.'

'How's your gut feel? Do you still believe we're barking up the wrong tree going after Malice?'

'Still there.'

'Don't lose focus.'

'I won't.'

'Sorry, I have to go I'm late for a dinner appointment. See you tomorrow.'

'It's alright for some, I have a dinner appointment with the takeaway.'

'I'm just lucky, I guess.' He turned to walk away.

'Not that lucky. You might want to clean the dogshit off your shoe before reaching the restaurant.'

Pietersen walked back to her car, more conscious of skirting around the puddles than when she arrived. She rounded the bend to find a Ford Mustang parked next to her car. Malice was leaning against the bonnet.

A lump jumped up in her throat, she swallowed it down.

'Bloody hell, Mally, what are you doing here?'

'Whoever you're looking for… it's not me.'

Chapter 52

Elsa is preparing dinner in the kitchen. I've retired to the office for the afternoon where I'm pretending to work. My email box is filling with updates and briefing papers. To be honest, I can't be arsed, all I have in my head right now is how to make my wife disappear.

After the coppers left, I tried to keep the conversations light and airy; all the while plotting and scheming. Adrenaline is coursing through me and my shoulders ache from swinging that bloody axe.

My mind is running amok with a macabre to-do list.

This could work.

I have to be smart — I have to be clever. Fortunately I'm both.

It's a risk, but I cannot allow her to pursue DS Malice without consequences, and I'm afraid that only means one thing.

I can make her disappear. Her car disappear. A sizeable chunk of our bank balance disappear. That's no problem. The rest relies on my acting abilities and the plausibility of my scripted pleas. Given my recent court performances I'm feeling confident on all counts.

My problem is one of timing. I can't gauge how the police investigation into Belinda's disappearance is progressing. In one breath I don't believe they're getting anywhere, then in another I can envisage them knocking on the door and taking us to the station under caution.

I reach the conclusion that if I'm going to do it, I need to do it soon.

I've made my mind up. But my heart keeps holding me back.

Should I throw away all those years of marriage? There are moments when I talk myself out of it. Elsa is the love of my life and I'm unlikely to find another — not one like her anyway. Do I really want to do this over one man?

Then my rage kicks in. He is an Ugly. She's breaking the contract.

But then I think — *she hasn't done anything yet*. It's her intention that is driving me to the brink. My head is flipping from one to the other.

Elsa comes in holding two coffees.

'Just to let you know food won't be long. Are you working?' she asks, handing me a mug and perching herself on the edge of the desk.

All of a sudden, I'm starving. Plotting your wife's murder is hungry business.

'The trial has stalled which means our clerk of chambers has a hole in the billing for this month. He's jumping around trying to get me engaged on another case while the Bairstow work is on hold,' I push myself away from my work and cradle the cup on my belly. The coffee tastes good and takes the edge of my grumbling stomach.

'What did you do while I was with DS Malice?' Elsa asks.

'The woman detective was interested in my work.'

'What, being a criminal barrister?'

'No, she was asking about the pottery. Apparently, she did a fine arts degree and has a keen eye for detail.'

'You showed her?'

'Yes, most of the competition pieces. She was very complimentary.' I take another slug of coffee, it's definitely hitting the spot.

'Fancy that. A copper with an arts degree.'

'What about you? What did DS Malice want to talk about?

'Nothing really. He went over a load of questions he'd already asked.'

'You'd think they'd have better things to do.'

'He wanted to know how long we'd had an association with Belle. Ha, that made me laugh. *Association.* I love the way Brits dance around language. He asked about the Mexborough and quizzed me again about their new line of enquiry where they had her on CCTV getting off the train at Fallgate.'

'It's a good job I took care of that camera at the station.'

'You're always good at taking care of things. No loose ends, eh?'

'That's right,' I say, wagging my finger in her direction. 'It's all about staying one step ahead and thinking things through.'

'He also asked me about the swinging website and I gave him the web address.'

'He already had that. I gave it to him.'

'I told you he was going over old ground.'

'Sounds like a complete waste of time.'

Elsa turned her bottom lip out and tilted her head to the side.

'Not entirely, he fucked me on the desk.'

Chapter 53

Malice and Pietersen were sitting in the Mustang, both of them staring straight ahead, both wondering how they should start the conversation. It was cold inside the car; they were rubbing their hands and shivering in the silence.

Malice sighed, then slapped both of his palms on to his knees.

'Okay, I'll start. So, what are you?' He turned to her, his lips pursed. 'Anti-Corruption, DPS, IOPC?'

Pietersen faced him, her eyes squinting.

'What you talking about?'

He slapped a hand to his forehead while he sniffed a laugh out of his nostrils.

'Oh, come on, Kelly. Either you're on the game and do an early-bird special in that underpass or that's where you meet your handler.'

'I come down here because it's quiet, it gives me a chance to think. I have a lot of stuff going on outside of work. You've seen some of it at first hand.'

'Are you telling me that standing in a mouldy concrete tube, stinking of piss and God knows what else, helps the intellectual juices flow? I don't think so.'

'It's true,' she held her hands out, palms facing up.

'I'm not buying that, Kelly, give me some credit,' Malice snorted and shook his head.

'Credit for what! For following me!'

He stroked his stubbled chin, casting his eyes up the roof.

'My guess is you're new to it. This is your first or second assignment. The way you grilled me about Wrigley and Bullseye wasn't merely professional curiosity. There was an intensity which you couldn't hide. You're a bloody good detective but a crap undercover officer.'

'You've lost me.' It was her turn to laugh.

'I reckon someone has fingered our department for corruption. It's the latest fashion along with professional misconduct.'

'Mally, I have no idea what you're talking about. I know you fly a little off the mark at times but this is ridiculous,' she twisted around in her seat, staring out front and folding her arms across her chest.

Malice did the same.

'Okay if you want to play it like that. Let's start with your car,' he said.

'What about it?'

'It's registered to an Eleanor Pietersen.'

'Eleanor is my Christian name.'

'It doesn't say that on your pass.'

'Kelly is my middle name and I prefer it. This is stupid, Mally,' she felt as though she was being scolded by her father.

'I'm not angry, not even disappointed, you have a job to do and I know I fit the profile. You've been pointed at me because of my disciplinary record and personal circumstances – I get it. If I was going to look for a bent copper in our division I'd shine the spotlight on me too.'

'I don't have time for this, I'm going home,' Pietersen yanked on the door handle. 'I'll see you tomorrow.'

'I need your help.'

'What?' she had one foot out of the car, allowing a cool breeze to blow in.

'You're the only one I can trust.'

'With what?'

'This,' Malice reached under his seat and brought out a file containing a wad a paper. 'Listen to what I have to say and then I'll ask you again.'

'What the hell is this?' Pietersen pulled her foot back inside and closed the door.

'Just listen. A heavy-hitter drug boss called Lubos Vasco has been muscling in on people's patches. My guess is he murdered Burko along with Wrigley and Bullseye. A low-level dealer I know got absorbed into his organisation, well, it was more of a case of work for us or join the others if you know what I mean. By all accounts Vasco is the real deal and has a slick operation and plenty of contacts.'

'Why the hell don't I know about this?'

Malice put his hand up to stop her, 'Just listen. Okay? My guy showed up for a meeting with Vasco to find him and four other people dead.'

'Shit.' Pietersen's face dropped, she chewed on her bottom lip. 'The bodies in the warehouse.'

'That's right. When he finds them he panics, it's obvious this is gang related and he doesn't want to end up the same way, so he does a runner. But not before be rifles through the place in search of cash, drugs and anything else he can get his hands on. One of the items he takes is a briefcase.'

'Why haven't you told Waite?'

'Hear me out. My guy is pissing in his pants and asks me to help him disappear. I tell him to take a hike but when he says he's got information and wants to do a trade I have second thoughts. So, I help him and he gave me this. He found it inside the briefcase.' Malice handed Pietersen the file. She opened it to reveal a set of printouts, each one showing a screenshot of a spreadsheet. She flipped through the pages.

'What is it?'

Malice heaved a huge sigh. 'I believe it's a payment schedule. Look, each of these tabs is a police force. Down the left are codenames and the figures represent payments made on these dates.'

'And you think these are bribes Vasco made to police officers?'

'Look at the tabs. The busiest docks in the country are Teesside and Hartlepool, Merseyside, the port of London, Grimsby and Immingham and Felixstowe. These … are the police forces who cover those areas.'

'He's bringing in the drugs through the ports.'

'Exactly. The other forces are probably where he operates his supply and distribution network.'

'Fuck, this is dynamite.' She tore her gaze away from the printouts, her eyes wide.

'This …' Malice took the file, rifled through the papers and handed Pietersen a sheet, 'is our force. There's one entry: Komodo. Does that mean anything to you?'

'No.'

'Whoever it is received fifty-five grand, which in my book would suggest the person is not at the bottom of the food chain; the information they provide must be valuable. When Vasco moved in he was clinical, he knew exactly who to hit and what to target. He had inside information, no doubt about it. Now check out the payment dates.'

Pietersen ran her finger down the column of figures.

'All made in the last nine months,' she said under her breath.

'Okay so this is where I go out on a limb. My man told me Vasco was a bit of a joker, he was a Slovak and loved the way Brits took the piss out of one another. I think these are nicknames for people. What do you think of when you see the word Komodo?'

'It's a dragon thing, found on some island or another?'

'Very David Attenborough. It's the Komodo Dragon. Who do we know that reminds you of a dragon and who began working for the force nine months ago?'

Pietersen's eyes widened even further.

'Superintendent Waite.'

'And that's the answer I get. Now, let's start again … are you going to help me?'

Chapter 54

It takes a while for Elsa's comment to land in my brain. I stare down at the square of green leather inset into the top of the desk. I run my hands across the cool surface and imagine Elsa sitting on it with her legs wrapped around his waist while he bangs her. She's biting his shoulder to keep herself from screaming out.

'You bitch!' I slam my hands down hard and bolt through the door into the kitchen. The pots are simmering on the hob, but she's not there. I dash into the living room then up the stairs to check the bedrooms and bathroom. Nothing.

'Where are you? You fucking bitch.'

I tear back down and open the front door to see her car parked in the drive. There's one more place. I sprint down the hall, through the kitchen, into the garden and across the lawn to my workshop. The windowless walls don't help but there's a six-inch by four-inch piece of glass set into the door. I cup my hands and peer inside. Elsa is sitting at the table, sipping coffee.

I tug on the handle. It's locked.

'Elsa! Open this fucking door.'

'No Damien, not until you calm down.' Her thin voice carries through the wood.

I step back and slam the sole of my foot into the lock. The door rattles in the frame but holds firm. I step back and crunch my shoulder into it.

That fucking hurts.

I remember making the door with a double reinforced design to prevent any unwanted visitors when I'm busy. There is no way I'm going to bust the lock.

I squash my face against the window to see her sitting with her arms folded, watching the door. She mouths at me and shakes her head. 'No, Damien'.

I run across the garden to the wood pile and grab the spare axe. When I reach the workshop the head of the axe buries into the wood. I pull it out and slam it into the door again. The wood splinters. And again, and again.

The cacophony of banging echoes back off the house.

'Damien, stop. You'll hurt yourself,' I hear her call from inside.

'I'm gonna fucking chop you into pieces when I get hold of you,' I snarl through the window. The axe embeds itself into the wood and I twist the head to fracture the frame. The door still holds strong.

My arms and shoulders are burning with exertion so I drop the axe to the floor.

'You have to come out sometime, bitch, and when you do you're mine,' I screech at her, my face pressed hard against the narrow window.

'Don't be so dramatic, Damien,' she says, shaking her head

'I'll fucking kill you!' I punch my fist through the glass. My knuckles run with blood as I pull out my hand. 'He's an Ugly and I told you *no*! You can't stay in here for ever, Elsa, and when you come out I'm going to be right here waiting for you. Waiting with this fucking axe.'

I lift it up and brandish it for her to see. She just tuts and rolls her eyes.

I step back and bring the axe down hard. The wood grips the head and I struggle to free it. I work the handle up and down and back and forth, but it won't budge. Then with a jolt it springs free and I topple backwards.

I land on my back, staring up at the sky and try to get up. But I can't. My head is swimming and I can't seem to sit up. My legs feel like they belong to someone else and won't do as they're told.

'Elsa,' I shout out. 'I'm gonna—' The rest of the words dry in my mouth.

My body feels like it's glued to the ground. My limbs are heavy.

I tilt my head to see Elsa's face at the window. Through gritted teeth I try to yell at her, but nothing comes out.

She opens the door, walks over and kneels down beside me, stroking my forehead.

I look down and can see my right hand holding the axe handle. I strain every sinew and muscle, but nothing happens. And again — nothing.

Her face is festooned with a thousand flashbulbs popping around her head and her lips are the reddest-red I've ever seen. And her eyes are the bluest-blue. Her mouth is moving but I can't hear what she's saying. It's like trying to tune into a radio station on an old wireless, turning the dial and catching a brief song only to go too far and lose it.

'...so you see Damien, I had to have him. He was what I wanted and I always get what I want.'

The trees lining the garden are bending over into my gaze, their leaves fluttering with fluorescent greens and yellows. The sky crackles and fizzes like a kid's sparkler. And all the while a halo of popping lights frames Elsa's face.

'...and I knew when I had him there would be trouble,' she says. 'You're so predictable Damien, having your little play tantrums down in your shed, wielding that axe around. It was obvious who you were chopping into pieces.'

I stare down at the axe still in my hand. If I could just lift my arm...

Elsa reaches down and pulls up my top eyelid to expose my eyeball. The sky bursts into a riot of silver and gold.

'You've not yet fallen through the K-hole but it won't be long. I wasn't sure how much of the coffee you'd drink so I made it extra strong, just the way you like it. You were so preoccupied working out how you were going to teach me a lesson I knew you wouldn't notice. The problem was I would have found it hard to drag you all the way through the house to here, so I dashed to the shed and you did the rest.'

I can feel myself melting into the grass and Elsa's face is blurring in and out of focus. But I can hear her voice crystal clear, like she's coming through on expensive headphones. Each word chimes in a different key.

Elsa gets to her feet and grabs hold of my shirt collar with both hands and heaves me across the grass. The axe leaves my grip as I slip across the lawn and over the step into the workshop.

My vison is closing in and I can't work out if my eyes are open or closed.

'That was tougher than I thought,' Elsa says looping a chain across my chest and under my arm pits. She rolls me onto my front and I hear something snap in place, followed by the noise of chain links running through a pully. Next thing I know I'm sliding head first across the floor to the sound of heavy breathing. I feel myself rising up and I flop over the lip of the kiln. I can see Elsa at the end of a long tunnel pulling on the chain for all she's worth, the walls are a kaleidoscope of changing shapes and colours. She stops and locks off the chain when I'm hanging upright inside the kiln.

My eyes close and I'm drifting on the breeze down by the quarry. Sailing over the black, still water. I feel her hand under my chin and she lifts my head up. My eyes crack open and I'm gliding down a lazy river, the bumps and ripples are rocking me to sleep. Elsa's face is everywhere, floating all around me. Her voice chimes again.

'When the police come again, asking further questions about Belle, you'll be gone. The pressure of the investigation must have proved too much and you've done a runner. I will of course be distraught, because despite the years of coercion and abuse, I loved you. I adored you. I worshipped you so much I even slept with other people so you could get your kicks. I mean, no woman in her right mind would live that life if given the choice. Screwing total strangers in order for you to act out your fantasies. They will lap it up. I knew nothing of what you did to poor

Belle; how could I and say nothing? You know how persuasive I can be.'

My eyes close. A parade of fireworks explodes against the backs of my eye lids. Elsa's voice falls away to a whisper.

'This heralds a new chapter for me. It's exciting. I'm sure when he knows you're no longer around the nice detective will be back for second helpings. You've been planning this for days, I've been planning it for years. I've even made you a collection of trophies. I took the trouble of keeping the underwear of every Pretty that ended up in your glaze. Boxers, thongs, briefs, knickers... and of course your semen is on all of them. Each item individually wrapped to keep in all that goodness. As you always like to say, Damien — keep one step ahead and leave no loose ends.'

I'm falling.

Drifting down to a warm place.

A place full of colour and happiness.

A place where nothing hurts and nothing matters.

Elsa is dissolving. Her face is coming apart like a jigsaw.

'It was always going to end this way. We were good together, but our life was only ever a transactional arrangement based on a contract. And like all good contracts there's an opt-out clause. I'm choosing to exercise it. I need to go now my love. I have so much to do, you wouldn't believe. Busy, busy, busy.'

I feel her cool hand in mine and her lips brush against my cheek.

I hear the door close and the hiss of the gas valve.

Then the starbursts of colour fade to black.

Chapter 55

Pietersen nosed her car up the ramp to the top floor of the multi-storey and pulled up next to a white Audi. She stepped out in to the otherwise deserted car park, slammed the driver's door shut and then shuffled over to the Audi before sliding into the passenger seat.

'How was dinner last night?' she asked, screwing up her face while leaning sideways over to look at his shoes.

'Fine,' he huffed. 'How was your takeaway?'

'A touch on the greasy side. But at least it didn't smell of shit.'

Anderson turned and gave her his best scowl.

'You said it was urgent,' he replied, not happy at being reminded of the putrid cleaning job he'd endured the previous evening.

'It is.'

The back door flew open.

'DS Khenan Malice, but you know that already,' Malice announced, piling into the back seat.

'What the f—' Anderson jumped out of his skin. He spun around, his fist raised.

'I wouldn't advise it.' said Malice, settling back into his seat and pulling his jacket around him.

'Kelly?' Anderson turned to her, his hand still poised.

'I'd put that down, mate. I've seen her in action and she'll rip your arm clean off.'

'I said it was urgent, Ryan, and I meant it,' Pietersen returned his stare.

'What's going on here?' Anderson looked at Malice, then at Pietersen and back again, his mouth flapping open.

'Sit back and relax, Ryan,' Malice said, 'I've got something to tell you.'

Malice went through his well-rehearsed routine. He told Anderson about Lubos Vasco and the turf war, about how a low-level dealer known to him had been recruited by Vasco. About his suspicions regarding the deaths of Wrigley and the others, and about the contents of the briefcase. He handed over the printouts and waited for Anderson to absorb the gravity of what he was being told, then hit him with his theory about Waite.

Malice concluded with the words, 'Whoever you're looking for… it's not me.'

There was a long silence after Malice ended his monologue.

'You'll need to leave this with me,' Anderson said eventually, his eyes glued to the printouts. 'I have to check it out and get back to you.'

'That's what we thought,' replied Malice, pulling on the door handle. 'I'll leave you two alone. I'm sure you have lots to chat about. Oh, and one last thing, Ryan;

please don't think about pulling Kelly off the job. She's a damned good detective and I need her.'

He got out, crossed the concourse and down the steps to the level below. His car was waiting. It roared in the confined space as he powered back to the station.

The CCTV material had begun to arrive. Some of it was attached to emails while the older footage came in the form of CDs – boxes of them. There were masses of material.

'Bloody hell, this is going to take a week,' Malice said, clicking on one of the files in his inbox. He opened the attachment and looked at the runtime in the bottom righthand corner. It read nine hours forty minutes.

Make that weeks ... plural.

He slammed his laptop shut, hurried from his desk and popped his head around the door to Waite's office. Fortunately, she wasn't in.

'If she's not here to ask, I may as well take care of it myself,' he muttered under his breath. 'It's gonna have to be a personal invitation after all. Maybe a bit of the old Malice charm will do the trick.'

He ran down the stairs and out the main entrance to the building.

Shit, it's raining.

He cursed under his breath at failing to take the basic precaution of looking out of the window before leaving the safety of his office. The Administration block, was a brisk three minutes-walk away. He broke into a run. The rain soaked his hair and shirt by the time he reached the revolving doors. He shook water droplets onto the carpet.

Charm? Who am I kidding?

He took the lift to the third floor and headed for Imaging. He could see Marjorie Cooper hunched over a laptop at her desk. He wandered over. A sign was protruding from the top of the partition which read: Queen of CCTV. Malice had no argument with that.

While most people have photographs of their loved ones decorating their desk, not Marjorie Cooper — pinned to the partition running around her workspace were photographs of reptiles; lizards to be precise.

'Hey,' he arrived at her desk. 'How you doing?'

Marjorie pushed herself away from her computer, slipped her glasses to the end of her nose and eyed him up and down.

'Did you forget your umbrella?'

'Yeah, something like that,' Malice pinched the material of his shirt and gave it a shake.

'I'm nice and dry, thanks for asking, how are you?'

'Pretty good, apart from …' he wiped his hand along his sleeve and it stuck to his arm. He sidled over, placed both hands on the partition and leaned in. 'I was wondering—'

'Did you manage to find the woman I identified at Paddington station?'

'Not yet, we're still looking.'

'Not an easy job.'

'No we need to get a break.'

'Good luck with that,' she pushed her spectacles to the bridge of her nose and rolled her chair back into place.

'That's why I'm here. We could do with your help again.'

'Sorry, I'd love to but I'm completely snowed under at the moment.'

'I thought you would be which is why I came directly to you. I'm afraid we're in a bit of a pickle.'

'Oh?' she looked up, a glint in her eye.

Malice made a theatrical play of looking around the office, then leaned even further into her workspace. He beckoned for her to come closer.

'I'm not sure Superintendent Waite would be too happy if she knew I was here,' he whispered. 'You did such a great job finding the Garrett woman we need you to help us find more missing persons. We believe they're linked to her disappearance. Waite reckons we can handle it ourselves but we can't. Any time you could give us would be gratefully received.'

'That sounds intriguing, I might be able to squeeze in a few hours but that's all,' she responded in the same hushed tones.

'Marjorie, what can I say, that would be a massive help?' Malice dipped at the knees as if he was accepting an award.

'Okay, when you're ready give me a shout.'

'Thank you I appreciate it,' he straightened up. 'Hey, these look like dinosaurs,' He waved his hands at the pictures.

'In a way they are,' her face lit up.

'Are they yours?'

'I prefer them to people.'

'I know a few people like that.'

'This is Joey,' she pointed to a photograph. 'He's an Iguana and this is Mitzy she's a Leopard Geko.'

'Wow, they look very cool.'

'They are but unfortunately I had to donate Joey to a zoo a few months back. He got too big for me to look after properly and it wasn't fair on him.'

'How big was he?'

Marjorie leaned back in her chair and opened her arms wide, she let out a low whistle.

'He was over three feet from nose to tail and weighed around twelve pounds. He was very strong and had sharp claws. The trouble was he was only going to get bigger, they grow to around seven feet in length.'

'Shit that's huge. I bet you miss him.'

'Yeah, he was a real character.'

'I take it Mitzy is a lot smaller,' Malice had decided it was certainly worth going the extra mile.

'She's my little darling. I might get another iguana at some point but right now I'm kind of pining for my boy.'

'I didn't know iguanas grew that big — they're monsters.'

Cooper rushes her hands to her keyboard, closed down the image on the screen and typed into an internet browser. 'They're not monsters, these guys are monsters.'

A collage of pictures came up on the screen showing massive creatures with forked tongues darting from their mouths. Marjorie was beside herself with excitement at finding a new-found enthusiast.

'Bloody hell!' crowed Malice, throwing his hands in to the air in mock surprise.

'These are my favourites. The biggest and most powerful lizard on the planet. They can grow up to ten feet in length, weigh one hundred and sixty pounds and have been known to eat people. The female doesn't even need a male to reproduce, now that's what I call a step forward in evolution.'

'What is it?'

'The Komodo Dragon.'

Chapter 56

Pietersen elbowed open the door, tossed her bag on the floor and then shuffled into the lounge carrying a bulging plastic bag. She dumped it on the coffee table. Malice followed behind her. He took one look at the apartment and bent down to remove his shoes.

She flicked a switch and a tall free-standing lamp radiated a warm glow across the room.

'Make yourself at home,' she said on her way to the kitchen. 'Plates or bowls?'

'What?' Malice fought with one of his laces; failed and prised the shoe off his foot.

'Do you want a plate or a bowl?'

'Oh, err, either is fine.'

'I like a bowl, it makes it more authentic.'

Malice wandered over and leaned against the archway, leading into the galley-style kitchen.

'That bag of food came from a takeaway around the corner where the Chinese bloke who served us is called

Derek. I'm not sure a bowl is going to raise the authenticity.'

'You leave Derek alone, he likes me.'

'I'm sure he does, given the amount of free stuff he chucked in,' Malice shuffled back into the lounge. The flat was modern and stylish with magnolia coloured walls and a grey leather suit. The smell of new carpets hung in the air.

'Do you want a beer?' she called out.

'Yeah, that would be good, just the one,' He removed his jacket and tossed it over the arm of the sofa, then slumped down against the array of cushions. He pushed his hands into the soft upholstery, for the first time in a long time he felt relaxed.

Pietersen appeared from the archway, her arms filled with cutlery and crockery plus two beers gripped between the fingers of her right hand. She offloaded them onto the table.

Malice picked up a fork and studied it, turning it over and over in his hand. He furrowed his brow.

'What's wrong?' she asked.

'Do you have any chopsticks?'

'Umm …'

'Only it makes it more authentic.'

'Sod off,' she handed over a beer and unpacked the plastic cartons and brown paper bags. 'Do you always order so much?' she said running out of space.

'What can I say, I'm a growing boy,' Malice took a slug of beer. 'Nice place you have here.'

'Yeah, it's convenient for work too.'

'Where's home? I mean real home.'

'Here,' Pietersen prised the tops off the containers to reveal a brightly coloured banquet. 'When me and Martin broke up we sold the flat, and since then I've been staying with friends until I got myself sorted.'

'Then you were assigned this job and the flat came with it.'

'Something like that. I've been here a little over a month now.'

'Nice.' Malice picked out a prawn cracker, dipped into an orange sauce and crunched it in his mouth. He leaned forward to take another swipe at the sauce.

'No double dipping,' she covered the carton with her hand.

'What?'

'I said no double dipping, I can't stand that. Martin used to do it all the time, it drove me mad.'

'Kelly where I come from double dipping was never an issue. We had bugger-all to dip anything into once, let alone twice.'

They laughed and chinked their bottles together. Malice glanced down to see his toe sticking out of his sock. He reached down and pulled at the material.

Bugger!

'Thanks for saying what you did in the car,' she handed him a bowl and put serving spoons into the cartons

'Which bit?'

'When you told Ryan that you needed me on the case. Nothing is ever good enough for him, it came a welcome relief to hear I was doing something right.'

'That's a fact. There's no way I'm starting fresh with someone else and besides, I meant what I said, you're a good detective.'

'But not such a good UCO.'

'How long have you been in the job?'

Pietersen reached over and piled food onto her plate.

'I joined the force straight from Uni. I'd been a Special and enjoyed it, and it was a natural transition for me to make it a career. I started in uniform then passed my detective exams and after a few years went into anti-corruption. Eight years' service all told.'

'I know coppers with twice that much who don't have your instincts,' Malice's bowl was at risk of overflowing onto his lap.

'Now you're making me blush.'

'The same colour as this?' Malice held up a battered pork ball covered in fluorescent red sauce.

'Eat it and stop moaning.'

He popped it into his mouth. He had to admit that despite its garish appearance, the food was damned good.

'Marjorie Cooper, who'd have thought it?' he held up a fork full of noodles.

'No one, and that's the genius of it. She operated across homicide, burglary, drugs, prostitution, you name it she saw it. She was in a perfect position to know what was happening on the ground. Vasco needed intelligence about what to expect when he moved in on the patch and she was in a prime position to tell him.'

'I'm surprised Ryan took the latest news as well as he did,' Malice said.

'I told him about Cooper and he seemed to take it in his stride. He said that it simply meant they had two people to look into instead of one.'

Malice winced at the thought of Anderson still having him in his sights. He pushed the thought to the back of his mind.

'He didn't strike me as a guy who responds well to surprises,' he said.

'He isn't, and anyway we don't know if it's her yet. Twelve hours ago, you thought it was Waite.'

'True.'

'The boxing and the enthusiasm for cars – is that all true? Or is it a cover?' Malice asked, wanting to change the subject.

'Yes, that's the real me. I found Crosley's gym the first week I was here and signed up.'

'Still reckon it's a bloody dance class.'

'I preferred it to the *Rocky* gym you go to. The place stinks.'

'The place kept me from going off the rails as a kid.'

'What's the next steps with the Von Trapps?'

'Hopefully the CCTV footage will turn up something we can use. But we're still running on circumstantial and nothing else. We need a break,' Malice said.

'We have to get inside their house with a warrant to look for evidence that Belinda Garrett was at the property,' Pietersen downed the rest of her beer and headed to the kitchen for another.

'If we go to Waite with what we have she'll show us the door.' Malice took the opportunity to double dip his prawn cracker. 'There's no way we'll get a warrant.'

'We need something concrete,' she reappeared with a bottle, none the wiser of his transgression.

Malice shovelled food into his mouth. He glanced across at his jacket to see a piece of paper sticking out from inside the lapel. He put down his bowl and fished it out.

'What's that?' Pietersen asked.

He unfolded the paper and stared at a series of numbers scribbled across it in black pall-point pen. The cogs whirred as he tried to remember how it got there.

'Elsa gave me her mobile number when I visited the house,' he said, his memory clicking into gear. 'She wrote it on an envelope.'

'I bet she did,' Pietersen stifled a giggle.

'I didn't screw her, you know?'

'I know, you said.'

Malice folded it into a square and was just about to return it to his jacket. A bombshell exploded in his head.

'Fuck,' he said, staring at the paper.

'What is it?'

'We've got an early start in the morning.'

'To do what?'

'Pick up the Von Trapps and bring them down to the station while Waite obtains a warrant.'

Chapter 57

Malice and Pietersen were milling about outside Interview Room Two; both nursing a cup of strong coffee.

'For a woman who couldn't wait to tell us every salacious detail of her home life, she clammed up pretty fast,' Pietersen says, swigging from her cup.

'She doesn't look good either.'

'By the look of her eyes she's either got conjunctivitis or has been crying all night.'

Waite bustled down the corridor holding a wad of paper. She handed it to Malice.

'Ma'am,' they said in unison.

'We have the warrant and I've lined up a search and CSI team. Go see what she has to say,' Waite said. 'This had better be worthwhile.'

'Yes, guv,' Malice said, putting his hand on the door handle.

'Oh, and good work, the pair of you.'

'Thank you, ma'am.'

Malice opened the door. Sitting at the table was Elsa, her face ashen grey and her hair a matted mess. The oversized sweatshirt hung from her slumped shoulders.

She looked up.

Pietersen pressed the button and the machine let out a long buzzing sound. When it finished she said, 'Interview commencing 10.25 a.m. Present is DS Malice, Detective Pietersen and Elsa Kaplan. I need to remind you that you are not under arrest, Elsa, but you are under caution and you have waved the right to have a solicitor present. Do you understand?'

'Yes I understand,' Elsa replied, staring into her lap.

'Elsa, when we came to your house this morning you—'

'I don't have to answer your questions, do I?' She straightened herself in her chair.

'No Elsa, you don't,' Malice said, 'but it would be helpful if you did.'

'I understand.'

She returned her gaze to her lap.

'When we arrived at your house this morning we asked you where Damien was and you told us you thought he was at work,' Malice paused.

'No comment,' replied Elsa.

'We've checked and his office says they've not seen or heard from him in a couple of days and he's not returning emails. Where is he Elsa?'

'No comment.'

Malice continued.

'His car is not at the house and it's not at the train station car park either. Where has he gone?'

'No comment.'

Pietersen took up the challenge.

'When we arrived, we found a suitcase on the bed half-filled with clothes. Where were you going?'

'No comment.'

'Were you planning to meet your husband?'

'No comment.'

'When we last spoke you told us that Belinda Garrett had never been to your home. I told you that we believe she got off the train at Fallgate station on the day she disappeared and you insisted she had not visited you or your husband. Is that correct?'

'No comment.'

Malice slid the papers in front of Kaplan.

'We have a warrant to search your home, Elsa. What do you think we'll find?' he said, studying her face.

'For the tape, DS Malice is showing Elsa Kaplan the warrant,' Pietersen chipped in.

Kaplan's eyes widened. 'No comment.'

'Do you think we'll find evidence that Belinda Garrett was at your house?' Malice said.

'No comment.'

'Do you think we might find articles of clothing?'

'No comment.'

'Or a red suitcase. The one she was pulling behind her when she got off the train at Fallgate?'

'No comment.'

'Garrett was at your home, wasn't she, Elsa? What happened to her?'

'No comment.'

'We can play this game all day if you like and wait until the search team comes back with something. Or you can talk to us.'

'No comment.'

'Do you remember this?' Malice slid a plastic evidence bag in front of her. 'This is the envelope you used to write down your mobile number. You plucked it from a pile of correspondence which was on the worktop in the kitchen. Do you remember, Elsa?' Kaplan edged the evidence bag towards her. 'That's your writing, isn't it? and your mobile number.'

Kaplan screwed her face up.

'No... no comment.'

'You handed me this when we were standing in your kitchen. Does that jog your memory?'

'No comment.'

'Your number is written on the one side and on the other side is this ...' Malice turned over the envelope. 'The front has an address written on it, but it's not your address is it Elsa? Do you recognise it?'

Elsa studied the writing.

'No... no...'

'This is Belinda Garrett's address. The postmark is dated four days before she went missing. It was posted in London with a first-class stamp. How did this envelope end up in a stack of mail sitting on your worktop?'

'I... I don't know.'

'What was in the envelope, Elsa?' asked Pietersen.

'No comment.'

'Belinda Garrett probably received this three days before she goes missing and it winds up in your kitchen. How does that happen?' Pietersen pressed her question home.

'No comment.'

'I believe you sent something to Garrett and she brought it with her when she visited your house. You carelessly swept up the envelope with the other mail. What was in the envelope and how did it end up at your house?'

Pietersen and Malice leaned forwards with their elbows on the table.

Tears began to fall into Elsa's lap. She wiped her nose on her sleeve and began to quake. Her arms and shoulders trembled.

'Elsa, are you okay?' Pietersen asked. 'Do you want to stop the interview?'

'It was a phone,' she blurted out, her whole body swaying back and forth as she sobbed. 'Damien said she had to leave her mobile at home because he didn't want to risk her being tracked. He had to be extra vigilant because of his job. Belle said she didn't like the thought of travelling without one so he sent her one of ours.' She straightened up, her face red. 'I didn't want to do it. I didn't want any of it.'

'Any of what Elsa?' Pietersen asked.

'The screwing, the fucking, the sleeping with total strangers,' she snarled the words through gritted teeth, droplets of spit peppered the surface of the desk. Her balled up fists hit the table. 'The more we did the more he wanted. Every day another suggestion, every day a new face to look at. On and on and on, it was never ending.'

'Are you telling us you never wanted the swinging lifestyle?' said Pietersen.

'Of course, I didn't want it,' she shrieked. 'Would you? Year after year of fucking the men and women he paraded in front of me while he... he... he got his rocks off. But it was never enough, he wanted more and more. What about this one; I've met so-and-so and he's interested; I saw a woman today that would be right up your street – it was never ending!'

'Did Belinda Garrett come to your house on that Saturday?' asked Pietersen.

'Yes, she did. Damien picked her up from the station and she arrived around noon. I'd prepared a nice lunch but Damien wanted us to perform straightaway. He was scaring both of us so we did as we were told and went upstairs. We eventually came back down around four o'clock and had something to eat. Then Damien wanted us to go again. Belle was tired and wanted a rest but he was insistent, offering her money. We went to bed and I eventually fell asleep exhausted. I woke about three in the morning and Belle had moved into the spare room. In the morning Damien said she'd gone, caught the first train back to London. I never saw her again.'

'Why didn't you tell us this at the time?' Malice asked, scribbling notes into his book.

'Damien said he would hurt me if I didn't do as he said.'

'Had he hurt you before?'

'Nothing serious, a slap here and a punch there. Nothing to cause lasting damage.'

'What happened to Belinda Garrett?' Pietersen asked in soft tones.

'I don't know,' Kaplan sobbed into her sleeve. 'You have to believe me. Damien made me screw other people so he could jerk his tiny dick. It was the only way he could get off. I wanted to please him, he's my husband and I love him. I don't know what happened to Belle, I really don't.' Elsa collapsed on the desk with her head on her forearms, her whole body rocked as she sobbed. 'I didn't want to do it, but what else could I do?' She straightened up. 'I have no money of my own and he threatened to throw me out on the street if I didn't do as he said. He would pack my bags and put them in the car until I agreed to do what he asked. Other times he would dump my clothes in a pile in the garden and threaten to set them on fire. Then he'd tell me I had one more chance and buy me flowers, can you believe that – fucking flowers.' Elsa banged her fists down on the table, the coffee cups jumped. 'I had no one to turn to, no one to tell – he made sure of that. He drove my friends away. I have nobody. I didn't know what to do.'

'How long had this been going on for, Elsa?' asked Pietersen.

'Years.' She rubbed her eyes in her jumper. 'So many years. I've lost count. He's going to come back and hurt me, I know it. You need to help – please help.'

'Were there others, Elsa?' Malice said. 'Other people like Belinda Garrett who you slept with and then they disappeared.'

Kaplan slouched her shoulders and nodded her head. Tears landed in her lap.

Malice flashed a look at Pietersen who took the hint.

'Interview suspended at 10.45,' she pressed the button and the red recording light went out. 'Would you like to take a break, Elsa? Another coffee perhaps?

Elsa nodded, her head bowed.

Outside in the corridor Pietersen turned to Malice, 'We need to bring in specialist support. This is domestic abuse, gaslighting, coercive control the whole nine yards.'

'I'll talk to Waite.'

Malice went to walk away and Pietersen grabbed his arm.

'Tell me again you didn't shag her.'

Chapter 58

Eight months later

Malice unwrapped a sweet and popped it into his mouth, then offered the packet to Pietersen. He looked around at the sea of earnest faces, each one eager for the show to start. The room was a buzz of whispered conversations. The crackle of expectation hung in the air.

'My mouth is dry,' she said, removing the paper.

'Yeah, mine too. I don't do well at this waiting game.' The heel of his foot was tapping up and down.

'I can see that, you can't sit still.' She reached over and placed her hand on his knee. 'Stop, you're making me nervous.'

'Sorry,' he twisted in his seat to look over the heads of those sitting behind him. 'It's standing room only at the back.'

'Not surprised, I bet the majority of them are reporters. The steps outside are going to be awash with cameras when this is over.'

'It might be best if we sit tight for a while to let things die down.'

'Good idea.'

'I honestly don't know which way this will go.' His foot started tapping again.

'Nor me. What do you think?'

He put his own hand on his knee to stop the damned thing jerking up and down.

'It doesn't matter what I think, it's what they think,' Malice nodded in the direction of the nine women and three men of the jury who were waiting for proceedings to kick off. The same way they had sat every weekday for the past seven weeks as the terrible events that had taken place at the home of Damien and Elsa Kaplan were laid before the court.

Early on in the trial the judge had taken the unusual step of bussing them to the house so they could view for themselves the secret enclosure behind the drying room. One woman had to be helped away from the workshop when she felt faint having seen the butcher's hooks suspended from the ceiling. And all twelve had suffered a joint recoil of revulsion when shown pictures of the underwear found under the floorboards in the office.

All the while Elsa Kaplan had maintained her demeanour of a broken woman, sitting in a crumpled heap, working her way through a box of tissues a day.

On the day she gave her testimony, the judge was forced to order numerous adjournments due to her breaking down. For five hours she took the stand while the prosecution tore apart her lifestyle and her character. The harder he pushed the more she'd dissolved into a pool of her own tears.

That was five days ago, this was verdict day.

The court fell silent as a sound of footsteps could be heard coming up the stairs from the holding cells below The head and shoulders of Elsa Kaplan appeared above the rail running around the dock, flanked by a uniformed officer. She took her seat, folded her hands in her lap and stared at the floor. She was wearing the same beige tracksuit as yesterday. The same tracksuit she'd worn for most of the trial.

The judge took his seat in the high-backed leather chair, taking pride of place underneath the crest of arms hanging high on the far wall. He gathered his robes around himself and adjusted his notes, then the clerk of the court rose to his feet and addressed the courtroom.

'Will the defendant please stand?' His monotone voice filled the room. Elsa got to her feet and steadied herself by holding onto the rail, her knuckles white. The clerk turned to face the jury. 'Would the chairperson please stand.' A tall woman wearing a dark suit got to her feet. 'Have you reached a verdict on which you are all agreed?'

'We have.'

The clerk looked down at his papers.

'On the first count: Do you find the defendant, Elsa Kaplan, guilty or not guilty of the charge of accessory to the murder of Belinda Mary Garrett?'

The woman straightened herself and clasped her hands behind her back. She tilted her head back slightly. The whole courtroom leaned forwards in their seats.

'Not guilty.'

Her voice was clear and crisp.

A gasp rippled around the courtroom. People held their hands up to their mouths. Elsa Kaplan pulled out a hankie from her sleeve and continued to stare at the floor as tears streamed down her face. Malice lasered the jury chairperson and shook his head, grinding his teeth. Pietersen dropped her head and closed her eyes.

'On count two: Do you find the defendant, Elsa Kaplan, guilty or not guilty to the charge of accessory to the murder of Brendan Anthony Bairstow?'

The silence was deafening.

'Not guilty.'

A second gasp washed through the room.

'On count three: Do you find the defendant, Elsa Kaplan, guilty or not guilty to the charge of accessory to the murder of Melissa Cromwell?'

'Not guilty.'

Elsa collapsed to her knees, her hands still grasping the rail. The sound of sobbing filled the courtroom. The officer stepped forward to help her back into her chair. Elsa's forehead was resting on her knees, her hands covering her head. Her shoulders shook.

The courtroom burst into a cacophony of voices.

Pietersen stared into the middle distance, her face expressionless. Malice cast his eyes up to the ceiling and balled his fists.

The judge demanded silence and then dismissed Elsa and the jury. The uniformed officer wrapped her arm around Elsa's shoulders and led her away.

People dashed from their seats to claim a prized spot outside the courthouse in order to get the best photograph. Malice and Pietersen remained seated.

'Thirteen people!' she hissed under her breath, still gazing straight ahead. 'Thirteen people!'

'I know,' replied Malice, he scraped his fingers through his cropped hair.

'There were thirteen items of underwear and we could only join the dots on three of them.'

'If the forensics isn't there, there's not much we can do about it. We found multiple human remains in the cess tank and the drains but couldn't identify them. We could speculate but…'

She snapped out of her thousand-yard stare to face Malice.

'I feel as though we've let them down,' her voice was shaking, tears of frustration in her eyes. 'Those people who died will never see justice. Their families will never see justice.'

'It's all about what we can prove, and today we proved nothing.'

'That's shit.' She slapped the palms of her hands against the vacant seat in front. Malice put his hand on her arm.

'We did our best,' he said. 'But without Damien Kaplan it was always going to be an uphill battle.'

'I can't help feeling she played us.'

'Once the specialist unit got involved it was no longer our case. You can't blame yourself. If it wasn't for you we would not have got this far. There is little doubt that Damien Kaplan murdered those people, there is some closure in knowing that.'

'But no justice,' she rubbed her eyes.

'The defence did a brilliant job of portraying Elsa as a victim in all of this. And let's face it she gave them plenty of ammunition.'

'You're not making me feel any better.'

Malice unwrapped another sweet.

'You got Marjorie Cooper, that was a result,' he said, trying to sound up-beat.

'Yeah, after all her ducking and diving she made a full confession last week. Ryan is walking around like a dog with two dicks. He's got enough leads on bent coppers to keep him busy for the next eighteen months. And, no doubt, a promotion to look forward to.'

'When does your transfer come through?' he asked.

'Should be anytime now. I think Ryan is pleased to get rid of me. We never hit it off.'

'His loss is our gain. You're a good detective.'

'But a shit UCO.'

'Well, I wouldn't put it quite like that.'

'Anyway, I'm not cut out to work in anti-corruption.'

'Why's that?'

'Because it turns out I'm complicit in it.'

'Complicit?' Malice screwed up his face.

Pietersen turned in her seat and looked at Malice squarely in the face.

'If we're going to be working together I want you to promise me something.'

'Since when did we get engaged?' Malice sniggered.

'No, I'm serious. I want you to promise you won't lie to me again.'

'I told you, I didn't screw–' he shook his head.

'Not that. There's been something bothering me about the Cooper investigation. Nobody walks around with a set of printouts in a briefcase showing screenshots of a spreadsheet. That just doesn't happen.'

'What do you mean?'

'That information would have been held on a flash drive and protected with a password.'

'Don't know anything about that,' Malice pursed his lips and folded his arms across his chest. His foot started dancing again.

'No? I'm not sure about the drug dealer friend of yours who happened to stumble across the bodies in the warehouse - that may or may not be true - but I do think is there was a memory stick that contained the payment schedules. So why would you not hand that over?'

'I can assure you–' Malice went to stand up, Pietersen tugged the sleeve of his jacket pulling him back down. She leaned in.

'You didn't hand it over because the digital forensics team would be all over it and they'd find there'd been a deletion,' her voice no more than a whisper.

'The briefcase was full of papers.'

'I reckon a name was deleted from the file – your name.'

'Kelly, you're talking rubbish.'

'We're going to be working together so I thought it was best to get things clear. You're a good man, and a damned good copper, and you took a major drug dealer off the streets. So, that's why I don't think I'm cut out for that line of work. Come on, I'll buy you a coffee.'

She got up to leave, Malice stayed in his seat, looking up at her.

'I don't know what to say,' he said.

'Then say nothing, that's what I'm going to do. As you said, I'm a crap UCO but a good detective.'

Chapter 59

Six months later

The plane touched down in Hamburg thirty minutes late. Elsa Kaplan let go of the armrests when she heard the brakes and could feel the aircraft slowing down. For all her experience with international travel, she hated landings.

She looked out to see the rain driving horizontally past the window.

The plane taxied to the stand located at Terminal 2 and the stewards opened the front door. She collected her coat and bag from the overhead locker, filed out with the other passengers and showed her passport to the bored looking guy who waved her through. She paid a visit to the Ladies to change her clothes while she waited for her suitcase to appear on belt No.6. It was only a three-night stay but she could never do that with anything under fifteen kilograms of luggage.

The taxi queue outside arrivals was short and the driver hopped out to put her case in the back.

'Hotel Reichshof in der Kirchenallee bitte,' she said sliding into the back seat and brushing her hair back.

'Na sicher,' the driver replied looking into his rear-view mirror. He pulled away from the concourse and headed for highway B433. The driver turned left into Kirchenallee and pulled up outside the arched frontage of the hotel. He jumped from his cab to retrieve her case.

'Stimmt so,' she said, handing him more euros that he'd asked for. He tipped his head in a shallow bow.

'Vielen dank.'

The concierge almost fell over himself as he dashed to her assistance. He smiled broadly, took the handle of the case and steered it through the glass doors leading to reception. Four grey check-in desks sparkled under the vast chandelier hanging in the vaulted ceiling. Three fresh faces looked in her direction.

She took out her phone and fired off a message to the agency to say she had arrived safely. They in turn were grateful for the confirmation that the €150 booking fee would be deposited into their account by close of business tomorrow. She tapped at the screen to send another text.

'Einchecken, madam?' asked the concierge.

'No thank you,' she said lapsing into English. 'I'm waiting for Mr Madison. Could you look after my case?'

'Ah, of course, madam.'

Elsa's high heels clipped on the marble floor as she wandered into the next room to take a seat at the bar. She slipped her coat from her shoulders and eased herself onto a black leather bar stool. The hem of her dress rode up her thigh. She made no attempt to correct it.

The barman came over with a glass of champagne.

'Forgive the familiarity, madam. You must be Elsa. Welcome to our hotel.'

'Nice to be here, Vince,' she said, pointing her finger towards his name badge. 'Thank you.'

'Mr. Madison said he won't be long?'

'Cheers,' Elsa raised the glass.

'Cheers, madam.'

She glanced around the bar. An older couple were sitting in a half-moon booth in the far corner and two men in business suits were pretending to be deep in conversation, when actually they were stealing furtive glances at the latest arrival.

Elsa sipped her drink and smiled at them. She wore nothing under her dress save for a splash of expensive perfume and body glitter. A €100 request with which she was only too pleased to comply.

'Elsa!' a voice boomed out. 'Elsa, how lovely to see you. Sorry to keep you waiting.' A tall slim man in his early thirties dressed in chinos and a blue shirt rushed over and took her hand. He leaned in and kissed her once on each cheek. 'I was stuck on a damned conference call. Such a bore. Have you been waiting long?'

'My flight got in late so, no, I've just got here. Vince has looked after me well.'

'I've been so looking forward to this. A long weekend with my favourite woman.'

Elsa grasped the front of his shirt, pulling him close and planting a kiss on his lips.

'I've been looking forward to it too, Xavier.'

This was their fourth meeting in seven weeks. Each time in a different hotel and each time in a different country. Xavier Madison was the only son of a stockbroker, his dad had long since decided that it was better to divorce his wife and jet about the world making millions rather than be a father to his son. In retaliation, Xavier had made it his life's ambition to prove that whatever his father could do, he could do better and was now a hedge fund manager and VC of a private equity firm. His net worth was not what his father had accumulated, but he was closing the gap fast.

'Vince, another drink, please,' he said, putting his arm around Elsa's waist. She put her hand on his and slid it down to her hip.

'This is what you wanted?' she said looking into his eyes.

Xavier held her gaze while the blood rushed from his head. It took him a while to realise his drink had arrived.

'Cheers,' Elsa lifted her glass. 'Here's to the next three days.'

'Cheers. Let's hope the weather clears up,' he chinked his glass against hers.

'I'm not sure you'll be going outside.'

Madison looked like a child who'd just been told he could have a BB gun for Christmas. 'Okay,' he croaked.

'Do you want to finish these here or would you rather show me where we'll be staying?'

Xavier snapped his fingers, 'Vince would you have these taken to my room along with the rest of the bottle,' he said, placing a €10 note on the bar.

'My pleasure, Mr Madison. Have a good evening.'

Elsa slid from the barstool and pressed herself into Xavier. She could smell his cologne — the one she'd bought for him last time. He picked up her coat in one hand and put his other hand in the small of her back.

'I booked a suite, I hope you like it,' he whispered into her ear.

'I'm sure I will, after all, it has you in it.'

They walked through into reception and he deposited another note into the hand of the concierge.

'Please take care of the lady's case.'

'Certainly, sir,' he beetled off to the service elevators, intent on reaching the room before his tipping guest.

Madison pushed the button and they waited for the lift.

'Any requests?' Elsa said.

'You're more addictive than any chemical rush.'

'I know.'

The lift doors dinged open and they stepped inside. Once the doors closed he pulled Elsa close and kissed her.

There is a niche but lucrative market for those younger men who enjoy the pleasures of the more mature woman. Men who don't have the time to do the dance of silliness with women their own age, preferring instead the certainty and experience of an older model. Especially when they have the body of a professional tennis player and the sex drive of a rugby team on tour. Fortunately for Xavier, Elsa had both qualities in spades.

He pushed the keycard in the holder and the lock disengaged. The door opened to reveal a huge room with a massive bed. Elsa's bag was already on the case rack. The bottle was chilling in an ice bucket with two new glasses at the side.

'What would you like to do now?' Elsa hitched up her skirt and sat cross legged on the edge of the bed. 'More champagne or…'

'I… I don't know.'

Elsa crooked her finger and he obediently stood in front of her. She pulled him onto the bed and her nimble fingers unbuckled his belt.

His eyes closed as she slipped her hand inside his underwear.

'You lie back and relax, I have everything in hand.'

'Elsa, I was thinking...'

'Shhh,' she put her finger to his lips. 'Let me do the thinking. You're mine now — all mine.'

Acknowledgements

I want to thank all those who have made this book possible:

My family, Karen, Gemma, and Holly for their encouragement and endless patience. Plus, my magnificent BetaReaders, Nicki, Jackie and Simon, who didn't hold back with their comments and feedback. I'm a lucky boy to have them in my corner.

My fabulous ARC Group who have shouted about my books and made me blush with their unwavering support.

Also, my editor, David Lyons, my proofreader, Brigit Taylor, the fabulous Emmy Ellis @studioenp who stepped into the breach at the last minute to rescue the formatting and cheriefox.com who designed an amazing cover.

My wider circle of family and friends for their endless supply of helpful suggestions. The majority of which are not suitable to repeat here.

And last but by no means least, you the reader, for making this all worthwhile.

How to get in touch

I love hearing from readers. If you want to get in touch please use the links below. Subscribe to my Readers List on my website to receive further details of new releases, promotions and events.

Website: robashman.com

Email: info@robashman.com

Facebook: Rob Ashman Author

Twitter: @RobAshmanAuthor

Printed in Great Britain
by Amazon